Mrs. Bridge

* * * * * * * * * * * * *

Mrs. Bridge

BY EVAN S. CONNELL, JR.

NEW YORK   *The Viking Press*   MCMLIX

* * * * * * * * * * * * *

Portions of the text appeared in *The Paris Review*
under the title "The Beau Monde of Mrs. Bridge"
and in *Contact* under the title "Mademoiselle from
Kansas City."

P N B

SET IN THE BASKERVILLE TYPE FACE AND
PRINTED IN THE U.S.A. BY VAIL-BALLOU PRESS, INC.

TO

BARBARA AND MATTHEW ZIMMERMANN

Mrs. Bridge

But where is what I started for so long ago?
And why is it yet unfound?

—WALT WHITMAN

* * * * * * * * * * * * * *

1

Love and Marriage

Her first name was India—she was never able to get used to it. It seemed to her that her parents must have been thinking of someone else when they named her. Or were they hoping for another sort of daughter? As a child she was often on the point of inquiring, but time passed, and she never did.

Now and then while she was growing up the idea came to her that she could get along very nicely without a husband, and, to the distress of her mother and father, this idea prevailed for a number of years after her education had been completed. But there came a summer evening and a young lawyer named Walter Bridge: very tall and dignified, red-haired, with a grimly determined, intelligent face, and rather stoop-shouldered so that even when he stood erect his coat hung lower in the front than in the back. She had known him for several years without finding him remarkable in any way, but on this summer evening, on the front porch of her parents' home, she toyed with a sprig of mint and looked at him attentively while pretending to listen to what he said. He was telling her that he intended to become rich and successful, and that one day he would take his wife—"whenever I finally decide to marry" he said, for he was not yet ready to commit himself—one day he would take his wife on a tour of Europe. He spoke of Ruskin and of Robert Ingersoll, and he read to her that evening on the porch, later, some verses from *The Rubáiyát* while her parents were preparing for bed, and the locusts sang in the elm trees all around.

A few months after her father died she married Walter Bridge and moved with him to Kansas City, where he had decided to establish a practice.

All seemed well. The days passed, and the weeks, and the months, more swiftly than in childhood, and she felt no trepidation, except for certain moments in the depth of the night when, as she and her new husband lay drowsily clutching each other for reassurance, anticipating the dawn, the day, and another night which might prove them both immortal, Mrs. Bridge found herself wide awake. During these moments, resting in her husband's arms, she would stare at the ceiling, or at his face, which sleep robbed of strength, with an uneasy expression, as though she saw or heard some intimation of the great years ahead.

She was not certain what she wanted from life, or what to expect from it, for she had seen so little of it, but she was sure that in some way—because she willed it to be so—her wants and her expectations were the same.

For a while after their marriage she was in such demand that it was not unpleasant when he fell asleep. Presently, however, he began sleeping all night, and it was then she awoke more frequently, and looked into the darkness, wondering about the nature of men, doubtful of the future, until at last there came a night when she shook her husband awake and spoke of her own desire. Affably he placed one of his long white arms around her waist; she turned to him then, contentedly, expectantly, and secure. However nothing else occurred, and in a few minutes he had gone back to sleep.

This was the night Mrs. Bridge concluded that while marriage might be an equitable affair, love itself was not.

＊

2

Children

Their first child, a girl, curiously dark, who seldom cried and who often seemed to want nothing more than to be left alone, was born when they had been married a little more than three years. They named her Ruth. After the delivery Mrs. Bridge's first coherent words were, "Is she normal?"

Two years later—Mrs. Bridge was then thirty-one—Carolyn appeared, about a month ahead of time, as though she were quite able to take care of herself, and was nicknamed "Corky." She was a chubby blonde, blue-eyed like her mother, more ebullient than Ruth, and more demanding.

Then, two years after Carolyn, a stern little boy was born, thin and red-haired like his father, and they named him Douglas. They had not wanted more than two children, but because the first two had been girls they had decided to try once more. Even if the third had also been a girl they would have let it go at that; there would have been no sense in continuing what would soon become amusing to other people.

*

3

Preliminary Training

She brought up her children very much as she herself had been brought up, and she hoped that when they were spoken of it would be in connection with their nice manners, their pleasant dispositions, and their cleanliness, for these were qualities she valued above all others.

With Ruth and later with Carolyn, because they were girls, she felt sure of her guidance; but with the boy she was at times obliged to guess and to hope, and as it turned out—not only with Douglas but with his two sisters—what she stressed was not at all what they remembered as they grew older.

What Ruth was to recall most vividly about childhood was an incident which Mrs. Bridge had virtually forgotten an hour after it occurred. One summer afternoon the entire family, with the exception of Mr. Bridge who was working, had gone to the neighborhood swimming pool; Douglas lay on a rubber sheet in the shade of an umbrella, kicking his thin bowed legs and gurgling, and Carolyn was splashing around in the wading pool. The day was exceptionally hot. Ruth took off her bathing suit and began walking across the terrace. This much she could hardly remember, but she was never to forget what happened next. Mrs. Bridge, having suddenly discovered Ruth was naked, snatched up the bathing suit and hurried after her. Ruth began to run, and being wet and slippery she squirmed out of the arms that reached for her from every direction. She thought it was a new game. Then she noticed the expression on her mother's face. Ruth became bewildered and then alarmed, and when she was finally caught she was screaming hysterically.

✻

4

Marmalade

Her husband was as astute as he was energetic, and because he wanted so much for his family he went to his office quite early in the morning while most men were still asleep and he often stayed there working until late at night. He worked all day Saturday and part of Sunday, and holidays were nothing but a nuisance. Before very long the word had gone around that Walter Bridge was the man to handle the case.

The family saw very little of him. It was not unusual for an entire week to pass without any of the children seeing him. On Sunday morning they would come downstairs and he might be at the breakfast table; he greeted them pleasantly and they responded deferentially, and a little wistfully because they missed him. Sensing this, he would redouble his efforts at the office in order to give them everything they wanted.

Consequently they were able to move to a large home just off Ward Parkway several years sooner than they had expected, and because the house was so large they employed a young colored girl named Harriet to do the cooking and cleaning.

One morning at the breakfast table Carolyn said petulantly, "I'm sick and tired of orange marmalade!"

Mrs. Bridge, who was mashing an egg for her, replied patiently, "Now, Corky, just remember there are lots and lots of little girls in the world who don't have any marmalade at all."

*

5

Christmas Basket

That there should be those who had marmalade, and those who did not, was a condition that appealed to Carolyn. She looked forward to Christmas, at which time the newspaper printed a list of the one hundred neediest families in Kansas City. Every year Mrs. Bridge adopted one of these families, seeing to it that they had a nice holiday, and Carolyn now took a definite interest in this annual project. Each needy family was described in the paper—how many children, how old, what they needed particularly, and so forth—and Carolyn helped her mother decide which family they should adopt. Ruth and Douglas did not seem to care very much.

A bushel basket, or perhaps two, would be filled with canned goods, possibly some clothing, and whatever else the poor family could obviously use—a smoked ham, a bag of flour, a bag of salt—and the basket would then be topped with candy canes and a paper angel or a Santa Claus, and the edges trimmed with scallops of red and green crepe. Then on the day before Christmas Mrs. Bridge and the children would deliver the basket to the address furnished by the newspaper.

During the preparations Mrs. Bridge would sometimes ask the children if they could remember the family they had adopted last year. Ruth, being the oldest, usually could, but it was always Carolyn who could describe most sharply the details of poverty.

Douglas, possibly because he was so young—or so Mrs. Bridge reasoned—did not enjoy these trips. Each Christmas when he saw the basket being filled and trimmed he grew restless and obstinate; she did not know why, nor could she get him to explain. He did not want to go, that was clear, but she wanted him to appreciate his own good fortune, and not to grow up thinking he was better than someone else, so she insisted he go along to visit the poor family; he would ride in the back seat of the Reo with one arm resting on top of the Christmas basket, and he never said a word from the moment the trip started until they were home again. But he, like Ruth, remembered. This was why he hated to go. He could remember the very first visit. He had been just three years old when he first joined his sisters on the annual expedition to the north end of the city—had it been to Strawberry Hill, where he had expected to see a bowl of strawberries on top of the hill?—no matter, he remembered how he had been sitting in the back of the Reo when the door was opened and a man leaned in and took the basket away. Then, while the door was still open and snowflakes were falling on his knees, someone else leaned in—he could not remember whether it was a man or a woman—and quickly, neatly touched the cushion of the Reo.

Although many years were to pass before Douglas could understand why someone had wanted to touch the cushion, or why the memory of that gesture should persist, each Christmas thereafter when he saw the basket being filled and trimmed he grew restless and obstinate.

*

6

Dummy in the Attic

On a winter morning not long after one of these excursions Mrs. Bridge happened to come upon Douglas in the sewing room; he was standing quietly with his hands clasped behind his back and his head bent slightly to one side. So adult did he look in the depth of his meditation that she could not resist smiling. Then she saw that he was staring at the dummy of her figure. She had kept the dummy there near the sewing machine for a long time and had supposed that no one in the family paid any attention to it, but after this particular day— unless she was using it to make herself a dress—the dummy stood behind an up-ended trunk in the attic.

7

Alice Jones

That summer Carolyn began playing with Alice Jones, the daughter of the colored gardener who worked next door.

Every Saturday morning he would appear from the direction of the streetcar line, his daughter Alice capering wildly around him. As soon as they came in sight of the Bridges' house she would rush ahead, pigtails flying. In a minute she would be at the back door, pressing the bell with both hands. Often Mrs. Bridge would be in the kitchen polishing silver or planning the week-end menu while Harriet did the heavy cleaning somewhere else in the house, so Mrs. Bridge would answer the door.

Alice Jones was always out of breath from the run and her eyes were shining with expectation as she inquired if Corky could come out and play.

"Why, I think she can," Mrs. Bridge would say, and smile. "Providing you two behave yourselves." About this time the gardener would come walking up the neighbor's driveway and she would say through the screen door, "Good morning, Jones."

"Mornin', Mrs. Bridge," he always answered. "That child bothering you all?"

"Not a bit! We love having her."

By this time Carolyn would appear and the two children would begin their day. In spite of Carolyn's excellence at school she was not very imaginative, and no matter what she suggested they do that day Alice Jones had a better idea. Carolyn was a little stunned by some of the suggestions, and for a few minutes would grow petulant and arrogant, but when she found that Alice could not be intimidated she gave way and enjoyed herself.

One morning they decided to take apart the radio-phonograph and talk to the little people inside the cabinet; another morning they made sandwiches and filled a Thermos jug with milk because they planned to leave on a trip to Cedar Rabbits, Iowa. Again, they composed a long cheerful letter to Sears, Roebuck & Co. in which Alice told how she murdered people. Some Saturdays they would stage extremely dramatic plays

which went on for hours—with time out for other games—
the leading part always being taken by Alice Jones because,
at her grade school in the north end of the city, she was invariably the Snow Queen or the Good Fairy or some other
personage of equal distinction. Carolyn, whose stage experience had been limited to a Thanksgiving skit in which she
had been an onion, seldom objected and in fact had some
difficulty keeping up with the plot.

Long before noon they were at the back door, wanting to
know if it was not yet lunchtime, and when at last Harriet, or
perhaps Mrs. Bridge, set up the breakfast-room table for them
they would turn on the radio so that during lunch they might
listen to the livestock reports, which Alice Jones found hilar-
ious.

One day a fire truck went by the house and Alice, wagging
her head in amazement, exclaimed, "There they go again!
Who they going to burn down this time?" Dismayed by the
wickedness of the firemen, she rolled her eyes and sighed and
helped herself to more caramel pudding.

Mrs. Bridge, who was making up a grocery list, paused and
smiled affectionately at both children, pleased that Carolyn
was not conscious of the difference between them.

Alice and her father appeared every Saturday, and the two
children, occasionally joined by Ruth—who more often spent
the day lying on the porch swing—would play together as
comfortably as on the first Saturday they met. The gardener
never failed to ask Mrs. Bridge if Alice was a nuisance; Mrs.
Bridge always smiled and assured him she was not.

For a month each summer the Bridges went to Colorado;
they hired Jones for this month to water the grass after he had
finished working for the neighbors, and so Alice amused herself on the familiar grounds and frequently asked her father
how soon Corky would be back.

"Soon enough," was his usual reply, but one day he paused,

and as if considering the future, he told her, cryptically and a little sadly, "She liable to not come back, child."

But at last the vacation ended and Carolyn returned, full of sunshine and sophistication.

"The mountains are awfully big," she said primly, and, echoing her mother, "It was just grand."

Then Alice Jones said, "You know what I got in this here pocket?"

Carolyn, reluctant to become once more the planet instead of the star, affected disdain.

"Who cares?" she announced, coolly turning away.

"A human gizzard," murmured Alice with a mysterious expression, and before much longer Carolyn was convinced a summer in Kansas City would have been much more exciting than the mountains. She said as much to her mother, who replied a trifle brusquely, being harried at the moment, "Don't be silly, dear." And Mrs. Bridge was about to add that there must be other girls besides Alice to play with, but she did not say this; she hesitated, and said, "Corky, you know perfectly well you enjoyed Colorado." Soon, she knew, the girls would drift apart. Time would take care of the situation.

8

Who Can Find the Caspian Sea?

As time went on it became evident that Douglas was the most introspective of the three children, but aside from this—to his father's disappointment—he appeared to be totally unremarkable. Mr. Bridge had hoped for a brilliant son, and though he had not yet given up that hope he was reluctantly adapting himself to the idea that his son was no prodigy. If Douglas amounted to anything in later life, he concluded, it would be less the result of brilliance than of conscientious effort.

Ruth, even more obviously, had no intention of relying on her brains; but Carolyn, as soon as she entered kindergarten, began to make a name for herself, and very shortly was known as the brightest child in the class. Furthermore she appeared to understand her own superiority and when, through some mischance, another child equaled or exceeded her for a moment, Carolyn would grow furiously vindictive, and was not above lying or cheating in order to regain her position at the head of the class, so that by the time she was in the third grade she was beginning to be envied and disliked by her classmates and carefully observed by her teachers. It was no surprise to anyone when she was allowed to skip the second half of the third grade.

The teacher of Carolyn's fourth-grade class was a young lame woman named Bloch, who wore eye shadow and mascara and had one rather strange habit: every day she would call one of the children to her desk, give the child a comb, and then, bowing her head and shutting her eyes, she would instruct the child to take the pins out of her hair. Her hair was thick and greasy and hung down to her waist.

"Who can find the Caspian Sea?" she would murmur, and the child behind her would begin combing.

"Who knows where to find the Caspian Sea?" she would ask again, and without opening her eyes she would say, "Albert Crawford knows."

Then the boy she had named would walk to the great green and blue map pulled down over the blackboard, and with the pointer he would locate the sea.

"Carefully, dear," she would whisper if the comb snarled, but even then she seemed not displeased.

Although the children did not like this curious task they seldom thought of it once they were out of class. Carolyn, however, happened to mention at home that she had been chosen that morning. Mrs. Bridge was aghast; she had never heard of Miss Bloch's habit. After questioning Carolyn and becoming convinced it was the truth, she resolved to telephone the school and report the incident to the principal, and yet, for some reason, she could not do it. Several times she picked up the telephone, shivering with disgust, but each time she put down the receiver with an expression of doubt and anxiety; she decided it would be better to visit the principal's office, and yet this, too, was beyond her. She did not know why. In the end she told Carolyn that if she was ever again called upon to comb the teacher's hair she was to refuse. Having done this, Mrs. Bridge told herself the teacher was no longer a threat and the entire affair, therefore, was closed. And so it was. Carolyn was not called upon for the remainder of the term, and the following September she had a different teacher. There were times later on when Mrs. Bridge wondered if she had done the right thing; she wondered if Miss Bloch was still calling children to comb her hair, and when Douglas entered fourth grade she waited anxiously to learn who his teacher would be. It was not Miss Bloch; if it had been she would have gone to the principal and demanded that something be done. But it was not, and Mrs. Bridge, who disliked making trouble for anyone, was greatly relieved, and found that she was no longer obliged to think about the matter.

*

9

Of Ladies and Women

For semi-annual housecleaning Mrs. Bridge hired additional help. Carolyn answered the back door and reported to her mother, "The cleaning lady is here."

"Oh, fine," Mrs. Bridge said, and put away her sewing basket and went to the back door, smiling and saying genially, "How do you do? Come right in, won't you?"

That evening she instructed Carolyn. "You should say the cleaning 'woman.' A lady is someone like Mrs. Arlen or Mrs. Montgomery."

*

10

Table Manners

Mrs. Bridge said that she judged people by their shoes and by their manners at the table. If someone wore shoes with run-over heels, or shoes that had not been shined for a long time, or shoes with broken laces, you could be pretty sure this person would be slovenly in other things as well. And there was no better way to judge a person's background than by watching him or her at the table.

The children learned it was impolite to talk while eating, or to chew with the mouth open, and as they grew older they learned the more subtle manners—not to butter an entire slice of bread, not to take more than one biscuit at a time, unless, of course, the hostess should insist. They were taught to keep their elbows close to their sides while cutting meat, and to hold the utensils in the tips of their fingers. They resisted the temptation to sop up the gravy with a piece of bread, and they made sure to leave a little of everything—not enough to be called wasteful, but just a little to indicate the meal had been sufficient. And, naturally, they learned that a lady or a gentleman does not fold up a napkin after having eaten in a public place.

The girls absorbed these matters with greater facility than Douglas, who tended to ask the reason for everything, sometimes observing that he thought it was all pretty silly. He seemed particularly unable to eat with his left hand lying in his lap; he wanted to leave it on the table, to prop himself up, as it were, and claimed he got a backache with one arm in his lap. Mrs. Bridge told him this was absurd, and when he wanted to know why he could not put his elbow on the table she replied, "Do you want to be different from everyone else?"

Douglas was doubtful, but after a long silence, and under the weight of his mother's tranquil gaze, he at last concluded he didn't.

The American habit of switching implements, however, continued to give him trouble and to make him rebellious. With elaborate care he would put down the knife, reach high across his plate and descend on the left side to pick up the fork, raising it high over the plate again as he returned to the starting position.

"Now stop acting ridiculous," she told him one day at lunch.

"Well, I sure bet the Egyptians don't have to eat this way," he muttered, giving "Egyptians" a vengeful emphasis.

"I doubt if they do," she replied calmly, expertly cutting a triangle of pineapple from her salad, "but you're not an Egyptian. So you eat the way Americans eat, and that's final."

*

11

Alice Jones Again

It seemed to Mrs. Bridge that Saturday came around quite often. She was selecting some sugar buns from the bakery man when Alice dashed up the driveway with a long piece of clothesline in her hand, and the first thing that came to Mrs. Bridge's mind was that the girl had stolen it.

"Good morning, Alice," she said. Alice dropped the clothesline on the back steps and ran directly into the house to find Carolyn. A few minutes later the gardener appeared and asked, as he always did, whether she was being a nuisance. Mrs. Bridge smiled briefly and shook her head, not knowing how to be truthful without hurting his feelings.

The children were in Carolyn's room playing jacks. Mrs. Bridge looked in on them after a while and asked why they didn't play out of doors, the day being so nice, and she thought—but could not be sure—that as she suggested this the little Negro girl gave her a rather strange look. In any event the suggestion appeared to take hold, because a few minutes later she heard them outside shouting with laughter about something.

Shortly before noon, while rearranging the handkerchiefs in her husband's bureau, Mrs. Bridge heard Carolyn singing at the top of her voice: "My mother, your mother, live across the way, eighteen-sixteen East Broadway! Every night they have a fight, and this is what they say—" Here Alice Jones took over the song: "Goddamn you, goddamn you, goddamn you, goddamn you—"

Mrs. Bridge rushed to the nearest window and looked down. One end of the clothesline was tied to the rose trellis. At the other end was Carolyn, churning the rope with both arms, and in the center was Alice leaping up and down.

Next week, when Alice came racing up the driveway and tried to open the screen door to the kitchen, she found it locked. Mrs. Bridge was in the kitchen and said, "Who is it, please?"

"It's me," replied Alice, rattling the door.

"Just a minute, Alice. I'll see if Carolyn is at home." She went into the living room and found her daughter looking at one of the movie magazines that Ruth had begun buying.

"Alice is here again. I'll tell her you're busy."

But at the first word Carolyn had jumped up and started for the back door.

About ten o'clock both of them came into the kitchen for a bottle of soda pop and wanted to know what there would be for lunch.

"Corky is having creamed tuna on toast and spinach," said Mrs. Bridge pleasantly.

Alice observed that she herself didn't care for spinach because it was made of old tea bags.

"I believe you're supposed to have lunch with your Daddy, aren't you?"

Alice heard a note in her voice which Carolyn did not; she glanced up at Mrs. Bridge with another of those queer, bright looks and after a moment of thought she said, "Yes'm."

✽

12

Agreeable Conversation

The Van Metres were no more Egyptian than Douglas was,
but in a sense they were quite foreign to Mrs. Bridge. She
thought them very odd. The Van Metres, Wilhelm and
Susan, were about fifteen years older than the Bridges; they
were rather pompous—particularly Wilhelm—and they were
given to reading literary magazines no one had ever heard of
and attending such things as ballet or opera whenever a company stopped in Kansas City. Mrs. Bridge could not quite recall how she and her husband became acquainted with the
Van Metres, or how they got into the habit of exchanging
dinners once in a while. Nevertheless this situation had developed and Mrs. Bridge was sure it was as awkward for the
Van Metres as it was for them—each couple felt obligated to
return the other's hospitality.

On those occasions when the Van Metres were hosts they
drove over to the east side of the city to a country club that
had gone out of fashion ten years before. Wilhelm Van Metre
never drove faster than about fifteen miles an hour, and he
sat erect and tense with both hands firmly on the wheel as
though expecting a fearful crash at any instant. He came to a
dead stop at almost every intersection, ceased talking, and examined the street in both directions. Then, unless his wife
had something to say, he would proceed, the result of all this
being that they seldom reached the club before nine o'clock.
Once there he would drive the old automobile cautiously

around the circular gravel drive and switch off the engine at the front entrance.

"Ladies," he would say, suggestively, in his rumbling and pontifical monotone, whereupon Mrs. Bridge and Mrs. Van Metre got out and walked up the steps to the club. He did not start the engine again until he had seen them pass safely into the clubhouse; then, driving in low gear, he went on around the gravel circle to the parking lot.

"I see there are no other autos this evening, Walter," he said. "I wonder where everyone can be."

Mr. Bridge, already bored and thinking of an important case at the office, made no attempt to answer.

The women were waiting for them in the deserted lobby.

"It seems," Van Metre chuckled, "we have the place to ourselves this evening."

"I do get so sick of crowds sometimes," Mrs. Bridge answered brightly.

The four of them began to walk along the corridor toward the rear of the building, where the dining room was. There was a series of rugs along the length of the corridor so that they would be walking in silence, then on the hardwood floor, then in silence, and so on. Whenever their heels struck the floor the noise echoed ahead of them and behind them as though they were being preceded and followed.

When the silence became unbearable Mrs. Bridge looked over her shoulder, smiling, and said, "Everyone says the chef here is the best in the city."

"We feel he's competent," said Wilhelm Van Metre, who was walking directly behind her with his head slightly bowed.

On they went, two by two, down the long corridor. Small tables of various shapes had been set against the wall at intervals in a desperate attempt to conceal the length of the corridor. On one of the tables was a wreath, on another was an unlighted candle, on another was a silver bowl, another held a telephone book in a gray leather binding. There were half a dozen mirrors along the wall. Mrs. Bridge did not dare look into any of the mirrors, and as the four of them marched along she wondered if she was about to lose control of herself. Where are we going? she thought. Why are we here?

"What lovely tables," she said.

Van Metre cleared his throat. "Tables are appropriate here."

"We really should get together more often," she said.

"Yes. Susan and I often say, 'We really should stop by to visit Walter and India.' "

Finally they came to the frosted glass doors of the dining room.

"Ladies," Van Metre said, holding open the door.

There were two people in the dining room.

"Susan, I believe that's young Blackburn over there with his father."

"He must be home from the university."

"I believe I'll go speak to them. Walter and India, I'm certain you will excuse me." He walked slowly across the dining room, said something to them, and they looked around at Mr. and Mrs. Bridge.

In a few minutes he returned, rubbing his hands. "Now, let's have a look. Which table shall we sit at? Anyone feeling particular?"

"I don't think it makes a bit of difference," said Mrs. Bridge. All the tables had been set. There was a candle burning on each table as though a great crowd of people was expected.

"As you probably know, the club was designed by Crandall."

Mrs. Bridge had never heard of this architect, but she thought his tone implied she should have. "Let me think," she said, touching her cheek, "is he the City Hall man? I really should know, of course. His name is so familiar."

Van Metre turned to stare at her. He smiled bleakly. "I'm afraid Crandall is not the City Hall man, India. No, I'm afraid not." After a pause he said, "In what connection have you heard of him?"

"He was mixed up in that USHA mess," said Mr. Bridge unexpectedly.

"You're correct about that, Walter," Van Metre said, "although that was hardly what I had in mind. Crandall also designed the famous Penfield house." He studied the empty tables, deliberated, and selected one, saying with a courtly gesture, "And now, ladies, if you will."

They seated themselves around an oval table in front of some French doors that opened onto the terrace. They could see a flood-lighted, empty swimming pool, a number of canvas-backed chairs, the flagpole, and a winding gravel path lined with white-washed rocks. In the distance above the dark wall formed by the trees, the sky was suffused with a chill pink color from the downtown lights of the city.

"What a lovely view," Mrs. Bridge exclaimed.

"I'm afraid you're being kind," Van Metre said, unfolding his napkin. "There isn't much to look at." He began to frown in the direction of the kitchen.

"I do think the pool looks awfully nice with the lights on it that way."

"Those rocks are absurd," said Susan Van Metre.

"Well, most places they would be a little too-too, but don't you think they look nice out here in the country? They seem to give such a homey touch."

"The club isn't precisely in the country, India," Van Metre said, and cleared his throat. Then he turned around in his chair and again frowned at the kitchen. "I am commencing to wonder if we have a waiter this evening."

"We're certainly in no hurry," said Mrs. Bridge.

Van Metre snapped his fingers, at which the father and son looked across the room.

"Don't we have any service?" Van Metre called with a note of joviality.

The father spoke to his son, who got up and walked to the swinging doors, pushed halfway through, and apparently spoke to someone in the kitchen. Presently a Filipino waiter came out with a napkin folded over one arm.

"What do you recommend this evening?" Van Metre asked him.

The waiter said the roast beef was especially nice.

"How does that sound? India? Walter? Susan? Roast beef, everyone?"

"Grand," said Mrs. Bridge.

"Four roast beeves," said Van Metre, and chuckled. "It sounds as though I'm ordering four beeves. Entire animals." He took a sip of water, removed his glasses, and while examining them against the light he said, "Possibly I have told you of my experience in Illinois last summer on the way home from my annual fishing trip."

"Why, no, I don't believe you have," Mrs. Bridge said attentively. "What happened?"

"I went fishing with Andrew Stoner," he said, and lifted his bushy white eyebrows in what appeared to be an inquiring manner.

Mrs. Bridge thought quickly. "Stoner Dry Goods?"

"No, no," he chuckled. "I should say not! Stoner Dry Goods, my Lord, no!" He continued to chuckle while he put on his glasses, and Mrs. Bridge noticed with a slight feeling of discomfort that the hair of his eyebrows actually touched his glasses.

"I've met that fellow," he was saying. "No, India, not Stoner Dry Goods, not by a damn sight, no sir. Andrew Stoner, not John Stoner. My man is in the winter-wheat business. In fact, I expect you've met him."

"A rather short man with quite an attractive wife?"

"You're probably thinking of Dr. Max Hamm. He wears gold-rimmed glasses and speaks with a German accent."

"Oh—well, I don't believe I know the Stoners."

"I'm sure you must have met him somewhere."

"Oh, I'm sure of it. I'm terrible about names."

"However, you may not have met him." Van Metre thoughtfully rubbed his chin and took another sip of water. "I believe, now that I think of it, Andrew's wife died before you moved into the neighborhood. Andrew went away for several years." He turned the water pitcher around; apparently he was inspecting the design etched into it. "At any rate, we were returning from our annual fishing expedition when we had occasion to put up for the night at a small hotel in Illinois. It was in the town of Gilman, as I recall. Not too far from Peoria." His expression was inquiring again.

"I don't believe I've ever been there. It must be nice."

Van Metre put the napkin to his mouth and coughed. Then he continued. "Well, India, I shouldn't care to live there. However, Andrew and I did stop there overnight, although at this moment I am unable to recall our reasoning. It was a mistake, you may be sure of that."

"Sounds dreadful."

"Well, I wouldn't say it was quite that bad."

"I didn't mean that exactly, it's just that those little farming towns can be awfully depressing."

"I wouldn't call Gilman a farming town."

"Oh, I didn't mean that it was."

"It's quite a little city. Good bit of industry there. In fact, Gilman may have quite a future."

"Is that so? I suppose it *is* altogether different than I imagine."

Wilhelm Van Metre stared at the tablecloth for a while, as though something had annoyed him.

"We stopped there overnight. We got a room in the hotel, not a bad room, though small, and as we were walking downstairs for supper Andrew said, 'Wilhelm, how about a drink?' Well, India and Walter, I said, 'That sounds like a good idea, Andrew. Let's have a drink.' We decided to have a martini.

I've forgotten just why. We didn't know if the bartender in that little hotel even knew what a martini was, but we decided we would try him out."

Mrs. Bridge, thinking the story was about a terrible martini, said, "That certainly was taking a chance."

"Well sir," Van Metre said, leaning back in his chair and all at once slapping the table, "that martini was the finest I ever tasted."

"What a surprise that must have been!"

The waiter was coming across the floor trundling a cart with the roast beef under a large silver bell. After he had served them and refilled their water glasses he returned to the kitchen. They began to eat.

"This beef isn't quite done," Van Metre observed.

Mrs. Bridge said it was just the way she liked it.

*

13

Guest Towels

Boys, as everyone knew, were more trouble than girls, but to Mrs. Bridge it began to seem that Douglas was more trouble than both the girls together. Ruth, silent Ruth, was no trouble at all; Mrs. Bridge sometimes grew uneasy over this very fact, because it was slightly unnatural. Carolyn made up for Ruth, what with temper tantrums and fits of selfishness, but she was nothing compared to Douglas, who, strangely enough, never actually appeared to be attempting to make trouble; it was just that somehow he *was* trouble. Invariably there was something about him that needed to be corrected or attended to, though he himself was totally oblivious to this fact, or, if he was aware of it, was unconcerned. Whenever she encountered him he was either hungry, or dirty, or late, or needed a haircut, or had outgrown something, or had a nosebleed, or had just cut himself, or had lost something, or was just generally ragged and grimy looking. Mrs. Bridge could not understand it. She could take him down to the Plaza for a new pair of corduroy knickers and a week later he had worn a hole through the knee. He was invariably surprised and a little pained by her dismay; he felt fine—what else mattered?

He was hostile to guest towels. She knew this, but, because guest towels were no concern of his, there had never been any direct conflict over them. She had a supply of Margab, which were the best, at least in the opinion of everyone she knew, and whenever guests were coming to the house she would put the ordinary towels in the laundry and place several of these little pastel towels in each of the bathrooms. They were quite small, not much larger than a handkerchief, and no one ever touched them. After the visitors had gone home she would carefully lift them from the rack and replace them in the box till next time. Nobody touched them because they looked too nice; guests always did as she herself did in their homes—she would dry her hands on a piece of Kleenex.

One afternoon after a luncheon she went around the house collecting the guest towels as usual, and was very much surprised to find that one of the towels in Douglas's bathroom had been used. It was, in fact, filthy. There was no question about who had used this towel. She found Douglas sitting in a tree in the vacant lot. He was not doing anything as far as she could tell; he was just up in the tree. Mrs. Bridge approached the tree and asked him about the towel. She held it up. He gazed down at it with a thoughtful expression. Yes, he had dried his hands on it.

"These towels are for guests," said Mrs. Bridge, **and felt herself unaccountably on the verge of tears.**

"Well, why don't they use them then?" asked Douglas. He began to gaze over the rooftops.

"Come down here where I can talk to you. I don't like shouting at the top of my lungs."

"I can hear you okay," said Douglas, climbing a little higher.

Mrs. Bridge found herself getting furious with him, and was annoyed with herself because it was all really so trivial. Besides, she had begun to feel rather foolish standing under a tree waving a towel and addressing someone who was probably invisible to any of the neighbors who might be watching. All she could see of him were his tennis shoes and one leg. Then, too, she knew he was right, partly right in any event; even so, when you had guests you put guest towels in the bathroom. That was what everyone did, it was what she did, and it was most definitely what she intended to continue doing.

"They always just use their handkerchief or something," said Douglas moodily from high above.

"Never mind," said Mrs. Bridge. "From now on you leave those towels alone."

There was no answer from the tree.

"Do you hear me?"

"I hear you," said Douglas.

*

14

Late for Dinner

Not long after the battle of the guest towels he came in late for dinner, and when asked for a suitable explanation he announced with no apparent concern, yet with a faint note of apology discernible in his tone as though he had let himself be tricked, "I got depantsed."

"You *what?*" Mrs. Bridge exclaimed, clutching her napkin. She and the girls were halfway through dinner, having decided not to wait on him any longer. Mr. Bridge was not yet home from the office.

Douglas stepped over the seat of his chair as if it were a hurdle and sat down astraddle. This was a habit that exasperated his mother; he knew it and she knew he knew it.

"Why must you do that?" she asked. She was relieved he had come home, but she could not help scolding now that she knew he was safe.

"Do what?"

"You know perfectly well what."

Every time they argued about the way he got into his chair he proceeded to explain that he did it in order to save wear and tear on the carpet. It was his theory that if he pulled out the chair every time, it would soon wear a groove in the carpet, and he was only trying to save things from wearing out because she was always telling him not to be so hard on the furniture. This was the way the argument went; it was quite familiar to everyone.

"Now," said Mrs. Bridge, settling the napkin in her lap and beginning to butter a hot biscuit, "let's start all over again." As soon as she said this she regretted it.

"They depantsed me," Douglas repeated cheerfully.

"What *are* you talking about?"

"They took my pants and threw them up on top of Goldfarb's garage."

"Who did?" she said, putting down the biscuit.

Carolyn, who often imitated her mother, also stopped eating and assumed a severe expression. Ruth quietly went on with dinner.

"Oh," said Douglas, "the guys. You know. Tim and Louie and those guys."

"But *why?*"

"I don't know." He was not greatly interested in the conversation. He began to help himself to everything on the table, building a mound of food just high enough to exceed the limits of good manners but not quite high enough to draw fire from his mother. He was quite conscious, however, that she was observing the size of the helpings.

"Well, for heaven's sake, they must have had a reason. Hadn't you done something to provoke them?"

"Nope. We were just wrestling in the vacant lot—sort of gang piling, you know—and I was on the bottom and then just all of a sudden they decided to depants me, that's all." He was ladling gravy onto his plate; he had built a semi-circular dam out of mashed potatoes and was making the lake with gravy.

"Now that's enough, do you hear?"

With a pained expression he put down the gravy and began looking around for something else.

"I simply can't understand why they would do a thing like that," she went on, half to herself.

"They just felt like depantsing somebody, I guess," Douglas went on obligingly, "and I was on the bottom, that's all. We depantsed Eliot Hoff a couple of weeks ago and he yelled bloody murder and cried all over the place."

"All right, all right, that'll do," said Mrs. Bridge. "I think we've covered the situation."

"How did you get them back?" asked Carolyn.

"Oh, I just climbed the telephone pole and there's a big cable that leads over to Shafer's garage, so after I got there I just took a run and jumped across to Goldfarb's garage." He was becoming voluble now. "Those garages look pretty close together from this side of the fence, but when you get up there, why, they're not, because I didn't think I was going to make it. I was just up there like the man on the flying trapeze without any pants and—"

"That will do!" Mrs. Bridge interrupted, looking him firmly in the eye.

"Well, gee whiz—"

"The subject is closed."

"Okay, okay," he muttered, and reached suddenly for the gravy.

15

Holiday News

On the fifteenth of each month there appeared in the south side of Kansas City a magazine called *The Tattler*. It was very thin—sixteen pages of coated ivory stock—but the format was large: it was about half the size of a newspaper. The typography, for reasons known only to the publisher, was in the style of 1910. *The Tattler* was Kansas City's magazine of society; it consisted of photographs of significant brides, of visiting celebrities feted at the homes of wealthy Kansas Citians, and pictures of subscribers, together with long lists of names of those who had either given or attended social affairs during the month. These lists of names were so long that it was found advisable to break them up into paragraphs and from time to time to insert a description of something—anything—that was reasonably pertinent.

A typical entry:

Seen wolfing the delicious hors d'oeuvres at the charming Lane Terrace residence of the Bob Brewers (she, née Nancy Page of Santa Barbara, California) a week ago Tuesday-last were Humboldt Aupp, Jr., Buzz Duncan with his captivating guest from Dixie, Lola Anne Sharpe in a positively stunning cardinal gown with net bodice; Nathalie Blakely, Gordon A. Spencer III home with Yule tidings from Yale, Jo Power with her sister-in-law from Gotham, Mrs. Andrew Koeppel and hubby (he the newly appointed chairman of the board of Koeppel, Koeppel & Ingle), the McKinney twins indistinguishable in saffron except for Wendy's rhinestone bracelet and Lt. Hal Graves, and last but far from least in stunning shell pink taffeta aglow with sequins, Mrs. Albert Tate fascinated by Mrs. Russ Arlen on the topic of Bermuda.

There followed a list of about thirty names, a description of the rumpus room, and more names.

The Tattler mentioned Mrs. and Mrs. Bridge whenever they were present at a major social function, and occasionally took their picture. The most memorable photograph of Mrs. Bridge was taken during a family vacation in Colorado. She had always been rather fond of horses, and before her marriage she used to go riding. In recent years, however, she had not had much to do with horses, partly because she was growing stout and was apprehensive that from certain angles she might not cut so sleek a figure in jodhpurs as she used to. In fact, at the time this picture was taken, she had not been on a horse for about ten years. The horse, unfortunately, had just sneezed and its head was down between his knees; Mrs. Bridge, her attention divided between the beast and the photographer, was leaning over its neck with a doubtful smile. The caption read, "Mrs. Walter G. Bridge, holidaying with spouse and young at Rocky Point Lodge, Estes Park, Colorado, likes nothing better than a canter on the bridle paths."

16

A Matter of Taste

At Christmas time *The Tattler* customarily published photographs of the lights in the Plaza shopping center and of various homes in the country club district that were more than usually decorative. There was a great deal of interest in Christmas decorations; Mrs. Bridge very much enjoyed them, but at the same time they presented her with a problem: if you did not put up any decorations you were being conspicuous, and if you put up too many you were being conspicuous. At the very least there should be a large holly wreath on the front door; at the most there might be half a dozen decorations visible, including the Christmas tree. In her annual attempt to strike the proper note she came to rely more and more on Carolyn, who possessed, she thought, better judgment than either Ruth or Douglas, although she was careful to keep this opinion to herself.

Every year, then, the Bridges' home was festive without being ostentatious. A strand of green lights was woven through the branches of a small spruce tree near the front porch, and there was a wreath in each of the first-floor windows and a large wreath with a red ribbon and a cluster of bells attached to the knocker of the front door. Inside, in a corner of the living room away from the heat of the fireplace, stood the tree, its topmost branches clipped or bent so as not to stain the ceiling, and a bed sheet draped around the bottom in order to conceal the odd-looking metal device that held the tree upright. Presents were arranged on the sheet and a few small presents tied to the limbs. There was tinsel on the tree, and there were peppermint-candy canes and popcorn balls and electric candles, and some new ornaments each year to replace the broken ones. On the mantel was a group of angels with painted mouths wide open and hymn books in their hands, and beside them a plastic crèche. Whatever pine boughs had been clipped from the top of the tree were laid along the mantel, with occasional tufts of cotton to simulate snow.

During the course of the holidays Mrs. Bridge would drive the children around to see how other houses were decorated, and on one of these trips they came to a stucco bungalow with a life-size cutout of Santa Claus on the roof, six reindeer in the front yard, candles in every window, and by the front door an enormous cardboard birthday cake with one candle. On the cake was this message: HAPPY BIRTHDAY, DEAR JESUS.

"My word, how extreme," said Mrs. Bridge thoughtfully. "Some Italians must live there."

17

Good-by Alice

Alice Jones was now appearing every month or so, though her father came to work at the neighbors' each Saturday as usual. On those occasions when she accompanied him she would spend the morning with Carolyn, but then, about noon, she would get on the streetcar and go home by herself. During the morning she and Carolyn would have a confidential talk, usually in Carolyn's room, that is, in the room that Carolyn and Ruth shared. Ruth was seldom at home on Saturday; nobody in the family knew where she went. So Alice Jones and Carolyn would shut the door to the room and converse in low tones or in whispers about school and clothes and friends and boys and how they intended to raise their children.

"How many are you going to have?" asked Carolyn.

"Eleven," Alice said firmly.

"Heavens!" said Carolyn. "That's certainly telling."

"What kind of talk is that?" Alice wanted to know. "How many are you going to have?"

"Two, I believe. That makes a nice family."

One Saturday at lunch time, shortly after Alice had started to the streetcar line, Carolyn said that Alice had invited her to come to a party next Saturday afternoon.

"Well, that was nice of Alice, wasn't it?" Mrs. Bridge replied, and with a tiny silver fork she ate a slice of banana from her fruit salad, and then a piece of lettuce.

"Where is the party to be?"

"At her house."

"Where does Alice live?"

"Thirteenth and Prospect."

Mrs. Bridge took up a little silver knife and began to cut a slice of peach which was rather too large to be eaten in one bite. She knew where Thirteenth and Prospect was, although she had never stopped there. It was a mixed neighborhood.

"Can I go?"

Mrs. Bridge smiled affectionately at Carolyn. "I wouldn't if I were you."

*

18

Never Speak to Strange Men

It was necessary to be careful among people you did not know. Mrs. Bridge did not wish to be rude, but, as her husband had more than once reminded her, and as anyone could see from the newspapers, there were all kinds of people in the world, and this, together with several other reasons, was why she did not want Carolyn running around in the north end of town.

Not long after Alice's invitation had been rejected Mrs. Bridge was downtown shopping, paying very little attention to the people around her, when all at once she was conscious that a man was staring at her. She could not help glancing at him. She saw only that he was in his forties and that he was not badly dressed. She turned away and walked to another counter, but he followed her.

"How do you do?" he began, smiling and touching the brim of his hat.

Mrs. Bridge grew a little frightened and began looking around for assistance.

The man's face became red and he laughed awkwardly. "I'm Henry Schmidt," he said. There was a pause. He added nervously, "Gladys Schmidt's husband."

"Oh, for heaven's sake!" Mrs. Bridge exclaimed. "I didn't recognize you."

They talked for a few minutes. He mentioned having seen Ruth coming out of a movie the previous week and commented that she was growing into quite a beauty, for which Mrs. Bridge thanked him. Finally he tipped his hat and said good-by.

"It's so nice to see you," she responded. "Do say hello to Gladys for me. We really should get together some evening."

*

19

Grace Barron

Grace Barron was a puzzle and she was disturbing. She belonged in the country-club district, for Virgil was a banker, and yet she seemed dissatisfied there. Mrs. Bridge could not altogether grasp whatever it was Grace Barron was seeking, or criticizing, or saying.

Grace Barron had once said to her, "India, I've never been anywhere or done anything or seen anything. I don't know how other people live, or think, even how they believe. Are we right? Do we believe the right things?"

And on another occasion, when Mrs. Bridge had passed a nice compliment on her home, Grace replied, "Virgil spent fifty thousand dollars on this place." It had not been a boast; it had been an expression of dissatisfaction.

At luncheons, Auxiliary meetings, and cocktail parties Mrs. Bridge always found herself talking about such matters as the by-laws of certain committees, antique silver, Royal Doulton, Wedgwood, the price of margarine as compared to butter, or what the hemline was expected to do, but since Grace Barron had entered the circle she found herself fumbling for answers because Grace talked of other things—art, politics, astronomy, literature. After such a conversation Mrs. Bridge felt inadequate and confused, if a little flattered and refreshed, and on the way home she would think of what she should have said, and could have said, instead of only smiling and replying, "It does seem too bad," or, "Well, yes, I expect that's true."

Said Mr. Bridge, glancing over the edge of his evening newspaper while she was talking about Grace Barron, "Ask her if she wants one to marry her daughter."

Mrs. Bridge replied defensively, "They just have a son." She knew this was a silly remark and added hurriedly, "I suppose you're right, but—"

"If you doubt me, ask her and see what she says."

"Goodness," Mrs. Bridge said, picking up the latest *Tattler,* "suppose we drop the subject. I certainly didn't mean to provoke you so."

Yet she continued to think about many things Grace Barron had said and about Grace herself because she was different somehow. The first time she had ever seen Grace was one afternoon in October of the previous year, and she could remember it so clearly because it was the day of the first Italian air raid against Ethiopia. In Kansas City the sun was shining and the leaves of the trees were changing color. It was a beautiful day. The Barrons had just moved into the neighborhood and Madge Arlen, whose husband had attended high school with Virgil Barron, was going to stop by and get acquainted, and Mrs. Bridge went along. The Barrons had moved into an enormous Colonial home near Meyer Circle, and that afternoon as Mrs. Bridge and Madge Arlen drove up to the house they saw a gang of boys playing football in the street. Apparently Grace Barron was not at home because no one answered the bell; they were about to leave when one of the boys came running up from the street. He stopped and kicked the ball back to the other players, then jumped over a flower bed, and with a whoop and a wave came running straight across the lawn.

"That must be her son," Madge Arlen observed.

"His name will be mud if she catches him leaping over her flowers," said Mrs. Bridge.

They waited, a trifle critically, for him to approach. He was wearing a baggy sweatshirt, faded blue jeans, dirty white tennis shoes, and a baseball cap. He was a thin, graceful boy, about the same height as Douglas, and as he came nearer they could see that he had freckles and a snub nose. He was laughing and panting for breath.

"Hello!" he called, and at that moment they realized he was not a boy at all. It was Grace Barron.

And Mrs. Bridge recalled with equal clarity an evening when she and Grace attended an outdoor symphony. Music was one of the things Mrs. Bridge had always wanted to know more about, and so she was pleased, if startled, when Grace, whom she scarcely knew, simply telephoned one evening and asked if she would like to go to the concert in the park. They sat on folding chairs and listened, and it was like nothing else Mrs. Bridge had ever experienced. When the symphony ended, while the musicians were packing away their instruments and the conductor was autographing programs, Grace suggested they come to the next concert.

"I'd love to!" Mrs. Bridge exclaimed. "When is it?" And upon learning the date she said regretfully, "Oh, dear, the Noel Johnsons are having a few people over for cocktails—"

"That's all right," Grace interrupted. "I know how it is."

And there was an afternoon when they happened to run into each other downtown. Mrs. Bridge was looking over some new ovenware she had heard advertised on the radio. She decided not to buy, and in the course of wandering around the store she suddenly came upon Grace Barron staring fixedly at a gift item—an arrangement of tiny silver bells that revolved around an elaborate candlestick.

"Oh, isn't this tricky!" Mrs. Bridge said, having a look at the price tag. "But I think they're asking too much."

"I feel like those bells," said Grace. "Why are they turning around, India? Why? Because the candle has been lighted. What I want to say is—oh, I don't know. It's just that the orbit is so small." She resumed staring at the contrivance, which went slowly around and around and gave out a faint, exquisite tinkling.

20

What's Up, Señora Bridge?

Spanish was a subject she had long meant to study, and quite often she remarked to her friends that she wished she had studied it in school. The children had heard her say this, so for her birthday that year they gave her an album of phonograph records consisting of a lethargic dialogue between Señor Carreño of Madrid and an American visitor named Señora Brown. Along with the records came an attractive booklet of instructions and suggestions. Mrs. Bridge was delighted with the gift and made a joke about how she intended to begin her lessons the first thing "mañana."

As it turned out, however, she was busy the following day, and the day after because of a PTA meeting at the school, and the day after. Somehow or other more than a month passed before she found time to begin, but there came a morning when she resolved to get at it, and so, after helping Harriet with the breakfast dishes, she found her reading glasses and sat down in the living room with the instruction booklet. The course did not sound at all difficult, and the more pages she read the more engrossing it became. The instructions were clear enough: she was simply to listen to each line of dialogue and then, in the pause that followed, to repeat the part of Señora Brown.

She put the first record on the phonograph, turning it low enough so that the mailman or any delivery boys would not overhear and think she had gone out of her mind. Seated on the sofa directly opposite the machine she waited, holding onto the booklet in case there should be an emergency.

"Buenas días, Señora Brown," the record began, appropriately enough. "Cómo está usted?"

"Buenas días, Señor Carreño," Señora Brown answered. "Muy bien, gracias. Y usted?"

The record waited for Mrs. Bridge who, however, was afraid it would begin before she had a chance to speak, and in consequence only leaned forward with her lips parted. She got up, walked across to the phonograph, and lifted the needle back to the beginning.

"Buenas días, Señora Brown. Cómo está usted?"

"Buenas días, Señor Carreño," replied Señora Brown all over again. "Muy bien, gracias. Y usted?"

"Buenas días, Señor Carreño," said Mrs. Bridge with increasing confidence. "Muy bien, gracias. Y usted?"

"Muy bien," said Señor Carreño.

Just then Harriet appeared to say that Mrs. Arlen was on the telephone. Mrs. Bridge put the booklet on the sofa and went into the breakfast room, where the telephone was.

"Hello, Madge. I've been meaning to phone you about the Auxiliary luncheon next Friday. They've changed the time from twelve-thirty to one. Honestly, I wish they'd make up their minds."

"Charlotte told me yesterday. You knew Grace Barron was ill with flu, didn't you?"

"Oh, not really! She has the worst luck."

"If it isn't one thing, it's another. She's been down since day before yesterday. I'm running by with some lemonade and thought you might like to come along. I can only stay a split second. I'm due at the hairdresser at eleven."

"Well, I'm in slacks. Are you going right away?"

"The instant the laundress gets here. That girl! She should have been here hours ago. Honestly, I'm at the end of my rope."

"Don't tell me you're having that same trouble! I sometimes think they do it deliberately just to put people out. We're trying a new one and she does do nice work, but she's so independent."

"Oh," said Madge Arlen, as if her head were turned away from the phone, "here she comes. Lord, what next?"

"Well, I'll dash right upstairs and change," said Mrs. Bridge. "I suppose the garden can wait till tomorrow." And after telling Harriet that she would be at Mrs. Barron's if anyone called, she started toward the stairs.

"Qué tal, Señora Brown?" inquired the record.

Mrs. Bridge hurried into the living room, snapped off the phonograph, and went upstairs.

21

The Leacocks

New people in the neighborhood never failed to provide a topic for discussion. As time went by and they became more familiar they became, naturally, less newsworthy; the Leacocks, however, seemed more remarkable with every passing day. The family consisted of Dr. Gail Leacock, who was not a physician but an academic doctor—an associate professor of psychology—his wife Lucienne, who was reputedly quite wealthy, and Tarquin. Tarquin was about the same age as Douglas but here all similarity ended. For one thing, Tarquin was said to have an IQ of 185. Mrs. Bridge had not the vaguest notion what Douglas's IQ might be, and she was not particularly anxious to have him tested; not that she thought he was dull, but it would be just like him deliberately to answer the questions wrong. The discrepancy between their intellects, whatever it might be, was only the focal point of the difference between them; Douglas and Tarquin were, to say the least, oil and water.

Dr. Leacock, like the majority of husbands, was seldom seen in the daytime, but Mrs. Leacock and Tarquin liked to visit about the neighborhood, and within a few weeks of their arrival it had become evident that for some reason they had chosen Mrs. Bridge as a special friend. Mrs. Bridge, somewhat disconcerted by Lucienne Leacock's progressive ideas and a little frightened by Tarquin's self-possession, nevertheless felt vaguely flattered at being the object of so much attention.

One afternoon, while the three of them were drinking iced tea on the back porch, Douglas came sauntering home from a baseball game. He was barefoot—his sneakers were tied together by the laces and were dangling around his neck so that the toes bumped against his chest—and he had an apple in his mouth, and as he approached it became obvious that he was trying to eat the apple without using his hands. He was twisting his head around and making agonized faces. He did not see the visitors until he had opened the screen door. Then he stopped dead, looked first at Tarquin, then at Mrs. Leacock, then at his mother, and then back at Tarquin. Unmistakably —Mrs. Bridge saw this—Tarquin's upper lip curled backward in a sneer. Slowly Douglas took the apple out of his mouth and said in a low voice, in which there was no ignoring the hostility, "How'd you like a punch in the snoot?"

Mrs. Bridge had trained her children to be courteous no matter what occurred, for she valued courtesy as highly as she valued cleanliness, honesty, thrift, consideration, and other such qualities. Douglas, though rebellious, had never failed her when, so to speak, the chips were down. She knew he disliked being polite to visitors, but he was, nonetheless; in fact, though he grumbled more than his sisters, Mrs. Bridge had noticed with some surprise that he was actually less apt to be rude to guests than were the girls. He did try hard to be decent, and she knew it was difficult for him. He had been doing so well recently that she was flabbergasted by his remark to Tarquin, and by the absolute antagonism apparent in his stance—he was now standing just inside the screen with his fists balled and his head thrust truculently forward. Mrs. Bridge was so amazed that for several seconds she was unable to speak. Upon recovering her wits she began to get to her feet but was restrained by Mrs. Leacock who had been smiling rather earnestly at Douglas from the moment he first wandered into view.

"What else would you do, Doug?" said Mrs. Leacock. "We'd like to hear."

Douglas then gave her a long, baleful stare. Mrs. Bridge had not been so shocked in years. Without a word, as though there were no one on the porch, Douglas put the apple in his mouth and slowly backed out the door and around the corner of the house.

"Young man," Mrs. Bridge began, furiously shaking a finger at him when she found him sitting in the rafters of the garage a few minutes after the departure of the guests, "I don't know what got into you and I honestly don't care, but you're most certainly going to hear from your father when he gets home."

Douglas stepped across to another rafter and peered into the corner where some wasps had built a nest.

"What in the world made you behave like that?" demanded Mrs. Bridge, who was as nonplused as she was humiliated.

Douglas mumbled; it was not clear what he said.

"Well, I don't care whether you like him or not," she continued, assuming he had made some reference to Tarquin. "When we have guests you'll treat them courteously. How would you like it if we visited them and Tarquin behaved as you did?"

"I'm not going to visit them," he answered, still looking at the wasp nest.

"Well," said Mrs. Bridge after a pause, "we're not going to have any more of that, and that's final. Now I mean business. I've never been so ashamed in my life."

Douglas was sorry he had embarrassed his mother, but he could not say so. With his arms outstretched for balance he began to walk the length of the rafter.

"You're going to fall and break your neck," said Mrs. Bridge.

Douglas did not reply. He teetered a little and his mother gasped. He had only meant to frighten her but he had gotten a little farther off balance than he intended and had scared himself, so he sat down and began to swing his legs.

"The next time they're here you're going to behave yourself, is that clear?" She spoke as severely as possible, but by this time she knew that somehow he had defeated her.

A small, affirmative noise came from him and she decided that was the most she could hope for, at least for the time being. She returned to the house, puzzled by the violence of his reaction. Tarquin of course had been extremely rude to sneer, and, in truth, Mrs. Bridge herself did not like Tarquin. Even so she was baffled by Douglas's extraordinary hostility, and she was quite apprehensive about the future.

The Leacocks continued to appear, unannounced, **every**

few weeks—Tarquin always with a book—and Douglas was unquestionably able to divine their approach, because he vanished a few minutes before they arrived and nobody could find him until shortly after they had gone. Mrs. Bridge, while disapproving of some of the things Tarquin did and said, was nevertheless impressed by his brilliance.

Progressive education was Lucienne Leacock's favorite topic of conversation; politics was second. Mrs. Bridge did not know a great deal about either. Mrs. Leacock was a Socialist who voted the straight Democratic ticket because, as she phrased it, "We poor bloody Socialists never have a chance." Mrs. Bridge had never before known a Socialist, and only a very few Democrats, moderate Democrats at that, and she felt slightly guilty as she sat on the porch or in the living room listening to Mrs. Leacock lambast the conservatives.

As for the public educational system, well, she could not speak of it without profanity, and at every word Mrs. Bridge inwardly flinched. Superior children, the same as Socialists, did not have a chance. The system was geared to bourgeois mediocrity. Tarquin, as anyone could guess, attended a private school and he was as voluble a critic of public education as his mother, despite the fact he had never been inside a public school. He seemed unusually scornful of the school Douglas attended. Mrs. Leacock listened with an intent, forceful expression to whatever he said, afterward suggesting how he might have expressed himself more vigorously.

Progressive education had certainly developed Tarquin's sense of being an individual, but some of the results were so startling that Mrs. Bridge was reduced to a bewildered silence. One April afternoon while they were enjoying the rose garden Mrs. Leacock suddenly threw back her head and gave a loud neighing laugh and then, fixing Mrs. Bridge with a forcible look, she said, "Priceless! I must tell you. About two years ago when we lived in—New Haven?" She looked at Tarquin to see if her memory was correct.

"New Haven," said Tarquin, grinning.

"This young monster threw a temper tantrum, and what a tantrum! He set fire to the garage."

"I used benzine," said Tarquin indifferently as he began to pull the petals from a particularly fine rose. "I should have used kerosene."

Mrs. Bridge often thought about that afternoon. She did not think the Leacocks had been joking; on the other hand it seemed impossible that Tarquin could be so irresponsible. She was puzzled and irked and could not finally decide how she felt toward the Leacocks: at times she was positive she disliked them, then a moment later she would feel ashamed of herself. If only Tarquin would not curse! Mrs. Bridge had no use for profanity; she had always considered it not only vulgar but unnecessary, and was distressed by the fact that Lucienne Leacock encouraged the boy to swear. Furthermore, Tarquin smoked cigarettes and was allowed to stay up as late at night as he wanted to; yet he was not an adult, he was a boy, a large, shambling fleshy boy with a flushed, freckled complexion and moist red lips the color of liver. His eyes were alert and glassy, yellowish-brown and luminous like the eyes of a dog, and very knowing; it was all Mrs. Bridge could do to look him straight in the eye, and, what was worse, she knew he was aware of this and relished it. He clearly enjoyed catching and holding her attention until she could hardly keep from shuddering.

"Why don't you tell India what you said to your science adviser yesterday?" his mother suggested. She was wearing moccasins and white wool athletic socks and a baggy skirt and sweater, so that she looked like a high-school girl, except for her face, which was creased and shriveled like the face of a very old woman.

"Lucienne, really!" said her son. "How can I possibly express myself in regard to a man so jejune?" And he drew on his cigarette with a look of boredom. Mrs. Bridge was fascinated and exasperated whenever he pulled out a cigarette; the whole thing was beyond her understanding.

Although Douglas was absent whenever Mrs. Leacock and Tarquin were around, he was evidently somewhere within earshot, because one evening during an argument with his father about the size of his allowance he blurted, "Jeez, how am I supposed to express myself with nothing but a measly fifty cents a week?"

"What's that?" demanded Mr. Bridge, lowering the newspaper through which the discussion had been carried on.

"Well, I gotta express my personality, don't I?"

"Express your personality?" asked Mr. Bridge, and gazed at his son curiously.

"That's what Tarquin does. He gets to express it whenever he feels like it."

Mr. Bridge and Douglas studied each other for a while, one of them bemused and the other defiant, and Mrs. Bridge waited uneasily to find out how it was going to end.

"You'll express yourself when I say you can," Mr. Bridge replied quietly. He shook up the newspaper and continued reading.

*

22

Victim of Circumstances

There was another expressionist in the neighborhood, a boy several years older than Tarquin Leacock, whom Douglas avoided with equal assiduity, though for a different reason. His name was Peters and he was a bully.

One evening it was long after dark when Douglas finally came home. He was exhausted and covered with dirt, although this in itself was not remarkable.

"Where *have* you been?" Mrs. Bridge cried, rushing toward him the moment he entered the house. "We've been looking high and low for you. I was just about to phone the police."

"It was that big Peters guy's fault," Douglas said in a low voice. He wiped his nose on the sleeve of his sweatshirt and trudged upstairs to his room.

"Well, thank heavens you're safe, at least," she resumed when he came down. He looked a little more respectable. "Where on earth were you?"

He replied that he had been on top of Pfeiffer's garage.

"Until twenty minutes to nine?" she asked with as much sarcasm as she could muster, and this was not much.

"I figured it was probably later than that," he muttered very glumly. "It felt like it was about midnight."

She followed him to the breakfast room, where Harriet was setting his place.

"What were you doing on Pfeiffer's garage? I'm sure they didn't want you up there."

He started to answer, then sneezed, started to wipe his nose with his hand and then, thinking better of it, took out his handkerchief.

"I was hiding," he said and sneezed again.

"Hiding! From whom, may I ask?"

"From that big Peters guy," he replied with some annoyance, as though she should have known. "What did you think I was going to do, stick my head up and get it blown off?"

"I think you'd better explain yourself, young man, or your father's going to hear about this."

"That's okay with me," he muttered.

"All right, now. Begin at the beginning."

"Well," he said, wearily buttering a slice of bread, "he just chased me up there, that's all there is to it."

"Who chased you? What *are* you talking about?"

He put down the bread and explained with elaborate emphasis. "That big fat slob Peters. He trapped me on top of Pfeiffer's garage and wouldn't let me come down. Every time I'd stick my head up he took a shot at me. He almost hit me a couple of times."

"Do you mean he had a gun?"

"Well, what did you think he was shooting at me with?" He glanced uncertainly at his mother, knowing he had been rather impertinent, knowing secondly that he was not supposed to end a sentence with a preposition, but he saw that this time he would get away with both. She had the shocked look she sometimes got.

"What sort of a gun?"

"Oh, it was a beebee gun, one of those pump guns. He'd pumped it up about seventy-five times, I guess, because every time he took a shot at me it'd knock off a piece of cement. I guess," he added thoughtfully, "you could just about kill a horse with a good pump gun if you pumped long enough."

Mrs. Bridge did not know exactly what he was talking about, but she did know that he knew what he was talking about.

"Why on earth was he shooting at you?" she asked, rather weakly. She had never come up against a situation like this.

Douglas shrugged. "He just wanted to. I don't know. I didn't ask him, you can bet on that. He'd of probably shot my block off."

"But you must have provoked him."

"Oh, sure! A guy about sixteen times as big as me that's got a pump gun. That's a big laugh. Hah!"

"I'm going to telephone the police," she said resolutely, because it did seem like something the police would be interested in.

"Okay by me," said Douglas. "I guess they can find him easy

enough if they just hang around Pfeiffer's garage. He's probably got somebody else up there by this time."

"Well, who is he? Does he live around there?"

"I don't know. All I know is he just hangs around that
garage."

"But *why?*" There was something nightmarish about the
whole affair.

Douglas, however, was not in the least mystified. "Well, because it's a good garage for trapping littler kids so they can't
get away. It's flat on top and it's got this kind of a little tiny
wall around the top. So he just hangs around there and usually
about the time school gets out he catches somebody on their
way home and starts shooting, so naturally they go up the
telephone pole and scrooch down behind the wall. He always
runs them that way," he added as a final explanation. After a
pause he said moodily, "I usually detour, but I guess today I
was thinking about something else and forgot. Then all of a
sudden *zing!*—and boy, I jumped about a thousand feet in
the air, believe me! So anyway I went up the telephone pole
like I said, because I figured he could probably outrun me
even if he is a big slob, and then there wasn't any way to get
down except the same way and he was there with that old
pump gun. I didn't think he was ever going to leave."

"Why didn't you call for help?"

"Well, because if I did he'd of probably got sore at me and
then I'd really've got fixed."

Mrs. Bridge had become so confused that she could not even
begin to understand this statement; she gazed at him in despair. "Well, don't you know where this boy lives?"

Douglas shook his head.

"He must go to school somewhere, doesn't he?"

Douglas didn't know. "He's one of those big high-school
guys, except he's probably too dumb. They probably expelled
him."

"But you must know something about him."

"He's a big fat slob!" Douglas said, flaring up. He was getting peeved with his mother for asking so many questions; he had been trapped on the garage, he had escaped, that was all there was to it. He hated Peters, but that was irrelevant. He wished his mother would drop the subject.

The case had begun to seem a little weaker to Mrs. Bridge. She was on the point of telephoning the Sixty-third Street police station, for she was certain Douglas was telling the truth and she knew perfectly well that a beebee gun could put out someone's eye, and yet she could not very well call the police station to report a high-school boy with a beebee gun—just that and nothing more.

"But can't you tell me anything about him? Anything at all?"

Douglas shook his head. He could have found out more about Peters, but there was no need to. He would avoid Pfeiffer's from now on and that was all there was to it.

"I'm going to tell your father about that boy," she said positively. "Something ought to be done about him."

"Okay by me," Douglas assented. "Can I have some more potatoes and gravy?"

"*May* I?"

"Okay, *may* I?"

*

23

Rock Fight

Mr. Bridge did hear about the next adventure.

On his way home from the public school one afternoon shortly before the start of summer vacation, Douglas came across Tarquin seated beneath a chestnut tree. There was a book in his lap and he seemed to be innocently reading. Douglas was carrying a weed he had pulled up, and was using it to whip the horse on which he was making an escape from some Indians.

"Whoa!" said Douglas softly, reining to a stop. Then, conscious that Tarquin knew about the fictitious horse and was snickering at him, he abandoned the game and dropped the weed.

"Hello," Tarquin said without moving.

After a pause Douglas said, "H'llo." After another pause, during which he gazed up into the branches of the chestnut tree and industriously scratched first one ankle and then the other, he added, "What're you doing here?"

"Haven't I a right to be here?"

Douglas was thinking this over when Tarquin suddenly threw a rock at him. He had kept the rock hidden under the book. Douglas saw it coming and ducked, but even so it scraped the side of his head.

"Okay," he said. "You asked for it," and ran forward with his fists doubled up.

When he got home later that afternoon, after stopping by the high school to watch the track team at practice, and having searched the bleachers for valuables, he was disconcerted to find not only that his father was at home but that he had heard about the fight with Tarquin. Mrs. Leacock had telephoned Mr. Bridge at the office.

"Well, he started it," said Douglas defensively, and when told to continue with his version of the fight he said, "Well, he sort of jumped up and took out across the streetcar tracks toward Wornall Road, so I took after him—and boy, I just about didn't make it—and he kept yelling over his shoulder how I better not touch him because he knew how to fight with jiu-jitsu and—"

"What do you mean you just about didn't make it? Didn't make what?"

"Boy, that streetcar just about got me. But anyway, he—"

"Tell this to me again," said Mr. Bridge. He had been standing up; now he seated himself and listened to the story with extreme attention. "Do you mean," he asked, "that Tarquin threw the rock at you and led you across the tracks in front of a streetcar?"

Douglas nodded enthusiastically. He had, in fact, come very close to being hit.

"I see," Mr. Bridge said. For a long time he was lost in thought, but finally he glanced up and said, "I understand you caught him."

"Oh, sure. He runs like a girl. That's because he's knock-kneed."

"So then what transpired?"

Douglas gazed at his father doubtfully.

"What happened next?"

"Oh. Well, let's see. I sort of punched him in the nose once or twice, I think."

"You think?"

"I guess I did."

"Was that the end of the fight?"

"Pretty much. I suppose you could actually say it was because he started to bawl like a little kid, so—uh—that's about
all."

"Go on."

Douglas groaned and made an agonized face. He was embarrassed about this next item because he knew he had not
behaved very well. Unfortunately it was impossible to distract
his father in the way he could usually distract his mother, so
he did not even try to change the subject. Reluctantly he said,
"I can't stand cry-babies."

"Go on."

Douglas heaved a deep sigh. "Okay, okay. I hauled off and
socked him one in the breadbasket."

"While he was lying down?"

"He was up. I mean he was up when I let him have it in the
breadbasket. Then he fell down again and wouldn't get up
any more even when I dared him to. He only lay there and
screamed about how he was going to stab me to death."
Scarcely had he finished saying this when he became aware of
a change in his father's attitude; inquiringly he looked at his
father, and next at his mother, who had been lingering in the
hall.

With modest pride he concluded, "I guess he won't bother
anybody any more, not after what I did to him." He was astonished when his father reached forward and grabbed his
arm. "I can fix his wagon any old day!" Douglas shouted. He
was frightened at finding himself caught like this and he did
not know what was going on.

"Listen, son," his father said earnestly. "If that boy starts
another fight I want you to do something. Are you listening
to me?"

"What do you want?"

"I want you to walk away. Don't take your eyes off him, just
walk away, that's all."

Douglas attempted to twist out of the grip on his arm. He was deeply surprised by his father's strength. His arm had begun to throb from the pain. He was confused and defiant, and all that occurred to him was that he was being asked to run away from a fight, and not only that but from a boy he knew he could lick.

"Do you hear me?"

"Well, why?"

"Never mind why."

"Okay," he responded grudgingly, but added, as soon as his arm was released, "only he better cut out throwing rocks at me."

"Under no circumstances. I want this clearly understood."

"All right," he said. He was resentful and ashamed. More than anything else he was afraid of being thought a coward.

After he had gone upstairs his parents were silent for a few minutes. Mr. Bridge was thoughtful and Mrs. Bridge was waiting for what he would say.

"That Leacock boy is going to kill somebody one of these days," he observed.

"I do think they let him run wild," she agreed, "but I'm certain he wouldn't do anything really wrong."

"You just watch," he said angrily.

"It *was* awfully strange about setting the garage on fire," she admitted. "And gracious, I certainly don't approve of fighting, but it does seem that Douglas can look out for himself."

"Douglas is a boy and thinks like a boy. Tarquin Leacock has the mind of an adult."

"Well," said Mrs. Bridge as she put on her reading glasses and opened the latest copy of *The Tattler*, "if that's the case, I shouldn't think there'd be much to worry about."

*

24

Advanced Training

Appearances were an abiding concern of Mrs. Bridge, which was the reason that one evening as she saw Ruth preparing to go out she inquired, "Aren't you taking a purse, dear?"

Ruth answered in a husky voice that whatever she needed she could carry in her pockets.

Said Mrs. Bridge, "Carolyn always takes a purse."

Ruth was standing in front of the hall mirror, standing in a way that disturbed Mrs. Bridge, though she did not know precisely why, unless it could be that Ruth's feet were too far apart and her hips a little too forward. Mrs. Bridge had been trying to cure her of this habit by making her walk around the house with a book balanced on her head, but as soon as the book was removed Ruth resumed sauntering and standing in that unseemly posture.

"And you're older than Corky," Mrs. Bridge went on with a frown; and yet, looking at her elder daughter, she could not continue frowning. Ruth really was quite lovely, just as Gladys Schmidt's husband had said; if only she were not so conscious of it, not so aware of people turning to look at her, for they did stop to look—men and women both—so deliberately sometimes that Mrs. Bridge grew uneasy, and could not get over the idea that Ruth, by her posture and her challenging walk, was encouraging people to stare.

"Is somebody coming by for you?"

"I'm only going to the drugstore."

"What on earth do you do in the drugstore?" asked Mrs. Bridge after a pause. "Madge Arlen told me she saw you there one evening sitting all by yourself in a booth. She said she supposed you were waiting for someone."

At this Ruth stiffened noticeably, and Mrs. Bridge wanted to ask, "Were you?"

"I really don't approve of you sitting around in drugstores," she went on, for she was afraid to ask directly if Ruth was going there to meet a boy—not afraid of asking the question, but of the answer. "And I don't believe your father would approve of it either," she continued, feeling helpless and querulous in the knowledge that her daughter was hardly listening. "Goodness, I should think you could find something else to do. What about playing with Carolyn and her friends?"

Ruth didn't bother to answer.

"I'll lend you my blue suede purse, if you like," said Mrs. Bridge hopefully, but again there was no response. Ruth was still admiring herself in the mirror.

"I shouldn't think you could carry much in those pockets."

Ruth stepped backward, narrowed her eyes, and unfastened the top button of her blouse.

"Really, you *need* some things," Mrs. Bridge remarked a trifle sharply. "And button yourself up, for goodness sake. You look like a chorus girl."

"Good night," said Ruth flatly and started for the door.

"But, dear, a lady always carries a purse!" Mrs. Bridge was saying when the door closed.

25

From Another World

Ruth was not particularly extravagant, in contrast to Carolyn, who spent her allowance the day she received it—usually on a scarf or a baggy sweater, despite the fact that her dresser drawers were filled with scarves and sweaters—but Mrs. Bridge did not approve of Ruth's taste. Her allowance was apt to go for a necklace, or a sheer blouse, or a pair of extreme earrings. The earrings were impossible. Mrs. Bridge, whose preference in earrings tended toward the inconspicuous, such as a moderately set pearl, tried to restrain herself whenever she caught sight of Ruth wearing something unusually objectionable, but there was one morning when she appeared for breakfast in Mexican huaraches, Japanese silk pajamas with the sleeves rolled up—displaying a piece of adhesive tape where she had cut herself while shaving her forearms—blue horn-rimmed reading glasses, and for earrings a cluster of tiny golden bells that tinkled whenever she moved. She might have gotten by that morning except for the fact that as she ate she steadily relaxed and contracted her feet so that the huaraches creaked.

"Now see here, young lady," Mrs. Bridge said with more authority than she felt, as she dropped a slice of bread into the automatic toaster. "In the morning one doesn't wear earrings that dangle. People will think you're something from another world."

"So?" said Ruth without looking up from the newspaper.

"Just what do you mean by that?"

"So who cares?"

"*I* care, that's who!" Mrs. Bridge cried, suddenly very close to hysteria. "I care very much."

*

26

Tower

Douglas did a peculiar thing.

Instead of building a cave, or a house in a tree, as most of his friends were doing, he chose to build a tower of rubbish.

"Sounds awfully exciting," Mrs. Bridge responded somewhat absently when he first told her of his project; then, because she knew children wanted their parents to be interested in what they were doing, she asked how big it was going to be. He was vague, saying only that it was going to be the biggest tower anybody ever saw. She smiled and patted him affectionately. He looked at her for a long moment, shrugged in a singular way, and returned to the vacant lot where he intended to build the tower.

In the lot he had found some two-by-fours and a number of old bricks and half a bag of cement. He did not know where these materials had come from; he waited several days to see if they belonged to anybody. Apparently they didn't, so he claimed them. He got a shovel and went to work.

Having dug a hole about four feet deep, he lined it with brick and cement, planted the two-by-fours solidly upright, and liberally sprinkled this foundation with water. He then waited for his friends, the trash collectors, and followed their truck around the neighborhood. There was a moment between the time a rubbish barrel was rolled to the curb and the time the truck stopped for it that Douglas made good use of; he grabbed anything he thought belonged on his tower. He collected a great quantity of useful objects, and, on the side, about forty or fifty cereal boxtops, which he mailed to such places as Battle Creek, where there was a cereal factory, getting in return all kinds of prizes.

Within a week he had accumulated enough junk to keep the construction going for a long while. Half-hidden in the tall grass and wild shrubbery of the vacant lot lay a bundle of brass curtain rods which the Arlens thought were now in the city dump, a roll of electrician's tape and a bent skillet from the Pfeiffers' trash barrel, a hatchet with a splintered handle, a cigar box full of rusty nails, a broken fishing rod, several lengths of clothesline and wire, coat hangers, bottles, two apple boxes, an old raincoat and a pair of worn galoshes, a punctured inner tube, some very old golf clubs with wooden shafts, the cylinder from a lawnmower, springs from an overstuffed chair, and, among other articles, thanks again to the unconscious generosity of the Arlens, a mildewed leather suitcase.

"My!" said Mrs. Bridge, when he told her he was working on the tower, "I can see you're going to be an architect or an engineer when you grow up. Now we're having an early lunch because this is my day for bridge club, so don't run off somewhere."

Douglas said he would be in the vacant lot.

During the next week he managed to steal a full bag of powdered cement from a house going up in the next block; he broke it open after the workmen left, shoveled the powder into a wheelbarrow, and eventually managed to push the wheelbarrow into the vacant lot, where he dumped the powder in the pit and gave it a thorough watering. Thereafter he stopped mentioning his tower, and if asked what he was doing in the lot he would reply laconically that he was just playing.

With the addition of jugs and stones, tin cans, tree limbs, broken bottles, and all the other trash he could find, tied or nailed or cemented to the uprights, the tower continued to grow, until there came a Sunday morning when a man named Ewing who lived on the far side of the lot saw the tower rising above his hedge. At this point it was nearly six feet high. Ewing went around for a better look, and, discovering Douglas watching him from behind a sycamore tree, said to him, "What have you got here, my friend?"

"Nothing," replied Douglas, coming out from behind the sycamore. "It's just a tower, that's all. It isn't hurting anybody."

Having inspected the tower from all sides, Ewing turned his attention to Douglas, because it was the builder, after all, and not the building which was remarkable; and Douglas, embarrassed by the speculative eyes, picked up a length of pipe and struck the tower a resounding blow to prove it was as substantial as it looked.

Shortly thereafter Mrs. Bridge saw it too—it rose jaggedly above the fence that divided their grounds from the lot—and went out to investigate. She looked at it for a considerable period, tapping a fingernail against her teeth, and that same afternoon she said lightly to her son, "My, but that certainly is a big old tower."

Douglas thrust his hands in his pockets and gazed with a distant expression at his shoes.

"Think what would happen if it fell over ker-*plunk* and hit you square on the head," she continued, ruffling his hair, and reflecting automatically that he needed another haircut.

Douglas knew his tower would stop a truck, so he only sighed and pursed his lips.

Mrs. Bridge was not overly concerned, being under the impression he was going to become bored with the tower and would dismantle it. But about two weeks later she realized he was still working on it, because she could see a cider jug and a chicken coop wired to the top of a broken chair, and she recalled that on her last visit this chair had been on top of everything. She had assumed this chair was his throne; she remembered how he liked to play king-of-the-mountain, and possibly he only built the tower in order to have a throne. Now, wondering how much higher he meant to go, she walked out to the vacant lot for another look, and this time she remained somewhat longer. Tentatively she pushed at the tower and was troubled by its solidity. She pushed again, with her palm, and again, much harder. The tower did not sway an inch. She began to wonder whether or not he would be able to destroy his creation—assuming she could convince him it ought to be torn down.

She intended to speak to him that same afternoon, but she did not know precisely how to begin because, like the tower, he seemed to be growing out of her reach. He was becoming more than a small boy who could be coaxed this way or that; the hour was approaching when she must begin to reason with him as with an adult, and this idea disturbed her. She was not certain she was equal to it. And so a few days, a week, two weeks went by, and though she had not spoken neither had she forgotten.

"Well!" she finally exclaimed, as though she had just thought of it, "I see that ugly old tower keeps getting bigger and bigger." It was, to tell the truth, quite a bit bigger. When he did not say a word, or even look at her, she wanted to grab him by the shoulders and shake loose whatever was growing inside him.

"It seems to me that a big boy like you wouldn't want to go on building a silly tower," she said, hopefully, and then he glanced at her in a way that was somehow derisive, as if he were reading her mind.

"I'll tell you what let's do!" She stooped in order to look directly into his face. "First thing after dinner we'll get some wire clippers and a hammer and a screwdriver and—well, just everything we need, and you and I together will tear it to bits. Won't that be fun?"

He turned his head away and said very softly, "No."

"No? Why not?"

After a while Douglas rubbed his nose and muttered that there was too much concrete.

"Oh, I'll bet we—" Mrs. Bridge hesitated. Her insights usually arrived too late to illuminate the situation, but this one was in time.

"You're probably right," she said, continuing with treacherous frankness, "I doubt if you or anybody else could tear it down."

She watched him almost fall into the trap. He was ready to defy her by saying he could if he wanted to, and if she could get him to say that she knew the battle would be half over. He was on the verge of it; she could see the defiance on his face and in the way he stood. But then, instead of answering, he paused to think, and Mrs. Bridge was dismayed. All her life she had been accustomed to responding immediately when anyone spoke to her. If she had been complimented she promptly and graciously thanked the speaker; or if, by chance, her opinion was asked on something, anything—the cost of butter, the Italian situation—no matter what, if she was asked she answered readily. Now, seeing her son with his mouth clamped shut like a turtle with a seed and his face puckered in thought, she did not know what to do. She gazed down on him expectantly.

After a long silence Douglas said, "Maybe."

And here, for the time being, the matter rested.

*

27

Sentimental Moment

Mrs. Bridge stood alone at a front window thinking of how quickly the years were going by. The children were growing up so rapidly, and her husband— She stirred uneasily. Already there was a new group of "young marrieds," people she hardly knew. Surely some time had gone by—she expected this; nevertheless she could not get over the feeling that something was drawing steadily away from her. She wondered if her husband felt the same; she thought she would ask him that evening when he got home. She recalled the dreams they used to share; she recalled with a smile how she used to listen to him speak of his plans and how she had never actually cared one way or another about his ambition, she had cared only for him. That was enough. In those days she used to think that the long hours he spent in his office were a temporary condition and that as soon as more people came to him with legal problems he would, somehow, begin spending more time at home. But this was not the way it turned out, and Mrs. Bridge understood now that she would never see very much of him. They had started off together to explore something that promised to be wonderful, and, of course, there had been wonderful times. And yet, thought Mrs. Bridge, why is it that we haven't—that nothing has—that whatever we—?

It was raining. Thunder rumbled through the lowering

clouds with a constant, monotonous, trundling sound, like furniture being rolled back and forth in the attic. In the front yard the evergreen trees swayed in the wind and the shutters rattled in the sudden rainy gusts. She noticed that a branch had been torn from the soft maple tree; the branch lay on the driveway and the leaves fluttered.

Harriet came in to ask if she would like some hot chocolate.

"Oh, no thank you, Harriet," said Mrs. Bridge. "You have some."

Harriet was so nice. And she was a good worker. Mrs. Bridge was very proud of having Harriet and knew that she would be next to impossible to replace, and yet there were times when Mrs. Bridge half wished she would quit. Why she wished this, she did not know, unless it was that with Harriet around to do all the work she herself was so often dismally bored. When she was first married she used to do the cooking and house-cleaning and washing, and how she had looked forward to a few minutes of leisure! But now—how odd—there was too much leisure. Mrs. Bridge did not admit this fact to anyone, for it embarrassed her; indeed she very often gave the impression of being distracted by all the things needed to be done— phone the laundry, the grocer, take Ruth to the dentist, Carolyn to tap-dancing class, Douglas to the barber shop, and so on. But the truth remained, and settled upon her with ever greater finality.

The light snapped on in the back hall. She heard his cough and the squeak of the closet door and the familiar flapping sound of his briefcase on the upper shelf. Suddenly over-whelmed by the need for reassurance, she turned swiftly from the window and hurried toward him with an intent, wistful expression, knowing what she wanted without knowing how to ask for it.

He heard the rustle of her dress and her quick footsteps on the carpet. He was hanging up his coat as she approached, and he said, without irritation, but a trifle wearily because this was not the first time it had happened, "I see you forgot to have the car lubricated."

*

28

Soft Gift

She reflected that her difficulties with Ruth and Douglas might be inevitable; after all, years had passed since she was their age.

Each of her own birthdays she celebrated without joy, with a certain resignation and doubt; it came and went as it was supposed to, and a few months later she would find herself depressed and unaccountably perplexed by how old she was. Thirty, thirty-five, forty, all had come to visit her like admonitory relatives, and all had slipped away without a trace, without a sound, and now, once again, she was waiting.

Someone was at the front door; the chimes were jingling sweetly. It was the postman with a package. It was from Memphis. She cut the masking tape, lifted the cardboard flaps, and underneath the excelsior she found a pewter tray in the shape of a clover. She took hold of the stem to lift it out, but the tray, instead of remaining rigid like all the other trays she had ever seen, began to droop. The alloy was much too soft to support its own weight, so that in a few seconds the tray was dangling almost straight down from the handle. Mrs. Bridge was not surprised. She pressed it back into shape, returned it to the box, carried the box to the attic, and that afternoon wrote her annual thank-you note to second-cousin Lulubelle Watts. In years past Mrs. Bridge had received from Lulu such birthday gifts as a bile green kitchen alarm clock, a long-haired pillow, a framed photograph of the Great Smokies, and a pair of heavy bronze balls which apparently should have had an instruction booklet. In thinking over these gifts she often tried to decide whether Lulubelle disliked her and was deliberately insulting her, or whether it was simply that Lulu had the world's worst taste. She also thought of picking out something just as grotesque to send in return, but minding the Golden Rule she always shipped to Memphis on Lulu's birthday some very nice gift in the nature of a leather-covered engagement calendar, guest towels, a cake knife, or a bisque figurine.

29

Nothing Spectacular

At his wife's suggestion Mr. Bridge had walked around to the vacant lot to examine the eccentric and mystifying memorial Douglas had built and which he had not yet abandoned; Mr. Bridge tried to topple it and then simply attempted to shake it. The tower did not move. Satisfied that it would not collapse while Douglas or his friends were clambering about, and that they had sense enough not to impale themselves on the outcroppings, he returned to his evening newspaper and thought no more about it.

Mrs. Bridge, however, was uneasy. She sensed that people in the neighborhood were aware of the tower. Even so, she did not become actively alarmed until a man at a cocktail party, upon being introduced to her, mentioned that he had driven over to see the tower.

"Oh, horrors!" she exclaimed as a means of registering her attitude. "Is it famous all over the city?" And though she was joking she was dead serious.

"A curious form of protest," the man replied, tucking his pipe with tobacco; then, after a sharp glance directly into her eyes, he added, "You *are* aware of the boy's motivation, are you not?"

To which she smiled politely, being somewhat confused, and made a mental note that the man had been drinking.

The next morning as soon as Douglas left for school she telephoned the fire department. Everyone called the fire department when there was a problem that defied classification. Shortly before noon a small red truck parked in front of the house and two firemen—she had never spoken to a fireman before and found the experience rather strange—two of them entered the house as though it were the most natural thing in the world, and listened to what she told them about the tower. Then they went out to have a look. Mildly amused at first, presently they were startled. However they had been called upon by housewives for many unnatural labors, and so they unhooked their tools of destruction and set to work. It took them until almost dark to turn it into a mound of rubble, but at last an area of several square yards was covered with splintered wood, broken glass, wire, great gritty chunks of lumpy concrete, and whatever else had gone into the creation of it, and the air was filled with dust as though there had been a peculiar explosion. The firemen said they would make a report of the tower and its destruction and that the lot would be cleaned up within a day or two.

Douglas, having come home a few minutes before the firemen left, stood watching them in grieved silence. Mrs. Bridge, seeing him from an upstairs window, went out to stand behind him with her hands resting on his shoulders, and occasionally rumpled his hair.

"It was just getting too big," she confided to him gently. "People were beginning to wonder."

* * *

*

30

The Search for Love

It seemed to Mrs. Bridge that she had done the necessary thing, and therefore the right thing, in regard to the monstrous tower. Again and again she thought about it, and the reason she thought about it so intensively was that she perceived a change in Douglas's attitude toward her. He was more withdrawn.

As time went on she felt an increasing need for reassurance. Her husband had never been a demonstrative man, not even when they were first married; consequently she did not expect too much from him. Yet there were moments when she was overwhelmed by a terrifying, inarticulate need. One evening as she and he were finishing supper together, alone, the children having gone out, she inquired rather sharply if he loved her. She was surprised by her own bluntness and by the almost shrewish tone of her voice, because that was not the way she actually felt. She saw him gazing at her in astonishment; his expression said very clearly: Why on earth do you think I'm here if I don't love you? Why aren't I somewhere else? What in the world has got into you?

Mrs. Bridge smiled across the floral centerpiece—and it occurred to her that these flowers she had so carefully arranged on the table were what separated her from her husband—and said, a little wretchedly, "I know it's silly, but it's been such a long time since you told me."

Mr. Bridge grunted and finished his coffee. She knew it was not that he was annoyed, only that he was incapable of the kind of declaration she needed. It was so little, and yet so much. While they sat across from each other, neither knowing quite what to do next, she became embarrassed; and in her embarrassment she moved her feet and she inadverently stepped on the buzzer, concealed beneath the carpet, that connected with the kitchen, with the result that Harriet soon appeared in the doorway to see what it was that Mrs. Bridge desired.

31

Treachery

Mrs. Bridge often referred to Harriet as a "gem," adding that she had been with the family for more than nine years and that she didn't know what she would do if Harriet ever decided to leave. Considering that cooks and chauffeurs in southside Kansas City often stayed with a family for twenty or thirty years, Harriet's nine years was nothing to boast about. Even so there were a good many matrons who knew her by sight at the bus stop and had been elegantly served by her during luncheons or cocktail parties, with the result that Harriet, though a comparative newcomer, had the reputation of being a catch.

Indeed there were few things about her to which Mrs. Bridge could object. The main thing was her smoking. She was an expert at smoking, expelling it through her nostrils and blowing rings like a man, and she had to be warned occasionally because she did not mind answering the door with a cigarette in her mouth. Otherwise Mrs. Bridge very rarely had to speak to her. On certain humid summer days when she was alone in the house she would take off her uniform and put on a halter and an alpine dirndl skirt, and once or twice she had been caught wearing this outfit. But she was not lazy, and she did not drink at all, she was an excellent cook, and not only the children but Mr. Bridge himself seemed to like her.

So it came as a blow to Mrs. Bridge when, altogether by accident, she heard Harriet flirting with Mrs. Ralph Porter. The Porters had never been close friends but were decidedly in the same circle as the Bridges. It was one cloudy afternoon in spring when Mrs. Bridge, who had a headache, decided to telephone her husband at the office and ask him to bring home some Empirin. She was upstairs in the bedroom at the time, so she walked into the hall and picked up the receiver. The line was busy. She was about to replace the phone in its niche when she heard Harriet asking, "How much do you all pay?" Some instinct warned Mrs. Bridge what the conversation was about, and for a moment she had not the strength of character to stop eavesdropping. Mrs. Porter's voice answered, "Whatever you're receiving there, Harriet, I'll pay you ten dollars a month more."

"Do tell," murmured Harriet, her voice not giving away her thoughts, and Mrs. Bridge, frozen to the upstairs phone, could almost see her seated on the pantry stool with her legs crossed, blowing smoke rings.

There was a crucial pause. Mrs. Bridge was now afraid to replace the receiver because the click would be audible; all she could do was hold her head and wait.

"I feel," Harriet murmured, "Mr. and Mrs. Bridge could not precisely survive too well should I depart here." With chilling poise she added, "However, it was extremely nice of you to call."

And that, as even such a bald soul as Mrs. Porter could tell, was the end of the matter.

*

32

No Scenes in Church

The Porters were regular church-goers, and after the telephone incident Mrs. Bridge felt a sense of exasperation whenever she saw Mrs. Porter in church. It was difficult to imagine how a person could be so devout and so conniving, but that was Mrs. Porter.

For better or worse Mrs. Bridge did not often encounter her there, the reason being that she did not like attending church alone and it was quite difficult to get Mr. Bridge to go. He had little enough use for dogma and would rather lie abed reading vacation brochures on those Sunday mornings when he did not go to the office, or, dressed in old clothes, he would spend the morning in the yard with a can of snail poison. Now and then she became worried about his apathetic attitude toward religion, especially after one of Dr. Foster's sermons on the consequences of atheism, and she would then half-fearfully go after her husband.

"When I need to know anything," he would reply with awful finality, "I go to someone who knows more than I do." This was quite a slam at Dr. Foster.

"But don't you think he has some very good ideas?" she would counter. "It certainly wouldn't hurt you to attend once in a while. And people do ask where you are."

So it came about that once or twice a year he would silently drive to church. They would climb to the balcony, for what reason she could never understand, and there with heads almost touching the stained-oak rafters, surrounded by stifling, humid air, they sat through the sermon.

One Easter, an unusually warm day, just as Dr. Foster began easing into the familiar narrative—the empty tomb, and so forth—the scent of lilies became overpowering. Or was it the sight of Mrs. Porter looking altogether righteous? In any event Mrs. Bridge felt herself swaying. She reached toward the balcony rail for support and whispered giddily that she was going to faint. Mr. Bridge had been dozing, but he woke up immediately and turned his head and glared at her severely.

"Not here! Wait until we get outside," he told her in a voice that was audible throughout the balcony.

"All right, I'll try," she whispered. She thought he meant to escort her outside, but apparently not, because he did not get up, and in a few minutes she realized he meant for her to wait until church was over. There was nothing to do but to try not to faint, and so she did try, and succeeded.

✽

33

Powerful Vocabulary

Dr. Foster had such an impressive vocabulary that Mrs. Bridge was moved to amplify her own. She intended to, she had been intending to for quite a while, but the opportunity never presented itself until she received as second prize at bridge club a little book on how to build a more powerful vocabulary in thirty days. The dust jacket, an eye-catching red, guaranteed that if the reader spent only a few minutes a day, his ability to express himself would so noticeably improve that within two weeks friends would be commenting. Tests had proved, so said the dust jacket, that the great majority of employers had larger vocabularies than their employees, which, the jacket hinted, was the reason for the status quo.

Although Mrs. Bridge had no more thought of becoming an employer than an employee, she was delighted with her prize; everyone else in Kansas City was reading it and she had, therefore, been planning on buying a copy if she could not get it from the rental library. She began to read it that same afternoon as soon as she got home. The next day she was busy, but the day after that she spent almost three hours studying, completing several lessons—filling in the blanks and doing the multiple-choice exercises at the back of the book. She spoke of it enthusiastically to her friends, most of whom had either read it or were definitely intending to, with the exception of

Grace Barron, who always read books no one else ever heard of.

At the end of two weeks she was on her thirteenth lesson, very nearly on schedule, when the telephone interrupted; Madge Arlen was calling to say that a delivery truck had run over their next-door neighbor's boxer. Dogs were always being run over by delivery trucks. The Bridges had lost a collie several years before, and some people named Ilgenfritz who lived in the next block had lost two dachshunds.

"Oh, not really!" Mrs. Bridge began. "What a shame!"

"I tell you I'm up in arms!" replied Madge. "When Edith told me about it I was so put out I simply couldn't speak."

Presently the conversation got around to the vocabulary book and Mrs. Bridge praised it and recommended it quite strongly to Madge, who answered that she'd just finished reading it.

Mrs. Bridge was very much surprised by this news. "You did?" she asked uncertainly, for the book had obviously not affected Madge's vocabulary.

"Yes, and it was marvelous! Every last one of us ought to read it."

Mrs. Bridge felt rather subdued after this talk with Madge; however she continued with her lessons whenever there was time. She did want to complete the book because she was always meeting people who asked if she had read it, and within the month she had reached the twentieth lesson, where one turned adverbs into nouns. So far none of her friends had commented as the dust jacket promised; consequently Mrs. Bridge was a little discouraged. The book began to wander around the house. It found its way from the coffee table in the living room to the window seat in the breakfast room; after that it lay in a dresser drawer in the upstairs bedroom for about a week, and briefly in the room shared by Carolyn and Ruth. From there it traveled again to the breakfast room, to the basement, and finally, its pages already turning a sulphur color and its jacket mended with Scotch Tape, it died on a shelf between T. E. Lawrence and *The Rubáiyát*.

*

34

Tobacco Road

Madge and Grace were so different; Mrs. Bridge felt drawn to them both, and was distressed that the two of them did not care for each other. Now and then she felt they were competing for her friendship, though she could not be sure of this, but if it was true it was both exciting and alarming. She often thought about them. She felt more comfortable with Madge, who liked everything about Kansas City, more secure, more positive; with Grace Barron she felt obliged to consider everything she said, and to look all around, and she could never guess what Grace would say or do.

Tobacco Road, practically uncensored, had come to Kansas City, and Madge Arlen—possibly jealous of Grace Barron's attentions—called to ask if Mrs. Bridge wanted to go to the Wednesday matinee. She had not thought about it, but there was no reason not to, particularly since almost everyone was going to see it in spite of its shady reputation, so she agreed.

The play had scarcely got under way when she received a brief but severe shock: one of the girls in the cast looked extremely like Ruth with her hair uncombed. For an instant she feared it truly was Ruth; it wasn't, of course, and as the play went on she could see that the actress was a few years older.

She did not enjoy the play, neither did Madge Arlen; they left after the second act. On the way out of the theater Mrs. Bridge remarked, "Frankly, I don't see why a play like *Tobacco Road* is necessary."

"We expected it to be earthy," Madge Arlen observed with some lenience, "however, I do agree with you. It went much too far."

35

One Summer Morning

It was very hot that summer.

For as long as she could remember, Mrs. Bridge had known that unless she was wearing slacks—slacks were worn only for gardening—she must wear stockings. In summer this could be uncomfortable, but it was the way things were, it was the way things had always been, and so she complied. No matter where she was going, though it might be no farther than the shopping center at Sixty-third Street, or even if she was not going out of the house all day, she would put on her stockings.

But one morning—and an extraordinarily hot day it promised to be, because by ten o'clock the tar in the street was glistening—she decided not to wear stockings. It was Harriet's day off, Ruth and Carolyn had gone swimming at Lake Lotawana, and Douglas had gone to a model-airplane meet in Swope Park, so nobody would ever know the difference. Having selected the lightest dress she could find in her closet, she put on a pair of blue anklets and the clogs she wore at the country-club swimming pool. Thus dressed, she considered herself in the mirror and shook her head at the sight, but went downstairs all the same. The Beckerle sisters, two elderly widows who were seldom seen about the neighborhood, chose that morning to come visiting.

"Oh, goodness," cried Mrs. Bridge as she greeted them at the door, "I look like something out of *Tobacco Road!*"

✻

36

Growing Pains

Having been repelled by *Tobacco Road* to the point where it obsessed her, she employed it as a pigeonhole: whatever she found unreal, bizarre, obnoxious, indecorous, malodorous, or generally unsavory, unexpected, and disagreeable henceforth belonged in *Tobacco Road,* was from there, or should have been there. So, finding her son in ragged tennis shoes, she let him know where he was from. He didn't mind. He had never cared about clothes one way or another, unless he had become attached to a particular garment, in which case he wore it until she threw it away. Whenever it became necessary to get him some new clothing there would be a quarrel, and after much wrangling the two of them would drive off to one of the young men's shops where he would be turned over to a clerk experienced in these situations, and finally, after all three of them were exhausted, the purchase was made. The argument in regard to the gray suit was typical:

"I've already got a suit."

"But that's a summer suit," she countered.

He looked in his closet and found another outfit. "What's the matter with this, I'd sure like to know?"

"You've outgrown it, and besides, it's time you got another."

"I never wore it anyway," he said triumphantly, his voice changing pitch during the sentence.

"This is absolutely ridiculous. We're going down to the Plaza right now and get you something to wear, so you might as well get used to the idea."

"This suit works all right. I don't want another one."

"Can you imagine your father going to work in old clothes? Why, he'd be laughed out of court!"

Douglas said he didn't think it was so funny, and furthermore he couldn't understand what difference it made; for her part she could not understand why he objected to having new clothes. But, as always, they ended by going to the Plaza, where a very nice gray suit was purchased, although on the way home he said bitterly that he would not ever wear it. He did, of course, as they both knew he would; it was just that he could not admit he liked the suit. In fact he decided it was necessary to claim the suit was giving him a heart attack. Mrs. Bridge was so startled by this announcement that she was temporarily unable to reply.

"Well, it is!" he said, and began to stagger and clutch his chest. "It's too heavy. I can't breathe."

"The only thing wrong with you, my young friend, is your big imagination."

"Okay, then," he retorted gloomily. And with his head lowered he walked slowly away, stopping every few steps to feel his heart. At the door he hesitated, and before going out he said truculently, "But I'm just telling you, if I keel over dead, don't be surprised."

"Very well," she replied, "I won't."

∗

37

Maid from Madras

Mr. and Mrs. Bridge were giving a party, not because they wanted to, but because it was time. Like dinner with the Van Metres, once you accepted an invitation you were obligated to reciprocate, or, as Mr. Bridge had once expressed it, retaliate.

Altogether some eighty people showed up in the course of the evening. They stood around and wandered around, eating, drinking, talking, and smoking. Grace and Virgil Barron were there—Grace sunburned, freckled, and petite, and looking rather pensive; the Arlens arrived in a new Chrysler; the Heywood Duncans were there; and Wilhelm and Susan Van Metre, both seeming withered, sober, and at the wrong party; Lois and Stuart Montgomery; Noel Johnson, huge and alone, wearing a paper cap; Mabel Ong trying to begin serious discussions; and, among others, the Beckerle sisters in beaded gowns which must have been twenty years old, both sisters looking as though they had not for an instant forgotten the morning Mrs. Bridge entertained them in anklets. Even Dr. Foster, smiling tolerantly, with a red nose, stopped by for a cigarette and a whisky sour and chided a number of the men about Sunday golf.

There was also an automobile salesman named Beachy Marsh who had arrived very early in a double-breasted pin-stripe business suit, and, being ill at ease, sensing that he did not belong, did everything he could think of to be amusing.

He was not a close friend but it had been necessary to invite him along with several others.

Mrs. Bridge rustled about her large, elegant, and brilliantly lighted home, checking steadily to see that everything was as it should be. She glanced into the bathrooms every few minutes and found that the guest towels, like pastel handkerchiefs, were still immaculately overlapping one another—at evening's end only two had been disturbed, a fact which would have given Douglas, had he known, a morose satisfaction—and she entered the kitchen once to recommend that the extra servant girl, hired to assist Harriet, pin shut the gap in the breast of her starched uniform.

Around and around went Mrs. Bridge, graciously smiling, pausing here and there to chat for a moment, but forever alert, checking the turkey sandwiches, the crackers, the barbecued sausages, quietly opening windows to let out the smoke, discreetly removing wet glasses from mahogany table tops, slipping away now and then to empty the solid Swedish crystal ashtrays.

And Beachy Marsh got drunk. He slapped people on the shoulder, told jokes, laughed uproariously, and also went around emptying the ashtrays of their cherry-colored stubs, all the while attempting to control the tips of his shirt collar, which had become damp from perspiration and were rolling up into the air like horns.

Following Mrs. Bridge halfway up the carpeted stairs he said hopefully, "There was a young maid from Madras, who had a magnificent ass; not rounded and pink, as you probably think —it was gray, had long ears, and ate grass."

"Oh, my word!" replied Mrs. Bridge, looking over her shoulder with a polite smile but continuing up the stairs, while the auto salesman plucked miserably at his collar.

✱

38

Revolt of the Masses

The evenings were growing cooler, September was here, autumn not far to the north, and the trees rustled uneasily.

Having ordered the groceries and having spent the remainder of the morning more or less listening to the radio, and being then unable to find anything else to do, she informed Harriet—who was in the kitchen furiously smoking one cigarette after another while cutting up dates for a pudding—that she had some shopping to take care of on the Plaza and would not be home until late that afternoon. She felt somewhat guilty as she said this because in reality there was no shopping to be done, but, with the children again in school and with Harriet to do the cooking and housekeeping and with the laundress coming once a week to do the washing, Mrs. Bridge found the days were very long. She was restless and unhappy and would spend hours thinking wistfully of the past, of those years just after her marriage when a day was all too brief.

After luncheon in her favorite tearoom she decided she might as well look at candlesticks. She had been thinking of getting some new ones; this seemed as good a time as any. On her way to Bancroft's, which carried the nicest things on the Plaza, she stopped at a drugstore for a box of aspirin, then paused in front of a bookstore where her eye was caught by the title of a book in the window display: *Theory of the Leisure Class*. She experienced a surge of resentment. For a number of seconds she eyed this book with definite hostility, as though it were alive and conscious of her. She went inside and asked to see the book. With her gloves on it was difficult to turn the pages, so she handed it back to the clerk, thanked him, and with a dissatisfied expression continued to Bancroft's.

39

Minister's Book

If she bought a book it was almost always one of three things: a best-seller she had heard about or seen advertised, a self-improvement book, or a book by a Kansas City author no matter what it was about. These latter were infrequent, but now and again somebody would explode in the midst of Kansas City with a Civil War history or an account of old Westport Landing. Then, too, there were slender volumes of verse and essays usually printed by local publishing houses, and it was one of these that lay about the living room longer than any other book, with the exception of an extremely old two-volume set of *The Brothers Karamazov* in gold-painted leather which nobody in the family had ever read and which had belonged to Mr. Bridge's grandfather. This set rested gravely on the mantelpiece between a pair of bronze Indian-chief heads—the only gift from cousin Lulubelle Watts that Mrs. Bridge had ever been able to use—and was dusted once a week by Harriet with a peacock-feather duster.

The volume that ran second to *The Brothers Karamazov*

was a collection of thoughts by the local minister, Dr. Foster, an exceptionally short and congenial man with an enormous head which was always referred to as leonine, and which was crowned with golden white hair. He allowed his hair to grow very long and he brushed it toward the top of his head so as to appear taller. He had written these essays over a period of several years with the idea of putting them into book form, and from time to time he would allude to them, laughingly, as his memoirs. Then people would exclaim that he surely mustn't keep them to himself until he died, at which Dr. Foster, touching the speaker's arm, and perhaps rising on tiptoe, would laugh heartily and reply, "We'll see, we'll see," and thereupon clear his throat.

At last, when he had been preaching in Kansas City for seventeen years and his name was recognized, and he was often mentioned in *The Tattler* and sometimes in the city paper, a small publishing firm took these essays, which he had quietly submitted to them several times before. The book came out in a black cover with a dignified gray and purple dust jacket that showed him gazing sedately from his study window at dusk, hands clasped behind his back and one foot slightly forward.

The first essay began: "I am now seated at my desk, the desk that has been a source of comfort and inspiration to me these many years. I see that night is falling, the shadows creeping gently across my small but (to my eyes) lovely garden, and at such times as this I often reflect on the state of Mankind."

Mrs. Bridge read Dr. Foster's book, which he had autographed for her, and she was amazed to find that he was such a reflective man, and so sensitive to the sunrise which she discovered he always got up to watch. She underlined several passages in the book that seemed to have particular meaning for her, and when it was done she was able to discuss it with her friends, all of whom were reading it.

This book came to her like an olive branch. It assured her

of God's love for man, of man's love of God: in the ever-lengthening shadow of Hitler and Mussolini her faith was restored, and the comfortable meditations of her minister found lodging.

*

40

Lady Poet

Quite a different sort of writer was Mabel Ong. There were persistent rumors that Mabel was a poet—supposedly quite good—and that one of her poems had been published in a magazine. Mrs. Bridge, having made discreet inquiries which failed to elicit either the name of the magazine or the title of the poem, was therefore pleased to hear Lois Montgomery announce that as a special treat immediately following the next Auxiliary meeting Mabel would read from her works. She was a vigorous, muscular woman of about thirty-five, with a sprinkling of moles on her forehead, and close-cropped hair, who generally wore a tweed coat and stood with her hands thrust into the pockets like a man. She had a positive manner of speaking, now and then turning her head aside to cough or to laugh; she spoke bitterly about capitalism and would relate stories she had heard from unquestionable sources about women dying in childbirth because they could not afford the high cost of hospitalization, or even the cost of insurance programs.

"If I should bear a child—" she was fond of beginning, and would then tear into medical fees.

On the appointed day Mabel Ong walked briskly to the front of the room, carrying a briefcase as though it were a book, and having placed this briefcase on a card table she unzipped it, spent several minutes shuffling through some papers, frowning, but eventually located whatever she was after. She poured herself a drink of ice water from the pitcher, lighted a cigarette, and with one eye closed against the smoke she shuffled through the papers again. Mrs. Bridge watched attentively, thinking that Mabel certainly looked capable of being a poet.

After another drink of water she crushed out her cigarette, ran her tongue over her teeth, and pensively frowned into space. All at once she began:

"Out of the wild womb weeping—"

Mabel was just a bit tongue-tied and Mrs. Bridge, in the back row, was not certain whether she had said "weeping" or "leaping," but decided not to inquire. When the reading concluded she applauded along with everyone else, and she stood around for a while and listened as various members of the Auxiliary asked Mabel about the significance of one line or another. Mrs. Bridge had not enjoyed the poems—they sounded quite free and not very poetic—and she hoped no one would ask for her opinion of them. No one did, though on a certain occasion she was rather surprised to hear herself volunteering the information that she had not cared for them; and being embarrassed by this critical observation, for she was conscious of her own limitations, she quickly added, "However, I'm sure I couldn't do half as well."

*

41

Voting

She had never gone into politics the way some women did, though she listened attentively whenever such topics as the farm surplus or public works programs were discussed at luncheons or at circle meetings; she felt her lack of knowledge and wanted to improve herself, and she often resolved to buckle down to some serious studying. But so many things kept popping up, always at the very moment she was about to begin, and then too she did not know exactly where to start. Once in a while she would be on the point of questioning her husband, but, after thinking it over, she realized she would be asking silly questions, and he was so overburdened with business problems that she did not want to distract him. Besides, there was not much she herself could accomplish.

This was how she defended herself to Mabel Ong after having incautiously let slip the information that her husband always told her how to vote.

"Don't you have a mind of your own?" Mabel demanded, and looked quite grim. "Great Scott, woman! Speak out! We've been emancipated!" She rocked back and forth, hands clasped behind her back, while she frowned at the carpet of the Auxiliary clubhouse.

"You're right, of course," Mrs. Bridge apologized, discreetly avoiding the stream of smoke from Mabel's cigarette.

"But don't you find it hard to know *what* to think? There's so much scandal and fraud everywhere you turn, and I suppose the papers only print what they want us to know." She hesitated, and then spoke out boldly. "How do you make up *your* mind?"

Mabel Ong, without removing the cigarette from her lips, considered the ceiling, the carpet, and squinted critically at a Degas print on the wall, as though debating how to answer such an ingenuous question, and finally she suggested that Mrs. Bridge might begin to grasp the fundamentals by a deliberate reading of certain books, the titles of which she jotted down on the margin of a tally card. Mrs. Bridge had not heard of any of these books except one, and this one because the author had committed suicide, but she decided to read it anyway.

The lady at her favorite rental library had never heard of the book, which was somehow gratifying; even so, having resolved to read it, Mrs. Bridge set out for the public library. Here, at last, she got it, and settled down to the deliberate reading Mabel had advised. The author's name was Zokoloff, which certainly sounded threatening, and to be sure the first chapter dealt with bribery in the circuit courts.

When she had gotten far enough along to feel capable of discussing it she left it on the hall table; however Mr. Bridge did not even notice it until it had lain there for three days. She watched him pick it up, saw his nostrils flatten as he read the title, and then she waited nervously and excitedly. He opened the book, read a few sentences, grunted, and dropped the book on the table. This was disappointing. In fact, now that there was no danger involved, she had trouble finishing the book; she thought it would be better in a magazine digest. But eventually she did finish it and returned it to the library, saying with a slight air of sophistication, "I can't honestly say I agree with it all, but he's certainly well informed."

Certain arguments of Zokoloff remained with her, and she found that the longer she thought about them the more penetrating and logical they became; surely it *was* time, as he insisted, for a change in government. She decided to vote liberal at the next election, and as time for it approached she became filled with such enthusiasm and with such great conviction and determination that she planned to discuss her new attitude with her husband. She became confident that she could persuade him to change his vote also. Politics were not mysterious after all. However, when she challenged him to discussion he did not seem especially interested; in fact he did not answer. He was studying a sheaf of legal papers and only glanced across at her with an annoyed expression. She let it go until the following evening when he was momentarily unoccupied, and this time he stared at her curiously, intently, as if probing her mind, and then all at once he snorted.

She really intended to force a discussion on election eve. She was going to quote from the book of Zokoloff. But he came home so late, so exhausted, that she had not the heart to upset him. She concluded it would be best to let him vote as he always had, and she would do as she herself wished; still, on getting to the polls, which were conveniently located in the country-club shopping district, she became doubtful and a little uneasy. And when the moment finally came she pulled the lever recording her wish for the world to remain as it was.

*

42

Oaths and Pledges

At one of the Auxiliary meetings a discussion arose as to whether it might not be a good idea to amend the constitution of the Auxiliary so as to include the words "under God." Throughout this debate Grace Barron gazed out the window. Everyone else got up to say it was a good idea, except Mabel Ong—being particularly severe in a tailored suit and a string tie—who argued against it, and it was common knowledge that Mabel, being an intellectual, argued against the majority rather than against the question. So, late in the afternoon, the resolution was passed. Of fifty-six ladies present, fifty-four voted to include God. Mabel was against. Grace abstained; in fact when her name was called she jumped and said, "What?"

Mrs. Bridge wished it could have been unanimous; unanimity was so gratifying. Every time she heard or read about a unanimous vote she felt a surge of pride and was reminded, for some reason, of the Pilgrims. She enjoyed all kinds of oaths and pledges and took them regularly, remaining cautious only if her signature was required; signatures were binding, this she knew, and she was under the impression that they were often photographed, or forged, or whatever it was that unscrupulous persons did with signatures.

Oral resolutions, however, seemed quite safe and gave

her a sense of participating, and she liked to discuss them. Often she could be heard urging ladies she scarcely knew to join with her and the others, saying, "It might help and it certainly can't do any harm."

*

43

Another Victim of Circumstances

Lois Montgomery was one of the most prominent members of the Auxiliary. Mrs. Bridge had known her for a good many years without regarding her in any way special until one afternoon when, not by accident, Mabel Ong let slip an allusion to the time when Lois had been raped. Mrs. Bridge's pleasantly neutral expression did not change, just as though she knew all about the case, or at least had had a good deal of experience with that sort of thing, but afterward she found out more. Lois Montgomery was now a tall, stately eagle of a woman with a deep snowy breast and rather overwhelming perfume. She wore her black hair in a huge ballerina knot, lacquered, through tiny cracks of which could be seen a tight roll of false brown hair. Mrs. Bridge would not have considered her the sort of person a sex maniac would attack, and yet the story, so far as she could ascertain, was true. It had taken place years ago when the Montgomerys were living in Butte, Montana, where Stuart had some kind of position with the railroad. How the story followed them from Butte to Kansas City so many years later there was no means of discovering.

Mrs. Bridge visualized the scene: Lois in her Fifth Avenue suit and silver fox boa striding imperially down a dark Montana street with the Canadian wind howling, and then the man rising from behind a bush, or stepping quickly around a tree—he was dressed in a shabby suit with the collar turned up, and he had not shaved, or he could have been wearing a leather jacket and a mask, a stocking cap perhaps. She tried to imagine Lois struggling with him in the darkness, shrieking for help; she wondered if the man had choked Lois with the silver fox boa. Afterward there was the ruined woman collapsed on the sidewalk and the man running away. Later she was lying in a hospital bed, having been given a sedative, and there were police lieutenants in their ill-fitting serge suits asking her embarrassing questions. After that there were relatives and friends who entered with flowers. The scene always ended in the hospital when the room was full of flowers and Mrs. Montgomery's perfume.

She also thought about Stuart Montgomery and how the affair must have affected him. She saw him in Kansas City as a tall, leathery man with a hard, bulbous face like those carved on bottle openers or on the knobs of canes. He did not have much to say if she chanced to meet him on the street with his odd yellow briefcase, and when he tipped his hat he seldom bothered to smile. She wondered if he had wept when he learned what had happened, and if he tried to apologize for having allowed her to go home alone that night, or whether he had been with her and had been frightened away by the man's gun. Or had he been struck over the head? Did he still respect her?

Mrs. Bridge wanted to make some gesture to tell Lois Montgomery how she sympathized, but, after all, what could be done when no one ever mentioned it and when Lois simply stood there smiling and chatting and eating crabmeat sandwiches like everyone else?

*

44

Leda

During one of the luncheons she got to talking with Grace
Barron about art, the result being that the two of them left
the clubhouse and drove to the William Rockhill Nelson
art gallery and stayed there till it closed. Mrs. Bridge felt
excited and guilty about the way they had gone off by
themselves, but it was how Grace did everything.

Goya, Holbein, Dürer, Corot—these names, at once so
familiar and so meaningless to Mrs. Bridge, were old friends
of Grace Barron. And before long Mrs. Bridge knew this was
a day to be remembered, like a day in February when, after
months of lowering skies, the clouds roll back.

A little self-conscious still, not yet ready to let Grace know
what she was intending to do, Mrs. Bridge enrolled in a painting class for adults at an art school near the gallery. She
bought a kit which contained some paints and brushes, a
palette—she had thought all palettes were of that peculiar
ornamental shape and was slightly disappointed to find
the one in her kit was plainly rectangular—and a bottle of
linseed oil and a bottle of turpentine, along with two metal
cups which the clerk told her were to be used for the turpentine and the oil. She also bought a sugar sack for wiping
the brushes, and a smock embroidered with bluebirds, and
thus equipped she began her art lessons three evenings a week.
She attended regularly for almost a month, skipped one night,

got to several more, skipped three, attended spasmodically
for another month, and finally dropped out altogether. But
while she did paint she painted with a certain gusto and feeling, and with not a bad eye. The instructor once or twice
gave her nice compliments and encouraged her to continue.
He was a morose and rumpled little man of about forty with
strong breath and bags under his eyes, who was in the habit
of scratching his head and saying, "Well, let's see, folks, to-
night why don't we sort of let ourselves go?"

Occasionally there would be a model in costume, often an
elderly immigrant in boots and a kerchief; sometimes they
would paint an arrangement of driftwood and wine bottles.
But one evening the instructor, whose name was Gadbury,
told them to try a subject from mythology and work from
imagination. He suggested Wotan as a subject, but added that
they might do anything they wished. Mrs. Bridge could not
recall anything about Wotan, but she did remember with
stark clarity the legend of Leda and the swan. She proceeded
to paint a small, zinc-white swan and a Leda standing stiffly
erect, with hands behind her back and ankle-deep in water
because hands and feet always gave her trouble, and she
clothed Leda in a flowered dressmaker bathing suit not unlike
her own.

Mr. Gadbury, making his rounds, stood for a while looking
over her shoulder at this Leda and at last said he thought
the lake was too blue.

*

45

The Clock

She spent a great deal of time staring into space, oppressed by the sense that she was waiting. But waiting for what? She did not know. Surely someone would call, someone must be needing her. Yet each day proceeded like the one before. Nothing intense, nothing desperate, ever happened. Time did not move. The home, the city, the nation, and life itself were eternal; still she had a foreboding that one day, without warning and without pity, all the dear, important things would be destroyed. So it was that her thoughts now and then turned deviously deeper, spiraling down and down in search of the final recess, of life more immutable than the life she had bequeathed in the birth of her children.

One fathomless instant occurred on a windy, rainy night when Harriet had gone to church, and the children were out, and only she and her husband remained at home. For some time, perhaps an hour or more, they had been reading, separately; he had the financial page of the newspaper and she had been idly reading of the weddings that day. The rain blew softly against the windowpanes, shutters rattled, and above the front door the tin weather stripping began to moan. Mrs. Bridge, with the newspaper in her lap, listened to the rumbling and booming of thunder over the house. Suddenly, in total quiet, the room was illuminated by lightning. Mr. Bridge lifted his head, only that and nothing more, but within Mrs. Bridge something stirred. She looked at her husband intently.

"Did the clock strike?" he asked.

"No, I don't believe so," she answered, waiting.

He cleared his throat. He adjusted his glasses. He continued reading.

She never forgot this moment when she had almost apprehended the very meaning of life, and of the stars and planets, yes, and the flight of the earth.

46

Countess Mariska

The one person she ever met who surely had experienced similar moments was a Russian-Italian-Hungarian countess who passed through Kansas City like a leaf in the wind.

"The Countess Mariska Mihailova Strozzi," was how Lois Montgomery, who was the newly elected president of the Auxiliary, introduced her at luncheon.

"Ladies," the countess began, and went on talking for an hour, but it was an hour that seemed like a minute. No one whispered, no one left the room. The countess was electrifying, and the women who missed hearing her were told about her for months afterward. She was born in Shanghai, the daughter of an elderly Russian diplomat who, until an intrigue at the court, had been a close friend of Czar Nicholas II. The family had been exiled, there had been murders, abductions, espionage, and no one knew what else. At fourteen she was married to an Italian millionaire who claimed direct descent from the great Renaissance family which opposed the Medici, but she had run away from him. Later she married a rich Greek. Now she was divorced and on her way to San Francisco at the invitation of a munitions maker. She talked of her experiences, but mostly of the Nazis, and there was a rumor that just before coming to America she had killed a Nazi colonel with his own revolver. Mrs. Bridge, sitting in the front row, looking up into the glittering violet eyes, could easily believe it.

The countess was quite small and chic, and wore a black sheath dress. Her only jewelry was a large star sapphire that accentuated a strange bluish-white scar across the back of her hand. Mrs. Bridge was certain everyone was dying to know what had caused the scar, but no one dared ask. It was only one of the mysteries of the countess. She was delicate and utterly feminine, but at the same she was as blunt as a man. It was clear she had been witness to many kinds of folly and wisdom and agony and joy. Once she paused and leisurely fitted a European cigarette into an ebony holder; several minutes must have gone by while she smoked and stared over the heads of her audience, but they were so transfixed that no one moved. Tamping out the cigarette, she continued in her perfect, heavy English, "We must destroy the Fascist. . . ."

Later Mrs. Bridge introduced herself to the countess, for that was what everyone else was doing, and for a minute or so they chatted. Two things Mrs. Bridge remembered about her: the first was a fresh red bruise on the tiny golden throat, a bruise such as a man's mouth would leave, and the second was that husky voice murmuring, "To be afraid is, I tell you, Madame, the most terrible thing in the world."

47

Tea Leaves

Not long after the countess left for San Francisco and the hospitable munitions maker, Mrs. Bridge was having lunch on the Plaza with Grace Barron. Grace seemed despondent, and Mrs. Bridge, thinking to cheer her up, looked into her tea cup and pretended to be studying the leaves. Laying one finger alongside her nose she said, "My gypsy blood tells me you—"

"My fortune?" asked Grace absently. "I know my fortune."

And then, while Mrs. Bridge stared at her in frightened amazement, two large tears came rolling down her cheeks.

48

Liberal

Whether it was in the pattern of the leaves, or in Grace herself, Mrs. Bridge could not be sure, but at a cocktail party honoring Mrs. Albert Tate, who was packing for a voyage around the world, Grace became unreasonable. The affair was held in the Arlens' new yellow brick Colonial on Shoat Drive and there were over one hundred people present. According to the invitations the party was to be from six till nine-thirty, but at ten o'clock the crowd was as thick as ever, and about that time the word began spreading that Grace Barron was in the basement recreation room having an argument with the host.

"—ethnocentricism, that's what!" Grace was saying just as Mrs. Bridge hurried anxiously down the basement steps.

Russ Arlen scowled and muttered. Grace took a long drink from a martini glass and smacked her lips.

"Furthermore," she announced to the crowd, "if we go to war again do you know who I accuse? The American press! Scare headlines sell copies. I accuse. Monsieur, j'accuse!"

Andrew Koeppel, who had been congratulated throughout the evening for having bought another hotel, suggested, "Let me put in a word. A few minutes ago you mentioned some Semite friend of yours who thought a pogrom was as likely in this country as in Germany. Let me tell you: Nazi Germany is the most fascistic nation on the face of this earth, and if your friend doesn't like it here, let her go back. I've fought the Jews for whatever I own and I intend to keep it. My father, mind you, came to this country without a penny in his pocket and by the time he was thirty-six years old—" Here he began a long and rather uninteresting story having to do with pulling up cornstalks for eleven cents a day.

Attention gradually was reverting to Grace when there came shouts from upstairs of "Fire! Fire!" and everyone crowded the stairway, cocktail glasses in hand. There was indeed a fire, but not in the house. Somehow the back seat of the Ralph Porters' Cadillac had begun to smoulder. An alarm was not turned in for quite a while because everyone assumed someone else had taken care of it, but eventually a fire engine came clanging up Ward Parkway and swerved into Shoat Drive, one of the ladders scratching the fenders of several automobiles, and the firemen broke the window of the Cadillac and began spraying the rear seat. Smoke billowed out while Mrs. Porter wept and begged them to stop. The firemen believed a cigarette stub had caused it, but the Beckerle sisters, who had been riding in the back seat, denied this. A few minutes later almost everybody had returned to the house, and Grace was at it again, this time in the library under a full-length portrait of Madge. Mrs. Bridge entered the library to hear Grace saying, "—and the Modocs and the Nez Percé! And the Mimbreno Apache, the Teton Sioux, and Custer's deliberate violation of the treaty of eighteen-sixty-eight and—"

"Shrimp, anybody?" It was Madge hurrying in to save the day, followed by her new maid, who was carrying an immense silver platter heaped with hors d'oeuvres.

"I want another drink," Grace announced. "And what about the Seminoles? They never harmed us but we invaded their swamps and cut them to ribbons."

Mrs. Bridge felt the discussion to be beyond her depth, but, in hopes of moderating what could turn into an unfortunate scene, she asked hopefully, "It does sound as though we've done some dreadful things, Grace, but isn't it possible that when you investigate fully you'll discover the Seminoles attacked us?"

The conversation continued for some time, Grace Barron being the center of it all, arguing now against censoring books, now against opening the mail of suspected Fascists and Communists. Once or twice Mrs. Bridge attempted to direct the conversation elsewhere, praising the somewhat regal portrait of Madge under which they were standing, and also trying the fire in the Cadillac, but at the very moment she was about to succeed, Grace herself would irritate someone all over again.

There were several echoes of this evening. The very next

night someone unbuckled the windshield wipers from the Barrons' automobile, which had been parked on the street in front of their home. The wipers were found in the gutter a few yards away, twisted out of shape.

The scoutmaster of David Barron's troop received an anonymous letter telling him to watch young Barron. The scoutmaster, who had never before gotten such a letter, did not know what to do with it, and being very much agitated he gave it to Dr. Foster, who telephoned the police and talked for a long time on various subjects before telling them why he had called. The letter had a postscript demanding to know how many years young Barron had been playing the violin and adding triumphantly that he had not been invited to join a high-school fraternity.

Days passed. It seemed the affair was being forgotten. Then Madge Arlen happened to remark that her husband had switched accounts from Virgil Barron's bank to the Security First.

"Oh, my word!" Mrs. Bridge breathed. "What did Virgil say?"

"Russ told me he didn't open his mouth." Madge paused to light a cigarette and shake out the match. After inhaling deeply she said, "We weren't the first to change."

Mrs. Bridge thought for an instant she was going to faint, and even as her head stopped whirling she heard herself remarking in a sympathetic tone, "—suppose it was the best thing."

✻

49

The Private World of Wilhelm and Susan

Quite possibly the only persons unaware of Grace Barron's indiscretion were Wilhelm and Susan Van Metre.

"We chanced to be driving this way," Wilhelm Van Metre said, having cleared his throat twice in the midst of the remark, "and I said to Mrs. Van Metre, 'Susan, as long as we are in this neighborhood it might not be a bad idea to stop for a nice little visit with the Bridges.'" He cleared his throat again. "I seem to be having some slight difficulty with my vocal apparatus. But at any rate, Susan agreed with me." He turned to smile at her.

"What a nice surprise!" Mrs. Bridge replied. "Here, let me take your coats." And going to the bottom of the stairs she called, "Walter! Guess who's here?" This meant he was to put away his detective magazine or his vacation brochures or whatever he was looking at, and get out of bed and get dressed and come down.

"Now!" she resumed, having gotten them seated and having told Harriet to fix some tea, "Now, tell me what's new with you all?"

Wilhelm chuckled and slapped his knee. "Susan, did you hear India? Now you tell me," he continued, addressing his wife, "does anything new or extraordinary ever happen to us? Not much, I'm afraid, not much." He leaned back and touched his nostrils one after the other as though to prevent himself from sneezing. "No, not very much, not much."

It was quite a while before Mr. Bridge came downstairs to join the conversation; he had recognized the voices and was in no hurry. Then, for about three hours, they sat in the living room with the pot of tea. Mrs. Bridge, who was afraid her husband might walk out of the room and go back to bed, attempted to keep the conversation going; she also tried to get them to play a horse-racing game which was quite popular, and then she suggested cards. Wilhelm had a better idea; he thought he might tackle Mr. Bridge for a round of dominoes. However there were no dominoes in the house. Wilhelm suggested chess; there was no chess set. For a moment it looked as though Wilhelm might drive home to get his own chess set. Finally Mrs. Bridge got him off this subject. Presently he asked their opinion of the ballet troupe that had just completed an engagement in Kansas City.

"Oh, goodness," she said quickly, "now let me see—the ballet—yes, it *was* in town, wasn't it, because Grace Barron called—"

"I found the interpretation of the premier danseur rather too old-fashioned," said Wilhelm, tapping his fingertips and frowning. "Although Susan, if memory serves, thought not, especially the 'Swan Lake.' We both enjoy 'Swan Lake.'" He also inquired if Mrs. Bridge agreed with the criticism of Kafka in the latest issue of a literary review.

"I'm afraid I missed that altogether," she replied. She had never heard of the magazine.

And eventually, inevitably, the conversation turned upon engineering because Wilhelm had been an engineer for thirty years. In spite of his experience, he said, "I have found it inexpedient to rely on memory. I place my faith in instruments. You may or may not, India, be familiar with the log-log duplex decitrix." He paused, lifting his bushy white eyebrows.

"I'm afraid I'm not," she said.

"Well, since you are not an engineer that is excusable," he said, chuckling. "But I can tell you that in a tight spot there is nothing to help a man out like the duplex decitrix."

Mrs. Bridge replied that it sounded dreadfully complicated, and later, as they were leaving, said she hoped they would stop by again before long.

*

50

Sir William and Sir Thomas

The Van Metres had a disconcerting habit of believing what people said. Mrs. Bridge, having expressed the hope they would stop by again, forgot about them. Yet two weeks had not passed before they came for another nice little visit. She pretended to be glad to see them. They drank several pots of tea and seemed not to be aware of the long periods of silence. Mrs. Bridge desperately tried to prevent silences, and ordinarily she succeeded, but with the Van Metres it was an awful job. She was grateful when either of them began to speak because it gave her a moment to rest and to think of another topic. Susan very seldom had a word to offer; Wilhelm would be lost in thought for half an hour, after which he might take the next half hour to tell an anecdote. On this occasion he took very nearly that long to relate a tale about two sixteenth-century gentlemen: Sir William Roper and the lord chancellor of England whose name was Sir Thomas More. It seems that Sir William came calling on Sir Thomas with a proposal to marry one of his daughters.

Sir Thomas, being agreeable to this idea, led Sir William to the bedside of his daughters and whipped off the covers. The two girls were lying on their backs with their smocks up as high as their armpits. They at once rolled over on their bellies. Sir William said, "I have seen both sides." He then patted one of the girls on the buttocks, and said, "Thou art mine."

"Well," observed Mrs. Bridge the moment the story ended, "I'm certainly thankful times have changed."

*

51

The Low-pressure Salesman

A few days after this visit with the Van Metres another old acquaintance turned up. Mrs. Bridge was in the breakfast room wondering what to do—how to occupy herself till noon—when Harriet entered to say there was a man at the back door.

"What does he want?"

"That's what I asked him, and he wouldn't say."

"Didn't he give his name?"

"No name," said Harriet, "and he looks suspicious."

Everyone looked suspicious to Harriet. Mrs. Bridge, after a moment of thought, got up and walked through the kitchen to the back door. It was snowing outside, and on the back step was a stoop-shouldered little man with a woeful expression who was shivering uncontrollably and stamping his feet. On seeing her he attempted a smile and his mouth formed the word "Hello." Mrs. Bridge could not think where she had seen him; then she remembered the art instructor in whose evening class she had done some painting. Opening the door, but leaving the glass storm door locked, she said, "Why, it's Mr. Gadbury!" For some reason he did look suspicious, and more lost and defeated than in his studio. He was attempting to speak; his words were inaudible through the storm door. Mrs. Bridge, conscious of Harriet's premonition, despite the familiarity of it, was therefore reluctant to let him in.

"Is there anything I can do for you?" she inquired.

A flurry of snow swept over him. He tried once more to smile. He was not a stranger, but on the other hand he was not exactly a friend who had come calling. He did not appear to have been drinking, in spite of his red nose, nor did he look violent; so she disregarded Harriet—who was standing with her arms crossed, emphatically shaking her head—and unlocked the door.

"Won't you step in, Mr. Gadbury? It must be cold out there."

Gadbury stepped in. His teeth were clattering and he walked with difficulty. He looked as though he had been out in the snow for hours. He followed her into the living room with his hat in his hands, glancing behind to see if he was leaving tracks on the carpet, and he was. She invited him to sit down. He did so, and finding no place to put his wet hat he hung it on his knee. He shivered constantly. He had turned a mottled yellow and grayish-blue color like a piece of sausage that had been in the refrigerator for several weeks, with the exception of his moist red nose. He twitched and jerked and did not seem to be breathing. He made no attempt to speak. His chin was tucked into his collar, his knees knocked together, and his feet occasionally sprang off the floor of their own accord.

Mrs. Bridge, having observed him, said, "I'm going to have

Harriet fix you some hot tea." She got up and walked across the room to the bell pull. The bell pull was a strip of material about eight feet long, resembling a sample of Persian rug, which was suspended from a lever near the ceiling. It hung down against the wall alongside the highboy. It was actually simpler to step into the kitchen and speak directly to Harriet, but whenever there were guests Mrs. Bridge used the bell pull. She took hold of it about two feet from the bottom and gave a slow, gentle tug; she could never quite get over the feeling that someday when the room was full of people she would pull it and it would fall down around her neck like a Catholic chasuble. Presently Harriet appeared, looking overly insouciant, as though she suspected an intrigue.

"I believe we would like some tea," said Mrs. Bridge.

She then returned to her chair and waited for Mr. Gadbury to speak, but he made no effort to do so. He continued to twitch and shiver. She heartily wished he would think of some way to stop his teeth from chattering.

Finding that she was observing him, Gadbury drew a handkerchief from the pocket of his coat and weakly blew his nose, and said, "I'm pretty cold."

"I'm sure you must be," replied Mrs. Bridge. "The paper says it got down to zero at six o'clock this morning."

Harriet reappeared wheeling the cart. She rolled it to a stop in front of Mrs. Bridge, who then poured out the tea. Harriet delivered a cup to Gadbury, who drank it at once and who then looked very hopefully and earnestly at the cart where the silver tea pot stood.

"Would you care for another cup, Mr. Gadbury?"

He said that would be nice, so he had another, and before long he had another.

"How's the painting coming along?" he asked.

"I haven't had a spare moment in weeks, Mr. Gadbury."

"I sure remember that malachite sherry bottle," he said. There was a pause. "You really let yourself go on that one."

Mrs. Bridge smiled courteously. She waited for him to state his business. Gadbury stared around the room. He began to squint at an etching of a cathedral that occupied the space above the sofa. No one in the family had looked at it for years.

"I don't know about that," Gadbury said, studying it intently. "Maybe, but then again maybe not. There's a quality, all right." He discovered the water which had been dripping on the carpet from his hat and his coat, and nervously placed his foot on a soggy spot. At length he became aware that she was waiting for him to explain the visit, so he worked out of his pocket a crumpled little magazine which was titled *The Doberman,* and he held this up for her to see.

"Oh?" said Mrs. Bridge.

"I don't guess you or Mr. Bridge'd be much interested in subscribing to this, would you?"

She had suspected he was selling something, and she knew that whatever it might be she would have no use for it.

"I really hadn't planned on subscribing to any more magazines, Mr. Gadbury."

He nodded in complete understanding. "You wouldn't want it unless you had a Doberman." Then an idea came to him and he sat erect and asked, "You don't have one, do you?"

"No, we don't."

"Nobody does," he said despondently. "They eat an awful lot, I think."

"Oh? Don't you have one?"

"No. But when I was a boy I used to have a dog." He looked to see if this fact would arouse her interest. Finding it did not, after wiping his nose on his sleeve, he considered his magazine and launched into a sales talk. "This issue tells about one who wouldn't eat anything except sirloin steak and worked for the police department in Toledo." He mulled over this information and added pertinently, "Its name was Lieutenant." Suddenly he opened the magazine to the center spread, which had snapshots of nine Dobermans, and he held this up for her to see.

"My, they're ferocious looking, aren't they?"

Gadbury then had another look at the photographs. "I guess so. I hadn't thought about it."

Mrs. Bridge tipped her head slightly to indicate she was considering the pictures further. Gadbury became enthusiastic.

"This magazine comes out every month," he said. He was overtaken by a chill; he shivered, sniffled, stamped his feet, and looked around wildly. "It tells how you train these dogs," he said, speaking with great rapidity, "and, ah, eeehe-he-ahha-*sha!*" sneezed Mr. Gadbury. "I've got a cold," he said feebly, and then the life went out of him and he sat with his head bowed, silent, while a few more drops of water sank into the carpet. "It isn't that the school doesn't pay a living wage," he went on without lifting his head. "It's just that my daughter got in trouble and now she's in the hospital. I didn't know hospital bills were so high." He rolled the magazine into a tube and began striking it against his palm.

"Do you sell many subscriptions?"

Gadbury made no attempt to answer.

"How long have you been at it?" she asked.

"About two months," he said quietly.

Mrs. Bridge took a deep breath and clasped her hands. "Tell me, Mr. Gadbury, tell me the truth. Have you sold any at all?"

"No. But there was a lady the week before last who said she'd ask her husband."

"All right," said Mrs. Bridge. "You may put me down for a subscription."

Gadbury raised his head and looked at her in grave astonishment.

*

52

Second Lesson in Spanish

While cleaning out the back-hall closet she came upon the phonograph records and the booklet on how to speak Spanish. The records were covered with dust and one of them was broken. On an impulse she let the closet remain as it was; she carried the records into the living room and placed the unbroken ones on the phonograph. Then she seated herself with the booklet to refresh her memory, and finding that she could recall the procedure with no difficulty she set the needle on the first record.

"Buenas días, Señora Brown. Cómo está usted?"

"Buenas días, Señor Carreño. Muy bien, gracias. Y usted?"

At the pause she was ready. "Buenas días, Señor Carreño," she said pleasantly. "Muy bien, gracias. Y usted?"

"Muy bien."

The record squeaked and clicked, clicked again, and continued. Señor Carreño remarked that Señora Brown was in Madrid. Señora Brown evidently realized this.

"Estoy en Madrid."

"Estoy en Madrid," Mrs. Bridge repeated.

From upstairs Carolyn called, "Mother!"

"What is it, dear?" Mrs. Bridge called.

"La gusta Madrid?"

"Sí, mucho."

"*Mother!*"

With a sigh Mrs. Bridge got up and walked to the bottom of the stairs. "What is it, Corky? I'm busy right now."

"I can't find my saddle shoes."

Mrs. Bridge returned to the living room, turned off the phonograph, and came back to stand with one hand on the newel post. "I couldn't hear you, dear. What did you say?"

"What happened to my saddle shoes? I left them out for Harriet to clean but they aren't here."

Mrs. Bridge began climbing the stairs, because there was bound to be an argument and she did not like shouting back and forth. "I gave them to the laundress. They were simply too filthy to be worn."

Carolyn moaned and rocked on her heels, this being the current method of expressing agony. "What am I going to wear to the mixer?"

Mrs. Bridge had stopped to catch her breath on the landing. Now she continued around the turn and up the remaining steps.

"Well, dear, you certainly can't wear saddle shoes to a dance."

Carolyn spoke slowly and distinctly. "It isn't a dance, Mother, it's a mixer. It's in the gymnasium after school."

"I thought you danced at a mixer."

"You do, but it's different. Totally." Carolyn was rocking on her heels again. "I mean, it's already practically the end of my free period and I've got to get back for Latin and obviously you don't expect a person to wear these Indian skins even if it is a mixer. Fortunately." She held out one small moccasined foot and wiggled the toe.

"I should think you'd want to wear your new brown oxfords. They certainly cost enough."

"Oh, ugh! I mean, you're so behind."

"I suppose so," Mrs. Bridge responded drily. "But I'll thank you not to be impertinent."

"Oh, I'm sorry, Mother, but after all this is utterly tragic. I mean, let's not be bland."

"Well, let's see, I suppose the only solution is to drive to the Plaza and get you a new pair of saddle shoes."

"There isn't time! I mean I have this pathetic Latin!"

"Oh, dear," said Mrs. Bridge wearily, for it seemed such problems were always arising. "I'm supposed to pick up Madge Arlen at two o'clock, but I suppose if you must have them I can run down to the Plaza right now and deliver them to you at school. I honestly believe half my life has been spent arranging the family schedule."

Carolyn, who did not want anyone to see her mother delivering a pair of shoes, said, "Just leave them in the principal's office."

*

53

Servant's Entrance

Everyone made use of the back door whenever it was convenient, but Douglas seemed to prefer it—she had noticed that when he came home from school, although approaching the house from the front, he was apt to go all the way around and come in through the back. From the window of her sewing room upstairs she had seen him do this. She was distressed by his habit because it was customary for members of the family and guests to enter and leave by the front, the back door being used principally by the laundress and the various delivery boys, and by Harriet.

One day at lunch, unable to stand it any longer, she abruptly asked, "Do you have back-door-itis?"

Douglas had just started eating chipped beef; he lowered his knife and fork and gazed at her in stupefaction.

"You need another haircut," she said automatically, noticing how shaggy he looked. "And take that pencil from behind your ear. People will think you're a grocery clerk."

"What?" said Douglas, blinking.

"What on earth possesses you to always use the back door?"

"I don't know," said Douglas.

"Well, then," said Mrs. Bridge, "why don't you do like everyone else?"

Douglas appeared to be thinking this over. Finally he said in the same vacuous tone, "I don't know."

"Well," said Mrs. Bridge, "as long as we have a front door we might as well use it."

Douglas said he guessed that was right, but he did not sound convinced.

*

54

Rumpy

There was no end to the problems of adolescence. Carolyn was beginning to blossom, not only in front but in back, and as she had gotten into the habit of walking with her spine unnecessarily arched she soon became known among the high school boys as "Rumpy." One of these boys, calling for the first time at her home, absently referred to her by that name. The next day Mrs. Bridge, who was crocheting a nice muffler in case anybody wanted one, asked her about the name.

"That's nothing. You should hear what they call Ruth," said Carolyn.

Mrs. Bridge resumed crocheting with a displeased expression.

*

55

The Chrysler and the Comb

Mrs. Bridge, emptying wastebaskets, discovered a dirty comb in Ruth's basket.

"What's this doing here?" Ruth inquired late that afternoon when she got home and found the comb on her dresser.

"I found it in the wastebasket. What was it doing *there?*" Ruth said she had thrown it away.

"Do you think we're made of money?" Mrs. Bridge demanded. "When a comb gets dirty you don't throw it away, you wash it, young lady."

"It cost a nickel," Ruth said angrily. She flung her books onto the bed and stripped off her sweater.

"Nickels don't grow on trees," replied Mrs. Bridge, irritated by her manner.

"Nickels don't grow on trees," Ruth echoed. She was standing by the window with her hands on her hips; now, exasperated, she pointed to her father's new Chrysler, which was just then turning into the driveway.

"Put the comb in a basin of warm water with a little ammonia and let it soak," Mrs. Bridge went on. "In a few minutes you can rinse the—"

"I know, I know, I know!" Ruth unzipped her skirt, stepped out of it, and threw it at the closet. She sat down on her bed and began to file her nails.

"So is a nickel going to break us up?" she asked, scowling.

"I wash my comb and I expect you to do the same. It won't hurt either of us," replied Mrs. Bridge. "Taking out without putting in will soon reach bottom," she added and left the room, shutting the door behind her.

For a few minutes Ruth sat on the bed quietly filing her nails and chewing her lower lip; then she snatched the comb and broke it in half.

56

No Evangelism

Christianity meant nothing to Ruth, at least so far as Mrs. Bridge could determine. Ruth went to church reluctantly, sullen and uncommunicative, until she was old enough to defy her mother, knowing her father did not care if she went or not; and when Mrs. Bridge pleaded with her, saying, "Goodness, anyone would think you were a South Sea Islander!" Ruth only sighed and murmured, "Mother, let me be."

Douglas reacted quite differently; he objected strenuously when he was a small boy, but later, discovering the church had a basketball team on which he might play if he attended with reasonable regularity, he became more manageable.

Carolyn was no trouble at all. As a child she seemed to enjoy Sunday school, and when she was fourteen she joined the choir. Before long she was reading her Bible at home during the week and, on Sundays, listening quite attentively to the mellow sermons of Dr. Foster. She also joined the Wednesday evening group of teen-agers who met in the church basement.

Mrs. Bridge customarily drove Carolyn to these Wednesday evening meetings and allowed one of the older boys or girls to bring her home. She felt a deep sense of pleasure, a pleasure that bordered on real happiness, whenever she thought of Carolyn's participation. She herself had never grown as close to the church as she would have liked, though she did not know quite why, and in consequence she blamed herself for Ruth's failure, and, to a lesser extent, for the fact that if it were not for the basketball team Douglas would drop out. Mrs. Bridge felt proud and reassured each Wednesday evening. There, on the church steps, she beheld a group of nicely dressed, clean, smiling, courteous young people. Invariably they appeared cheerful and confident. Surely, these faces told her, no evil can befall us. Surely, she thought, none would.

The choir, the Sunday sermons, the Wednesday evening group—all this failed to satisfy Carolyn's appetite for religious experience. She became insatiable. She spent hours reading the Bible; she read the Apocrypha; she had long talks with Dr. Foster. It was not enough. One evening she told her mother she intended to join a group of evangelists.

Mrs. Bridge immediately saw eight or ten lower-middle-class people on a downtown street corner, the women in bonnets and dark shapeless gowns and the men somehow reminding her of Mr. Schumann, who led the high-school band. Tubas in the rain, a tambourine being passed around —she had always looked upon these people with a mixture of pity and respect, and, if she could not avoid the tambourine, she put a quarter in it.

"Well," she said, "it's an awfully nice idea, of course. I just wonder if you'd be happy doing it. Let's see what your father says."

Mr. Bridge came home about nine o'clock. His briefcase was packed and he was harassed and short-tempered; he told Harriet to fix him a sandwich and some coffee and bring it into his study. Carolyn knew it was a poor moment to announce her decision, but she was too thrilled to wait.

"Nonsense," he told her when she stopped him on the stairs. "You'll continue with your schooling. I've already put in your application at the university."

That ended the matter. Carolyn was enraged, but, like every other member of the family, with the possible exception of Ruth, who seemed unafraid of him, she did not dare argue.

Mrs. Bridge sympathized with Carolyn, putting an arm around her waist and saying gently, "I expect Dad knows best. But you're an awfully sweet person, Corky, to think of an idea like that."

*

57

Chaperon

The telephone rang and it was Naomi Gattenberger, the fattest girl in the high school. She always wore a brilliant red coat that hung down to her ankles and a pair of shell-rimmed glasses studded with rhinestones. Her father had recently made a fortune in the used-car business.

"How are you, Naomi?" Mrs. Bridge asked.

"Just fine," said Naomi.

"I saw your mother the other day."

"That's what she said."

As this exhausted their common interests, Mrs. Bridge said, "I'll see if Corky's come home yet." She put down the receiver and went to look, but Carolyn had not returned from having her hair set.

"I didn't want to talk to her anyway," said Naomi. "I'm chairman of the Activities Committee for the sorority dance and we decided on you for one of the chaperons."

"Why, how nice! This is quite a surprise."

Naomi guessed maybe it was a surprise.

"Well—when is the dance to be?" Mrs. Bridge stalled.

"Two weeks from Friday from eight o'clock to twelve-thirty in the Elbow Room."

Still fighting for time to set up her defenses Mrs. Bridge asked about the Elbow Room.

"It's downtown. It used to be a pool hall, I think, only

they took out the pool tables." There was a pause. Naomi added hopefully, "Lots of fraternities have parties there, I think."

"It's very nice, I'm sure."

Naomi guessed probably it was.

Another pause ensued, a longer one, during which Mrs. Bridge could hear Naomi breathing. Obviously the question had already been put and some kind of an answer was expected.

"Well, just a minute, Naomi, I'll see if we're busy that evening." She slid the tabulator of her plastic engagement book to the proper date and pressed: up popped the cover and Mrs. Bridge found, to her dismay, that nothing was planned.

"I sure do hope you can do it," Naomi said miserably. "I already called up almost all the mothers."

Mrs. Bridge was a bit disconcerted by this confession, but she was touched by Naomi's despair. Then, too, Carolyn had been a sorority member for more than a year and during this time Mrs. Bridge had not been called upon to serve as a chaperon at any of the parties, so she said, "That'll be grand, Naomi. I'll make a note of it right now." And while jotting it down she asked, "What sort of decorations are you planning?"

Naomi said they hadn't gotten a majority vote on anything, but probably it would be a Hawaiian party.

"Well, you have lots of time. I'm sure it will be exciting."

Naomi sounded despondent. "I sure do hope so."

This seemed to conclude their business, so, after a pause, Mrs. Bridge said, "I'll tell Carolyn you called."

"She knows."

"Oh! Well, thank you for asking me, Naomi. I'm flattered."

"You're welcome," said Naomi phlegmatically. "Well, good-by."

Mrs. Bridge replaced the receiver and murmured, "Oh, dear!" for it sounded like a dull evening.

The Elbow Room was decorated with Chinese lanterns hung from the ceiling and with hundreds of yards of crepe paper lividly criss-crossing the windows, framing the doors, and connecting the lanterns. Mrs. Bridge, who was quite sensitive to odors, was certain the moment she entered that it had indeed been used as a pool hall, if not worse. The orchestra consisted of a piano, a complicated arrangement of drums, a bass viol, and five saxophones, all played by high-school boys. There was a girl about thirteen years old on the stage; she was wrapped as tight as a mummy in a piece of flowered silk and it was evident she intended to sing. Mrs. Bridge, surveying this scene, found there were three other chaperons, two of them high-school teachers of whom she had heard a great deal and whose photographs Carolyn had pointed out to her in the school yearbook, and a swarthy young man named De Falla who was the father of one of the sorority girls.

The first half of the evening moved along smoothly enough; Mrs. Bridge thought the orchestra played remarkably well, considering, and the dancers—some of them at least—looked as though they had been accustomed to this sort of thing for years. The boys in the stag line stood around with their hands in their pockets and did a great deal of staring and whispering. Later in the evening a fight broke out near the punch bowl, and shortly after this two boys in tuxedos began burning holes in a lantern with their cigarettes and had to be warned by Mr. De Falla that if they did it again they would have to leave. Naomi was there in white taffeta, enormous, alone, and wretched; Mrs. Bridge smiled to her and talked with her occasionally and wondered if, as a chaperon, she could flatly order one of the stags to dance with Naomi.

She had a feeling there would be trouble if she attempted this.

Carolyn danced by every few minutes; Mrs. Bridge waved and smiled and during the evening was introduced to a number of boys. Mr. De Falla asked her to dance, and though she did not want to she felt it might look rude if she refused. He danced with a rather wild, swooping motion, but otherwise proved to be more cultured than she had expected and she found herself half-hoping he would ask for another dance. But he did not; when the music ended he escorted her back to her chair and resumed talking to the female mathematics teacher, who was wearing a low-cut gray satin gown, with a gardenia looking quite mashed in the crevice.

About eleven o'clock a game of dice was discovered in the cloakroom by Mr. De Falla, because the sentinel was at the punch bowl, and the gamblers were dismissed from the party. Beyond this there were no incidents until shortly after midnight. This last affair was witnessed by Mrs. Bridge alone. She never mentioned it to anyone.

She had been sitting quietly, partly concealed by the piano, for quite a while when she noticed a couple dancing in the corner where the lantern had burned out. Their motions were definitely erotic, though in time to the music. In a lesser degree such dancing had been evident throughout the evening, modern dancing being more suggestive than the dancing of Mrs. Bridge's youth; but, because the other chaperons had taken it all without comment, she had not objected. This couple, however, thinking themselves unobserved in the darkened corner, were consciously beyond the limit: Mrs. Bridge knew it immediately from the girl's apprehensive eyes. The boy was dancing, shuffling, insinuating himself, with his eyes closed and his nose thrust into the flower she wore in her hair, and on his pimpled face lay a sleepy smile. The girl, too, was dreamily smiling, though she remained alert. Mrs. Bridge leaned forward in her chair and attracted the girl's attention; instantly the couple broke apart and went dancing rapidly to the other end of the room and on out the door. She saw them both look back to see if she had gotten up and was coming after them. She never saw them again and never learned who they were. She did not ask. This was the thing she remembered longest and most vividly about the sorority party, and the thing that caused her to look more carefully at the boys who came by the house for Carolyn. The horrifying part of it had been that the girl's back was turned to her partner.

*

58

Good Night

Carolyn was dating a clumsy, bumptious boy with crew-cut hair and an idiotic laugh whose name was Jay Duchesne, and about whom Mrs. Bridge had her doubts. Duchesne chewed gum with awful assurance and reputedly drove too fast, but because she wanted Carolyn to learn to judge people she said nothing, always greeting Duchesne with a neutral smile and saying, "Good evening, Jay. Won't you have a chair? Carolyn will be down in a few minutes."

"Why not?" Duchesne would answer, and after shaking his own hand in congratulation he would sit and twirl his hat on his index finger and chew gum with a loud snapping noise.

Until Carolyn got in at night Mrs. Bridge would lie awake

or would sit up reading. Carolyn knew this and consequently talked to Duchesne in very low tones at the front door; Mrs. Bridge could hear them murmuring because their voices carried much farther in the still night air than they realized. One evening, after they had been saying good night at the door for about an hour, she heard the next-door neighbor's fox terrier—which was often left out overnight—begin to growl, and she concluded that Duchesne must be molesting Carolyn. Throwing back the covers she hurriedly pulled on her robe and went to the banister, prepared to call out, but at that moment a cat hissed; with a sigh of relief Mrs. Bridge prepared to go back to bed. Then, however, she heard Duchesne ask Carolyn for a kiss.

"You're frequently mad," Carolyn responded.

"Nobody'll find out," Duchesne answered.

"You're an ogre," said Carolyn.

Duchesne didn't think that was a good reason.

"Then, because," said Carolyn.

"Why, because?" inquired Duchesne.

"Because, that's why."

"Because why?"

After this had gone on for several minutes Carolyn said her mother wouldn't approve. Duchesne apparently was thinking this over because his chewing gum snapped incessantly; then he muttered something Mrs. Bridge could not hear.

"But of course not!" Carolyn sounded shocked. "Are you mad?"

"Aw, why not?" Duchesne bleated. "Don't be a duchess."

In a very superior tone, then, Carolyn said distinctly, "Because, that's all. We won't discuss it any further. And besides, don't be excruciating."

Duchesne, sounding uncommonly like a musical saw, was heard to say, "Awwwww, awwwww, jeez!"

"I feel terribly sorry for you," Carolyn said with unnatural compassion. "I'd like to, you know. Really, *really* I would, don't you know? So terribly, terribly much, you mad child. Because you're good," she said earnestly, *"Good!"* And Mrs. Bridge, puzzled, tried to recall that particular inflection because it did sound familiar. She wondered if Carolyn was running her fingers through Duchesne's hair, or, considering how short it was, over the top. He was working on the chewing gum again. Mrs. Bridge sensed that Carolyn had him on the defensive.

"I am fond of you, Jay. Dreadfully so. I ache, actually. But—but—"

"Listen, Cork," growled Duchesne, man of action, and his big feet scraped on the doorsill. "You want to be a virgin forever?"

"Silly!" said Carolyn.

Mrs. Bridge, clutching the banister in horror, was gathering strength to speak out when the door bumped shut and Carolyn sighed, clearly alone. A moment later the engine roared and the tires squealed out of the driveway. Carolyn went into the kitchen. Mrs. Bridge, folding her robe more tightly, stood in the upper hall trying to regain her composure. If anyone had asked her such a question she was positive she would have slapped the boy with all her strength, but a moment afterward she thought of the night some twenty years ago when she had barely resisted the pleas of a boy whose very name she had long since forgotten. It was the moonlight that had weakened her, the moonlight and her own desire.

"Carolyn?" she called very softly through the silent house.

The refrigerator door closed. Carolyn walked into the downstairs hall and gazed upward.

"Are you all right, dear?"

"Natch."

"Did you have a good time?"

"So-so."

"That's nice," Mrs. Bridge said absently, drew the robe more tightly around herself, and started back to bed.

"Mother?"

"Yes, dear?"

"We're all out of peanut butter."

"Oh, thank God!" whispered Mrs. Bridge. Aloud, softly so as not to waken her husband, she called, "I'll tell Harriet to order some in the morning. Don't stay up too late."

✳

59

Suitor

When Harriet, who was at times inclined to insubordination, brought in the breakfast tray Mrs. Bridge exclaimed, "For Heaven's sake! What on earth happened to you?"

"Couperin," said Harriet, grinning.

"Oh, goodness! Is he the one with the motorcycle?"

"No, ma'am," said Harriet vehemently. "I took my last ride on a motorcycle, believe me. Approximately eight or ten weeks back." She began to feel tenderly about her jaw, on which there was a large purple bruise.

"I certainly hope this was an accident," said Mrs. Bridge.

"It came about," Harriet replied with regal poise, "because only last evening it so happened that I and that Couperin had a grave dispute. Couperin, he got the worst."

The evidence seemed to indicate Couperin had spoken the final word, but Mrs. Bridge decided not to get involved.

"What does he do?" she inquired, to change the subject.

"He is associated with the collection bureau of this city."

"Tax collectors, or—"

"Bureau of rubbish and trash. Then, too, he plumbs a bit. When he is inclined."

Mrs. Bridge, beginning to sense this would be one of Harriet's insolent days, sipped at the orange juice and then started to butter a slice of toast.

"Last evening," Harriet continued, wetting a finger and touching up her eyebrows, "I received his proposition."

This obviously demanded some sort of acknowledgment, even though Couperin or one of the other suitors proposed every Thursday night. What jarred Mrs. Bridge as much as anything was Harriet's referring to it as a proposition instead of a proposal, and every Friday when the subject was mentioned she was about to point out the difference.

"I hope you didn't accept," she said, pouring some cream in the coffee.

"Frankly, I was tempted," said Harriet. "However I declined, as you say. The reason being he chooses to get disgustingly drunk following on the heels of his pay check. I disapprove of that, don't you?"

"I most certainly do," agreed Mrs. Bridge, busying herself at the table somewhat more than necessary. Then, as Harriet appeared to be reflecting on the previous evening, she said, "Isn't that a new hair-do?"

"Well, it is, yes." Harriet pushed it lightly with her fingertips. "I believe it will prove suitable."

"You look very chic."

"Well, I find it pays to keep up appearances."

Mrs. Bridge had the feeling she was about to pull out a cigarette. "Perhaps you'd better look in the refrigerator and see if we're going to have enough whipping cream for the week end."

Harriet, holding her bruised jaw, turned to go into the kitchen.

Mrs. Bridge, who was very thankful that Carolyn had no Couperin to contend with, said, "I hope you won't be seeing him any more."

"I believe not until next week on the customary evening," replied Harriet.

60

Laundress in the Rear

Every Wednesday the laundress arrived, and as the bus line was quite a few blocks distant from the Bridge home someone would usually meet her bus in the morning. For years the laundress had been a withered old colored woman named Beulah Mae, who wore a red bandanna, a ragged velvet dress split at the seams, and a pair of tennis shoes with the toes cut out because her feet hurt. Mrs. Bridge was very fond of Beulah Mae, speaking of her as "a nice old soul" and frequently giving her extra money or an evening dress that had begun to look dated, or perhaps the cookies that she was obliged to buy from the Girl Scouts. But there came a day when Beulah Mae had had enough of laundering, extra gifts or no, and without a word to any of her clients she boarded a bus for California to live out her time on the seashore. Mrs. Bridge was therefore without a laundress for an interval of several weeks, during which the work was taken to an establishment, but at last she got someone else, an extremely large, doleful Swedish woman named Ingrid, who said while being interviewed in the kitchen that for

eighteen years she had been a masseuse on the island of Got-
land and wished she had stayed there.

When Mrs. Bridge arrived at the bus line the first morning Ingrid saluted her mournfully and got laboriously into
the front seat. This was not the custom, but such a thing
was difficult to explain because Mrs. Bridge did not like to
hurt anyone's feelings, so she said nothing about it and hoped
that by next week some other laundress in the neighborhood
would have told Ingrid.

But the next week she again climbed in front, and again
Mrs. Bridge pretended everything was satisfactory. However, on the third morning while they were riding up Ward
Parkway toward the house Mrs. Bridge said, "I was so attached to Beulah Mae. She used to have the biggest old time
riding in the back seat."

Ingrid turned a massive yellow head to look stonily down
on Mrs. Bridge. As they were easing into the driveway she
spoke. "So you want I should sit in the back."

"Oh, gracious! I didn't mean that," Mrs. Bridge answered,
smiling up at her. "You're perfectly welcome to sit right here
if you like."

Ingrid said no more about the matter and next week with
the same majestic melancholy rode in the rear.

*

61

Complexities of Life

The elegant Lincoln her husband had given her for her birthday was altogether too long, and she drove it as prudently as she might have driven a locomotive. People were always sounding their horns at her, or turning their heads to stare when she coasted by. Because the Lincoln had been set to idle too slowly, the engine frequently died when she pulled up at an intersection, but as her husband never used the Lincoln and she herself assumed it was just one of those things about automobiles, the idling speed was never adjusted. Often she would delay a line of cars while she pressed the starter button either too long or not long enough. Knowing she was not expert she was always quite apologetic when something unfortunate happened, and did her best to keep out of everyone's way. She shifted into second gear at the beginning of every hill and let herself down the far side much more slowly than necessary.

Usually she parked in a downtown garage where Mr. Bridge rented a stall for her. She had only to honk at the doors, which would soon trundle open, after which she coasted inside, where an attendant would greet her by name, help her out, and then park the formidable machine. But in the country-club district she parked on the street, and if there were diagonal stripes she did very well, but if parking was parallel she had trouble judging her distance from the curb and would have to get out and walk around to look, then get back in and try again. The Lincoln's cushions were so soft and Mrs. Bridge so short that she was obliged to sit erect in order to see whatever was going on ahead of her. She drove with arms thrust forward and gloved hands firmly on the wheel, her feet just able to depress the pedals. She never had serious accidents, but was often seen here and there being talked to by patrolmen. These patrolmen never did anything, partly because they saw immediately that it would not do to arrest her, and partly because they could tell she was trying to do everything the way it should be done.

When parking on the street it embarrassed her to have people watch, yet there always seemed to be someone at the bus stop or lounging in a doorway with nothing to do but stare while she struggled with the wheel and started jerkily backward. Sometimes, however, there would be a nice man who, seeing her difficulty, would come around and tip his hat and ask if he might help.

"Would you, please?" she would ask in relief, and after he opened the door she would get out and wait on the curb with an attentive expression while he parked the car. It was then a problem to know whether he expected a tip or not. She knew that people who stood around on street corners did not have much money; still she did not want to offend any-one. Sometimes she would hesitantly ask, sometimes not, and whether the man would accept a quarter or not she would smile brightly up at him, saying, "Thank you so much," and having locked the Lincoln's doors she would be off to the shops.

*

62

News of the Leacocks

She gasped when she saw the evening paper. On the front page was a picture of Tarquin Leacock taken a few minutes after he had been captured. The Leacocks had moved away from Kansas City about two years ago and no one had heard anything from them since that time. Every once in a while someone would ask what had become of them, for they had been such a remarkable family that it seemed they must be making news wherever they were. Now indeed they were.

"I saw it," Mr. Bridge said when he got home that night. He had been working late again; it was nearly midnight when his Chrysler turned in the driveway, but she had waited up.

"I simply can't believe it," she said.

"I can," said Mr. Bridge as he took off his overcoat. "You remember I warned you about that kid."

"Oh, yes, I know," she said faintly, "but this!"

He hung his coat in the closet, placed his Homburg atop the briefcase and returned to the living room, where he glanced with no particular interest at the picture of Tarquin, who had developed into a surly, hulking youth.

"Well," said Mr. Bridge quietly, and tapped the newspaper with his index finger, "I am sorry about this, but on the other hand those people had no one to blame but themselves. This doesn't surprise me in the least. They should have taught that youngster there are other people in the world besides himself." He shook his head and took off his glasses, as he did whenever he was exhausted. "It gets worse every day. These psychologists have bluffed parents into thinking nothing is more important than a child's right to assert himself. Lord knows where it will end. But I'll tell you this: Douglas is going to learn he's not the supreme authority. His personality can go to pot, so far as that's concerned, but my son is not going to run around pulling stunts like this!"

With which Mr. Bridge again tapped the paper, significantly, and headed for the kitchen. Mrs. Bridge followed him and began to warm the supper that Harriet had prepared and covered with oil paper and left on the drainboard, for it was Thursday night and she had stepped out with Couperin.

"Really, it just makes me ill to think about it," Mrs. Bridge said, and she lighted the oven and placed his supper in to warm.

"Society gets the crime it deserves," Mr. Bridge remarked with indifference. "I'll never forget that kid calling his parents by their first names."

"No, I don't approve of that either," she said.

Tarquin, having had a bellyful of psychology, or, perhaps, only feeling unusually progressive, had entered the bedroom of his parents while they were asleep and had shot them dead.

63

The Hat

Tarquin Leacock preyed on her mind and she therefore took to observing her son more closely, wondering if he, too, might unexpectedly go berserk. He was now in high school, and so far as she could tell he was less of an Apache than most of his companions, for which she was grateful, but he did become unpredictable, given to fits of introspection during which he dressed quite formally and stalked about with hands behind his back, followed by a grandiose kind of goodfellowship, and it was in this latter mood that the battle of the hat took place.

She was of the opinion that at certain ages one wore certain articles of clothing—each of the girls had received a girdle on her fourteenth birthday—and she now suggested to Douglas that he was old enough to begin wearing a hat.

"I don't need a hat," he said.

"It's time you started wearing one," she replied.

"They don't feel good on my head," said Douglas.

"Your father would look awfully silly without a hat," she argued.

"Who knows?" he countered, flinging up his hands.

So it went for a period of several weeks until finally they drove downtown and picked out a hat, a very nice conservative hat. She never expected to see it on his head, but strangely enough he began to wear it everywhere. He wore it to school and while playing ball after school, and he wore it around the house and in his room at night while doing homework. Very shortly she was sick of seeing the hat, but now he would not think of going anywhere without it. Furthermore there developed, somewhere between the high school and the drugstore where he played the pinball games, the habit of wearing it on the back of his head; not only this but on the crown he pinned a glazed yellow button saying: LET'S GET ACQUAINTED!

＊

64

First Babies

That summer the family was invited to the wedding of a relative named Maxwell who was a postal clerk in the nearby town of Olathe. Carolyn was the only one who wanted to attend the wedding, but because it was an obligation of sorts the entire family—except Mr. Bridge—drove to Olathe. When the bride came down the aisle they discovered the reason for the wedding.

After the ceremony they put in an appearance at the reception and then, in silence, drove home.

About three months later they received the traditional announcement concerning the birth of a child. It happened that Ruth, Carolyn, and Douglas were at home when this announcement arrived, and Mrs. Bridge, having exclaimed, in spite of her disgust, "Isn't that nice!" felt it necessary to add, "First babies are so often premature."

At this time Ruth was eighteen years old, Carolyn was sixteen, and Douglas, nobody's fool, a shrewd fourteen. A profound silence, a massive, annihilating silence, greeted her remark. Carolyn gazed out the window. Douglas became greatly interested in his fingernails. Ruth looked at Carolyn, then at Douglas, and she seemed to be considering. Finally she said, quietly, "Oh, Mother, don't."

None of them said anything further. The Maxwells were not mentioned again.

*

65

Who's Calling?

She was kneeling in the garden with a trowel in her hand when Harriet lifted the kitchen window to announce that some man who would not give his name was on the telephone asking for Ruth.

"I'll take it," Mrs. Bridge said, getting to her feet. She entered the house and approached the telephone with a feeling of hostility, and taking up the receiver more firmly than usual she said, "Hello. Ruth is not in Kansas City at the moment. Who's calling, please?"

"Where's she at?" a deep voice asked.

Mrs. Bridge signaled Harriet to stop running the vacuum cleaner.

"Ruth is visiting friends at Lake Lotawana. Who is calling, please?"

"What's the number out there?" the man demanded.

Despite his rudeness and obvious coarseness, if he had been inquiring about Carolyn she would have given him the number at the lake, but she had never liked or trusted the men who came after Ruth.

"I'm certain she would like to know who called."

There was a pause. Mrs. Bridge thought he was going to hang up, but he finally answered, "Tell her Al called." Then he added, "Al Luchek." And faintly, from wherever he was, came the clink of glasses.

For some reason Ruth's friends always had foreign names. Carolyn's companions were named Bob or Janet or Trudy or Buzz, but there was a malignant sound to Al Luchek, and to the others—the Louie Minillos and the Nick Gajadas. They sounded like gangsters from the north end. Mrs. Bridge had once or twice asked Ruth who they were, and how she met them, but Ruth replied evasively that she had simply met them at So-and-so's house or at a New Year's Eve party.

"But what do they *do?*" she asked, and Ruth would shrug.

"Tom Duncan was asking about you the other day," she would say, but Ruth would not be interested.

Now she said in cool and civil tones to the man on the telephone, "Thank you for calling, Mr. Luchek."

Immediately the vacuum roared.

Mrs. Bridge was disturbed. Ruth was incomprehensible to her and with every year she became more so, more secretive and turbulent, more cunning and inaccessible, more foreign. Where had she come from? How could she be Carolyn's sister? Mrs. Bridge was deeply worried and found it more and more difficult to call her by the pet names of childhood, and before long she was unable to call her by any name except Ruth, though it sounded formal and distant and tended to magnify their separation. Are you mine? she sometimes thought. Is my daughter mine?

*

66

Mademoiselle from Kansas City

It was to Carolyn, though she was younger, that Mrs. Bridge was in the habit of confiding her hopes for them all. The two were apt to sit on the edge of Carolyn's bed until quite late at night, their arms half-entwined, talking and giggling, while across the room Ruth slept her strangely restless sleep—mumbling and rolling and burying her face in her wild black hair.

Mrs. Bridge could never learn what Ruth did in the evenings, or where she went; she entered the house quietly, sometimes not long before dawn. Mrs. Bridge had always lain awake until both girls were home, and one evening during the Christmas holidays she was still downstairs reading when Carolyn returned, bringing Jay Duchesne, who was now considerably over six feet tall and was doing his best to grow a mustache. In certain lights the mustache was visible, and he was quite proud of it and stroked it constantly and feverishly, as if all it needed in order to flourish was a little affection. Mrs. Bridge liked Jay. She trusted him. There were moments when she thought she knew him better than she knew Douglas.

"What's new, Mrs. B.?" he inquired, twirling his hat on one finger. And to Carolyn, "How's for chow, kid?" So they went out to the kitchen to cook bacon and eggs while Mrs. Bridge remained in the front room with the book turned over in her lap and her eyes closed, dozing and dreaming happily, because it seemed to her that despite the difficulties of adolescence she had gotten her children through it in reasonably good condition. Later, when Duchesne roared out of the driveway—he still drove as recklessly as ever and she was still not resigned to it—she climbed the stairs, arm in arm, with Carolyn.

"Jay's voice has certainly changed," she smiled.

"He's a man now, Mother," Carolyn explained a bit impatiently.

Mrs. Bridge smiled again. She sat on the bed and watched as Carolyn pulled off the baggy sweater and skirt and seated herself at the dressing table with a box of bobby pins.

"Funny—it's so quiet," said Carolyn.

Mrs. Bridge looked out the window. "Why, it's snowing again. Isn't that nice! I just love snowy winter nights."

Large wet flakes were floating down and clasping the outside of the window, and the street light shone on the evergreen tree in the back yard.

"There goes a rabbit!" she cried, but by the time Carolyn reached the window only the tracks were visible.

"Is Daddy asleep?" Carolyn asked.

"Yes, poor man. He didn't get away from the office until after seven and insists he has to get up at five-thirty tomorrow morning."

"That's silly."

"I know, but you can't tell him anything. I've tried, goodness knows, but it never does any good."

"Why does he do it?"

"Oh," said Mrs. Bridge irritably, for the thought of it never failed to irritate her, "he insists we'll all starve to death if he doesn't."

"That'll be the day!"

Both of them were silent for a while, watching the snow descend.

"I do hope Ruth gets home soon."

"She can drop dead for all I care."

"You know I don't like you to use that expression."

Carolyn split a bobby pin on her teeth and jammed it into her curly blond hair. "Well, what's the matter with her then? Who does she think she is, anyway?" She leaned to one side and opened the cupboard that belonged to Ruth. "Look at that! Black lace bras. Mademoiselle from Kansas City."

Presently the grandfather clock in the hall chimed twice, and Mrs. Bridge, after brushing Carolyn's cheek with her lips, went downstairs and into the kitchen, where she made herself some cocoa and moodily watched the snow building up on the sill. After a while she went upstairs again, changed into her nightgown, and got into bed beside her husband. There she lay with her hands folded on the blanket while she waited for the faint noise of the front door opening and closing.

She believed she was awake but all at once, without having heard a sound, she realized someone was downstairs. She heard a gasp and then what sounded like a man groaning. The luminous hands of the bedside clock showed four-fifteen. Mrs. Bridge got out of bed, pulled on her robe, and hurried along the hall to the top of the stairs, where she took hold of the banister and leaned over, calling just loud enough to be heard by anyone in the living room, "Ruth?"

No one answered.

"Ruth, is that you?" she asked, more loudly, and there was authority in her tone. She listened and she thought some delicate noise had stopped. The dark house was silent.

"I'm coming down," said Mrs. Bridge.

"It's me," said Ruth.

"Is there anyone with you?"

"He's leaving."

And then Ruth coughed in a prolonged, unnatural way, and Mrs. Bridge knew she was coughing to conceal another noise.

"Who's there?" she demanded, unaware that she was trembling from anger and fright, but there was only the sound of the great front door opening and shutting and seconds later the crunch of auto tires on the crust of yesterday's frozen snow as whoever it was released the brake and coasted away.

A cold draft swept up the spiral staircase. Mrs. Bridge, peering down into the gloom, saw her daughter ascending. She snapped on the hall light and they met at the top step. Ruth was taking the last of the pins out of her hair. She reeked of whisky and her dress was unbuttoned. Idly she pushed by her mother and wandered along the hall. Mrs. Bridge was too shocked to do anything until Ruth was at the door of her room; there they confronted each other again, for Ruth had felt herself pursued and turned swiftly with a sibilant ominous cry. Her green eyes were glittering and she lifted one hand to strike. Mrs. Bridge, untouched by her daughter's hand, staggered backward.

*

67

Ruth Goes to New York

That was the year Ruth finally managed to graduate from high school. She was there five years and for a while they were afraid it would be six, though she had taken the easiest courses possible. Her electives were music, drawing, athletics, and whatever else sounded easy. She seldom studied, and even when she did study she did poorly. She had been a member of the swimming team and this was the only activity listed after her name in the yearbook: "member of girls' swimming team"—that and the desperate phrase "interested in dramatics." She had once tried out for a play, but gave a rather hysterical reading and failed to get the part. When she finished high school Carolyn was only one semester behind her, although they had started two years apart.

A few days after the graduation she said she was going to New York to get a job. She did not like Kansas City; she never had. She had not made many friends. She had never seemed happy or even much at ease in Kansas City.

Mrs. Bridge tried to become indignant when Ruth announced she was going to New York, but after all it was useless to argue.

"What on earth would you do in New York?" she asked, because Ruth had been unable to learn shorthand, nor could she operate a typewriter as efficiently as Douglas, who tapped out his English themes with one finger.

"Don't worry about me," Ruth said. She had grown tall and beautiful, and somehow—in the powerful arch of her nose and in her somber, barbaric eyes—she looked biblical, swarthy and violent.

"I'm putting a thousand dollars in the bank for you," said Mr. Bridge, "on one condition." This condition was that if she could not support herself by the time the money ran out she would agree to return to Kansas City. She laughed and put her arms around him, and no one in the family had seen her do this since she was a child.

Mrs. Bridge was disturbed that she did not want to go to college, being of the opinion that although one might never actually need a college degree it was always nice to have; and yet, thinking the matter over, she realized Ruth would only be wasting four years—obviously she was no student. But why New York? Why not some place closer to home?

Soon she was ready to leave. The entire family went to the station.

"You didn't forget your ticket, did you?" asked Mrs. Bridge.

"Not quite," said Ruth drily.

"Be sure to look up the Wenzells when you get there. I've already written them you're coming to New York, but of course they won't know where to find you." The Wenzells were people they had met one summer in Colorado and with whom they exchanged Christmas greetings.

"I will," said Ruth, who had no intention of getting in touch with them.

"Have a good trip," her mother said as they were embracing at the gate. "Don't forget to write. Let us know as soon as you arrive."

"Here are your traveling expenses," her father said, handing her some folded bills. "For God's sake, don't lose it. And behave yourself. If you don't, I'm coming after you."

"I can look out for myself," said Ruth.

He laughed, and his laughter rang out odd and bold, the laughter of a different man, a free and happy man, who was not so old after all. "That isn't what I said," he told her lightly, and Mrs. Bridge, glancing from one to the other, was struck by their easy companionship, as though they had gotten to know each other quite well when she was not around.

Once on the train Ruth kicked off her shoes and curled up in the seat. She unsnapped the catch of her traveling bag and reached in for a copy of *Theatre Arts* but felt a strange envelope. She knew immediately what it was—it was called a "train letter," and a generation or so ago they were given to young people who were leaving home for the first time. She withdrew her hand and sat motionless for quite a while. Tears gathered in her eyes and presently she was shaken with dry sobs, although she did not know whether she was laughing or weeping. Before long she dried her face and lighted a cigarette.

Much later Ruth took out the envelope, read the letter of advice, and seemed to see her mother seated at the Chippendale highboy with some stationery and a fountain pen, seeking to recall the guidance of another era.

*

68

Tornado at the Club

Not long after Ruth's departure a very familiar day rolled around for Mrs. Bridge.

Each year on her birthday she was distressed by the extravagance of her husband's gift. Invariably she protested to him, and meant it, but he was determined to give her costly presents and she could not dissuade him. Once he set his mind he was immovable. One year it had been the Lincoln, another year it was an ermine coat, another year it was a diamond necklace. She loved these things, to be sure, but she did not need them, and knew this quite well, and in spite of loving them she could not help being a little embarrassed by the opulence of her possessions. She was conscious of people on the street staring at her when, wrapped in ermine and driving the Lincoln, she started off to a party at the country club; she wanted to stop the car and explain to them that her husband was still at work in the office though it was nine in the evening, and that she had not asked for these expensive things but that he had given them to her for her birthday. But, of course, she could not stop to explain any more than she could stop people from staring.

This year, therfore, she was mildly surprised when her birthday arrived and all he said was that they were going to have dinner at the club. She supposed this was to be her gift. It was odd, considering the past, but she was not displeased; she was even a bit relieved.

And it came as an unforgettable shock when he remarked, slyly, pleased with himself, soon after they had been seated in the country-club dining room, that the two of them were leaving for Europe three weeks from Sunday. Mrs. Bridge at first thought he was joking. He was not. And she learned that all her friends had known about the trip for the past month, but not one of them had so much as hinted about the surprise in store for her. The tickets were already bought and he had reserved hotel accommodations in the countries they were to visit. They would be gone, he told her, for about six weeks.

"I feel giddy," said Mrs. Bridge. "I never dreamed of anything like this."

And when the waiter had taken their order Mr. Bridge proceeded to tell her of the cities they would visit, and as he talked she stopped listening, because she could not help thinking of another evening when he had told her of all he planned to do. He had said he would take her to Europe one day; she remembered having smiled at him fondly, not really believing, not caring, happy enough to be with him anywhere. How long ago, she thought, how very long ago that was! It seemed like eight or ten years ago, but it was more than twenty, and on this day she was forty-eight years old. She grew a little sad at this, and while he talked on and on—he was more excited than she—she gazed out the window at the gathering clouds. And the distant thunder seemed to be warning her that one day this world she knew and loved would be annihilated.

The clouds descended and the wind began to increase while they were eating. A few drops of rain spattered against the window. It was the season for tornados, and before much longer it had become evident that one was approaching. The club steward turned on the radio and listened to reports of the tornado's course; it was, he learned, bearing directly toward the country club at a speed of seventy miles an hour. The steward went from table to table explaining the situation and adding that if the storm continued to approach it would be necessary to take shelter in the basement.

"Thank you," said Mrs. Bridge. "Do you suppose there's much chance of it hitting us?"

The steward didn't know. The tornado was still quite a few miles west; the course of it might alter, or the funnel might degenerate before reaching Kansas City.

"Well, you'll let us know," said Mrs. Bridge.

The steward said he would keep them informed.

Soon the trees on the terrace were bending from the wind, and the rain poured down. She saw a metal chair go skidding off the porch as though someone were pulling it away with a rope. A few of the diners had begun to leave the room, and the steward was coming around again.

"Goodness, this *is* a storm," said Mrs. Bridge. "Do you think we should go to the basement?"

Mr. Bridge replied that the storm was not going to strike the clubhouse and that he, for one, intended to finish his dinner.

"There goes the mayor," she said, looking around. The mayor and his wife often ate at the club and the Bridges were acquainted with them.

"Good evening," said the mayor as he passed by, preceded by his wife.

"Good evening," said Mrs. Bridge.

The rain was coming down so heavily it was no longer possible to see through the window. There was no lightning and very little thunder, only the rain and a sense of terrible oppression as though something were lurking nearby.

Mrs. Bridge placed her napkin on the table and said, "Well, it looks like we're in for it."

Her husband continued eating.

"Steward, have you any further information?" she asked as soon as he had finished speaking to a couple at the next table.

The steward said the tornado was still approaching and he thought it would be a good idea to go to the basement.

"Thank you," said Mrs. Bridge, and looked expectantly at her husband.

"I'm going to finish this steak," said he.

The steward did not know quite how to proceed; he knew it was his responsibility to get everyone to the basement, and if Mr. and Mrs. Bridge should be swept up and carried away he would be called upon by the club directors for an explanation. On the other hand he did not care to begin giving orders to Mr. Bridge who, he knew, was not only short-tempered but very much aware of having been warned. He gazed earnestly at Mr. Bridge, who paid no attention to him, and at last, unable to decide whether he was more afraid of him or of the club directors, the steward hurried off to the radio in hopes that the decision would be taken out of his hands by the course of the storm.

The lights of the dining room looked extraordinarily bright because of the unnatural darkness outside. There was a curious stillness and the rain fell in waves. Mrs. Bridge, looking about, saw that except for her husband and herself everyone had left the dining room.

"Don't you think we should go?" she asked.

He was chewing and unable to answer at the moment. He swallowed, wiped his lips with his napkin, took a drink of water, and began to butter a piece of cornbread. Finding that he did not have enough butter he began to frown. He liked butter very much and at home he got all he wanted, but whenever they ate out he kept asking for more. Mrs. Bridge, who was on a diet, had already given him the butter from her plate, but this was not enough. Both of them looked around. There was not a waiter in sight.

"Well, I'll steal some from the next table," said Mrs. Bridge. "I don't suppose anyone will mind." And she got up and walked over to get a piece of butter for her husband. Fortunately there was an untouched square of it on the table and so she leaned across, holding her beads with one hand so they would not dip into the abandoned dishes, and picked up the butter plate. It was a small china plate with the crest of the country club stamped in gold and she thought as she picked it up how attractive it was. Just then the lights flickered. Apparently the tornado had struck a power line somewhere. Mrs. Bridge turned to go back to the table. She noticed the club steward standing in the doorway. He was watching them. He was wringing his hands and standing on one foot. She smiled politely, feeling a little foolish because of the butter plate in her hand. He smiled briefly and resumed staring at Mr. Bridge.

From the distance came a hooting, coughing sound, like a railroad locomotive in a tunnel; a very weird and frightening sound it was.

"Well, that must be the tornado," she said, listening attentively, but Mr. Bridge, who was eating the cornbread with great gusto, did not reply. She spread her napkin in her lap again although she had finished eating; she spread it because when she was a child her parents had taught her it was impolite to place her napkin on the table until everyone had finished, and the manners she had been taught she had, in her turn, passed on to her own children.

As the tornado approached the country club Mrs. Bridge remained seated across the table from her husband. She listened to the curious grunting and snuffling of the storm; although she had never been in the path of a tornado before, she knew this must be it, this must be the sound it made— the hooting, sucking roar of the vacuum. Now that it was so close it reminded her of a pig rooting on the terrace.

It did not occur to Mrs. Bridge to leave her husband and run to the basement. She had been brought up to believe without question that when a woman married she was married for the rest of her life and was meant to remain with her husband wherever he was, and under all circumstances, unless he directed her otherwise. She wished he would not be so obstinate; she wished he would behave like everyone else, but she was not particularly frightened. For nearly a quarter of a century she had done as he told her, and what he had said would happen had indeed come to pass, and what he had said would not occur had not occurred. Why, then, should she not believe him now?

The lights of the country club went out and she thought the breath was being drawn from her lungs. Short streaks of lightning flickered intermittently, illuminating a terrible cloud just outside—rushing toward them like a kettle of black water—and she caught the unmistakable odor of electricity. In darkness and silence she waited, uncertain whether the munching noise was made by her husband or the storm.

In a little while the lights came on again and the diners, led by the mayor, came up from the basement.

"There!" said Mr. Bridge, looking about for something else to eat. "I told you, didn't I?"

The tornado, whether impressed by his intransigence or touched by her devotion, had drawn itself up into the sky and was never seen or heard of again.

*

69

Non Capisco

They left for Europe, as he said they would, three weeks later.

In New York they saw Ruth, who had gotten a job as an assistant to one of the editors of a women's magazine, and who was living alone in a Greenwich Village garret. They went up four flights of steps to have a look at her apartment, though she seemed not overly anxious to show it, and Mrs. Bridge was relieved to find it was not quite so forbidding as it sounded. She was, however, surprised by the pictures on the walls—original oil paintings by one of Ruth's new friends —and by the other furnishings. The apartment was so un-like her room in Kansas City. It was neither so tidy nor so comfortable. There was not even a rug; the black wood floor was partly covered by a pattern of Oriental mats. And there were so many phonograph records! Mrs. Bridge had forgotten that she was so fond of music. The apartment, though slightly bizarre, was neatly balanced, she thought, except for one area where something was disturbing. She finally realized that a nail had been driven into the wall above the bed but no picture hung from it. She could not help staring at the nail, knowing Ruth had hidden what-ever belonged there. How strange! she thought. What was Ruth concealing? A moment later Mrs. Bridge became con-scious that she herself was being studied. Turning, then, to her daughter, she was greeted with a look of implacable defiance.

The Atlantic voyage did not agree very well with Mrs. Bridge, though she tried not to show that the motion of the sea was nauseating. She took some tablets and felt better, but could not truly enjoy the meals, and she looked forward to landing in England.

"I guess I'm just not cut out to be a sailor," she remarked more than once, not only to her husband but to some very nice people they had met aboard ship, and those who were feeling a bit queasy themselves were the first to sympathize.

She often noticed an old Italian woman from the tourist deck who, somehow or other, managed to get up to the first-class deck in the afternoons. The old woman would drag a chair into a secluded, sunny corner and would sit motionless for hours. No one ever spoke to her or came to see if she wanted anything. She did not look well. She was raggedly dressed, all in black, with shoes broken open at the seams, and a black scarf bound over her head. Mrs. Bridge, feeling better as the voyage progressed, thought that never in her life had she seen anyone so alone and wretched as this elderly woman, and so, resolving to help her, went one afternoon to the corner and bent over and gently touched her on the shoulder.

"Is there anything I can do for you?"

"Lei parla Italiano?"

"Oh, don't you speak English?"

"Non capisco," the old woman replied, gazing up at her in vast despair.

"I'm awfully sorry," Mrs. Bridge said helplessly. "I wish I knew what to do, but I just don't understand."

*

70

England

They landed at Southampton long before dawn and took the train to London. It was a rainy morning and most of the passengers dozed, but Mrs. Bridge stayed awake and stared out the train window, a trifle groggily, at the silent, stately, fogbound farmland. And as this train carried her across the English countryside, past cottages she had never seen and would never see again, where great birds nested in the chimney crook, and from the hedgerows smaller birds came fluttering in shrill desperation to circle twice, and then, finding nothing, to settle as before, and where the cattle in the mist grazed unperturbed by the train which rolled on and on beneath the somnolent English sky, as though there were no destination, past the rain-drenched, redolent fields, and the trees which cast no shadow, she thought to herself how familiar it was and that once this must have been her home. Yes, she said to herself slowly, yes, I was here before.

In London the hotel was just off Piccadilly Circus; they had some difficulty understanding the hall porter and the maid, and, in fact, at the desk or on the telephone they found it necessary to listen closely. Mrs. Bridge, unpinning her hat as she stood before the mirror in their room—a black straw hat it was, with a shiny cluster of plastic cherries on the brim—replied to her husband's comment, "I agree with you, but don't you suppose we sound funny to them, too?"

Next morning they hired a cab to the Tower of London, where Mrs. Bridge enjoyed the ravens and the colorful costumes of the Beef-eaters. Mr. Bridge spent a good deal of time investigating the instruments of torture and the chopping block, after which they got into the cab again and reached Buckingham Palace just in time for the changing of the guard. Mrs. Bridge used three rolls of color film on this but insisted it was worth every bit of it. After a very pleasant lunch they drove to Eton.

They also hired a car to Stratford-on-Avon, and to the Dover cliffs, to many historic spots throughout the city and around it, and yet, as they were leaving for Paris, it seemed to them both, and particularly to Mrs. Bridge, that they had hardly begun to get acquainted with England. While they were settling themselves on the train she told him she thought England was the nicest birthday present she had ever received.

71

French Restaurant

To Mr. and Mrs. Bridge it seemed that no matter where they went in Paris they ran into Americans; consequently it was no surprise when a young man named Morgan Hager, who was from Kansas City and whose father had written that the Bridges would be visiting, told them that in addition to tourists there were several thousand Americans who had taken up permanent residence in the city, mostly on the Left Bank. No, he did not know what all these expatriates did for a living; yes, he thought they were happy in France; he had no idea whether they intended to remain in a foreign country for the rest of their lives. Mrs. Bridge could not imagine anyone wanting to live outside the United States. To visit, yes. To take up residence, no.

"I should think they would get awfully lonely," she said.

"I guess so," said Hager. "I know I do."

"But then why do you stay?"

"Because I'm happier here."

This was puzzling and she wanted to understand. She observed him frankly and saw that he did not look happy; at least he seldom smiled. She did not think he was truly happy.

"If you have the time, Morgan," said Mr. Bridge, "I'd like to see some of this Bohemian life we hear so much about."

Hager looked at him doubtfully, for the request posed a problem. There were many things he could have shown them, but, even as certain murals in Pompeii are not open to casual tourists, so there were various Parisian experiences not listed in the guidebook.

"Well," said Hager modestly, "I really don't know of anything very Bohemian, but you might like to have dinner at a place on Montparnasse where a lot of art students eat. It's sort of dirty," he added thoughtfully.

Mrs. Bridge thought this sounded exciting. "Perhaps we should go back to the hotel and change," she said.

Hager did not know whether she meant to get more dressed up or less dressed up, so finally he said, "I don't think anybody will notice you." This had a peculiar ring, so he added, "You look all right." Somehow this was not what he had in mind either, so he cleared his throat, scratched his nose, and said, "The place is actually a real dump." He tried again. "I mean, you can get in with no trouble." Having run himself into a cul-de-sac he stopped to meditate. "Oh, well," he said at last, "let's go. I'm hungry as a sonofabitch."

It was the smallest restaurant Mrs. Bridge had ever seen. It was not much larger than her kitchen at home, but somehow or other there were a dozen oilcloth-covered tables jammed into it and every table was crowded. It reeked of cheese and wine and smoke and perspiration. Wedged between the door and a coatrack they stood and waited for three vacancies, and finally the waiter, who was a fat boy with crew-cut hair and a dirty apron, called through the smoke and the gabble, "Alors, vite! J'ai trois! Vite!"

"Okay, step on it," Hager muttered. "He's got three but they won't last," and he began pushing Mrs. Bridge into the confusion.

Finding no room on the table for her purse, and no other place to put it, she was obliged to hold it in her lap. The menu was scrawled on a blackboard on the wall and Hager translated and made recommendations and both Mr. and Mrs. Bridge accepted his suggestions. Seated next to her was an unusually ragged person wearing a short-sleeved shirt and a filthy blue beret.

"Bonjour, Claude," said Morgan Hager.

"Ah, mon ami!" said the dirty one. "Comment ça va?"

"Oh, ça va," replied Hager. "Claude, je vous présente Monsieur et Madame Bridge."

"How do you do?" said Mrs. Bridge.

"Enchanté!" said Claude, with his mouth full of bread. He looked at her speculatively. He plucked at his shirt and said, "C'est un cadeau."

"I gave him the shirt," said Hager.

"Oh. How nice."

"Oui," said Claude, still chewing and eyeing her. He

saw that her wine glass had not been filled, so he reached across the table for the community bottle and filled the glass for her, saying, "C'est bon, alors."

"Thank you," said Mrs. Bridge. The wine was bright red and had a few specks floating on the surface.

"It tastes like vinegar," said Hager as he saw her looking at it doubtfully. "We can get some better stuff. Claude's dead broke, that's why he drinks it. I mean, it's only about one cent a glass."

"Oh, I'm sure it's quite good," she replied, though she was sure it wasn't. She tasted it and smiled because Claude was watching.

"C'est bon, n'est-ce pas?" he demanded.

"Oh, yes, it's really awfully good," she replied, and took another sip to prove she meant it. Claude nodded approvingly. He was eating salad now. He paused, leaned forward, and pulled a limp, black, stringy object out of the bowl. Mrs. Bridge saw it was a spider. Evidently it had climbed into the salad, or had fallen in, and drowned. Claude indifferently dropped it into a shell half filled with ashes and cigarette stubs and continued eating. In a little while the spider recovered and crawled unsteadily out of the ash tray, across the table, and disappeared on the other side.

Presently the waiter arrived with the first course and stood around for a few moments to see if they would enjoy it. The spider had taken the edge from Mrs. Bridge's appetite, and as for salad, though she tried valiantly she could eat nothing more than a bit of tomato.

Back at the hotel that night Mr. Bridge observed that he had always heard so much about Franch cooking but if that was a fair sample he would rather eat in Kansas City.

"I thought it was very good," she said loyally.

"You didn't eat much," he said.

"Well, good heavens," she replied, "we didn't go there for the food."

✳

72

Winged Victory

To the Louvre they went as soon as they got down from
the Eiffel Tower. The Louvre was a symbol to Mrs. Bridge.
As Texas meant size, as Timbuktu meant the ends of the
earth, so did the Louvre have meaning. To be sure, there
were nice galleries in the United States; in Kansas City, for
example, there was the William Rockhill Nelson gallery and
although she had not been in it more than four or five times
in the last twenty years she was very proud that it was in
Kansas City. It had a national reputation, she knew, and
once in a while she thought of visiting it, for she remembered
that on the few occasions she had been there she had enjoyed herself. Once inside it was very nice and of course
remarkably interesting; it was just that getting there was
so difficult, not that it was out of the way, it was not far
from the Plaza, and there was plenty of parking space, but
somehow she could not bring herself to go there. Each time
the idea came to her she began to feel uncomfortably cool
and depressed, and would hear once again her footsteps
echoing from the marble. The few visitors she had encountered had ignored her, or at best seemed distantly courteous.
It was all so impersonal, a trifle ghostly. Now if there were
music and if the windows were open—yes, that was the
trouble. And if it could be nicely carpeted!—instead of
spending all that money on marble pillars. And if there were

a nice tea shop and a gift shop—perhaps Bancroft's could show the gallery directors how to make things more attractive. . . .

And so she meditated in the taxicab as they were on their way to the Louvre. It was a lovely afternoon. Men were fishing from the banks of the Seine, couples browsing along the bookstalls—what oddly shaped green boxes! she thought, with the lids propped up and so many maps and pictures on display. And in the Tuileries, with the Louvre in the background, ladies were knitting and children were rolling hoops across the grass. Balloons waved at the end of sticks, or clustered together, bumping against one another in the afternoon breeze, and she noticed, as the taxicab stopped in front of the famous French museum, how many people were going in and out; Paris was really altogether different from Kansas City.

In the Louvre she immediately recognized the Venus de Milo, even though they happened to approach from the rear, and of course the Mona Lisa was unmistakable; it looked exactly like the reproductions. The tapestries seemed familiar somehow; perhaps it was just that most tapestries looked alike, and most Greek vases, and all mummies.

At the end of an hour Mr. Bridge said he thought he would go outside and wait, with the result that she continued through the Louvre alone. It was tiring, but it was exciting, and she knew she would never forget this day; it was with a feeling of regret—despite the fact that she was so exhausted she could hardly walk—that at last she concluded it was time to leave. Her husband was probably bored to death waiting for her; she felt a little guilty about letting him wait, but knew he would understand. He knew how she had looked forward to visiting the Louvre.

She had not managed to see everything but she reflected as she walked toward the exit that she had seen all the most famous paintings and statuary—except the Winged Victory of Samothrace, she thought, and promptly stopped. It had been familiar to her as long as she could remember. There must have been a picture of it in one of her earliest schoolbooks. Even now she could imagine it so clearly: that imperial figure advancing and the drapery streaming backward. How impressive it must be!

"Well," she said, half aloud, "it may be ages before I'm in the Louvre again, so if I'm going to see it I'd better see it now."

She looked around, intending to inquire where it was, but for the moment there seemed to be no English-speaking people in the corridor, so she decided to continue to the exit where there should be an information desk, or at least a guard who would understand. She turned the corner and there, all of a sudden, was the Winged Victory. Mrs. Bridge gasped and took a step backward, for the great statue seemed to be bearing down on her and it was the very image of Lois Montgomery in a nightgown.

73

Strangers in Paradise

Next day they went window-shopping along the boulevards near the Opéra, and in the course of this stroll Mrs. Bridge became slightly separated from her husband. They were walking slowly up the rue Auber, stopping at whatever interested them, and she had drifted ahead, musing on the difference between Paris and Kansas City, observing the

French businessmen who seemed content to loiter for hours in sidewalk cafés, and whose attitude, she reflected, was certainly pleasure before business.

Finding herself alone, she looked back and saw him standing with his arms folded, staring into one of the shop windows. She waited a while, thinking he would be coming along, but whatever he saw had hypnotized him. Her curiosity aroused, she retraced her steps. He sensed her approach and looked around with a start. They wandered along as before, but she had seen the object of his attention: a black lace brassière with the tips cut off.

The more she mulled over this incident the more concerned she became. The French, after all, might do as they pleased; she need have nothing to do with the French, but she must live with her husband. She had lived with him for a long time now, and assumed she knew whatever was worth knowing about him. True, there were occasional surprises—once he had told her, and afterward seemed to regret having divulged the secret, that when he was a boy he used to dream of becoming a great composer—but the revelations of his nature had seemed meaningless, no matter how fascinating, and she was not apt to dwell on them, but now she did.

Why had he stood there looking? What had he been thinking? His expression had been so serious. Were there things he had never told her about himself? Who was he, really? From all the recesses of her being came the questions, questions which had never before occurred to her, and there on the foreign street she felt lost and forsaken, and with great longing she began to think of Kansas City.

*

74

Intellectual Café

The guidebook spoke of a café called Le Dôme as having been the haunt of famous intellectuals at the beginning of the century, so there they went to spend an hour or two.

"Picasso used to linger here," Mrs. Bridge read from the book, and she went on to read the names of other celebrated individuals who had taken their leisure on this very terrace.

"Here comes Picasso now," said Mr. Bridge.

"Oh, I don't believe it," she said, looking up nevertheless. In a moment she saw to whom he was referring; it was Morgan Hager, whom they had not seen for several days. Hager was carrying a portfolio under his arm and he was wearing a beret that for some reason made him resemble a fox. He looked startled when he saw them in the café, and for an instant seemed ready to flee, but then he smiled and nodded and came over to join them, placing his portfolio in a corner. Mrs. Bridge thought about asking to see his drawings, and after some hesitation she did so. He said the drawings were not much good and she did not press the matter.

"Well," he said, "I see you're still here." This was not what he meant to say, so he amended, "I figured you'd probably left." Since this was not right either he said, "I never did know what you were doing here." He saw Mrs. Bridge smiling courteously and steadily, and Mr. Bridge observing him with frank curiosity, so he took off his beret and scratched his head, gazed around Le Dôme in search of something whereby he might distract them from his inability to make conversation, and he exclaimed, "Oh! Look at that!"

Mr. and Mrs. Bridge turned and looked and they saw a shaggy girl, rather pretty in a gypsy sort of way—so Mrs. Bridge thought—who was wearing a silk blouse that was not tucked into her skirt but was simply tied in a loose knot so that a good deal of midriff was showing. She was laughing and shaking her head in response to the comments of two Frenchmen who were sitting at the next table. One of the Frenchmen took out his wallet and slipped a bill under the saucer of her coffee cup, and at this she promptly untied the knot in her blouse and straightened up, revealing her breast to her neighbors as well as to anyone else who cared to look, whereupon there was a burst of clapping and much laughter not only from the two businessmen but from everyone else in the café, with the exception of Mr. and Mrs. Bridge.

"Well," said Morgan Hager suddenly, "I guess I'd better be running along."

"Oh, must you go?" inquired Mrs. Bridge.

"Yes, there's a girl at the ho— ah, I mean, I've got some plans for the next few hours." He paused. "It's just that I'd forgotten about Kansas City—what the people were like, if you know what I mean." He stopped again. "Well," he said, picking up his portfolio, "it's sure been an experience!"

Mrs. Bridge was not certain what he meant, but replied courteously, "Good-by, Morgan. We'll tell your parents we saw you." To which Hager responded with an uneasy grin and vanished swiftly into the crowd on the street.

*

75

Sidewalk Artist

"I never knew there were so many artists," she observed as they wandered along the quay. "How do you suppose they keep from starving to death?"

Mr. Bridge had never been greatly interested in art, but if this was how she wanted to spend their final day in Paris it was all right with him. Some of the pictures in the book stalls he did rather like; then, too, it was a warm sunny afternoon near the end of August and he was pleased, and he made up his mind to buy her a painting. He said nothing, but he began to pay more attention, and near the cathedral of Notre Dame she paused to admire a watercolor of the city.

"Parlez-vous Anglais?" Mrs. Bridge politely inquired of the old gentleman who sat beside the stall in a canvas chair. He shook his head and went on smoking his pipe.

"Well, combien?" she asked, pointing to the one that struck her fancy.

"Vingt mille," he answered without looking around, and continued smoking.

"Vingt mille," she repeated, for she had been listening closely, knowing he would speak in French. "Now, let's see. Vingt is twenty, I believe. And mille is thousand. Well, that sounds like a lot." Whereupon she opened her handbag and took out a little booklet which equated American money with virtually everything on earth. Having learned how much it would cost in dollars, she exclaimed, "Oh, I'm afraid that's much too much," and shook her head and regretfully moved along, remarking to her husband, "I'm sure he's spotted us as tourists."

Mr. Bridge took a long, shrewd look at the picture so as not to forget it. He did not think it was very good—in fact he was of the opinion that Ruth had done better paintings when she was in high school—but he seldom offered an opinion on a subject with which he was not familiar. Later that afternoon, back at their hotel on the Champs Elysées, while she was packing the suitcases, he went out, hired a taxi, and drove to the quay, where he bought the painting and arranged to have it shipped to Kansas City. The next day as they were getting settled on the train for the trip to the Riviera he observed rather dryly that he thought he knew how the Parisian artists kept from starving, but since she had no idea he had bought the painting for her this remark meant nothing, and she replied as she took off her hat that she supposed they must manage some way.

76

Telegram

A telegram was waiting for them in Monte Carlo. Douglas, knowing the date of his parents' wedding anniversary, sent this message: MAY I TAKE THE OPPORTUNITY EXTEND FELICI-

TATIONS UPON MEMORABLE OCCASION AND IN BEHALF ENTIRE COMPANY EXPRESS HOPE YOUR CONTINUED SUCCESS.

Mrs. Bridge was touched by his thoughtfulness and wrote to him, "It was awfully sweet to hear from you on our anniversary, but I do think the American Express company must have gotten their messages mixed up. . . ."

77

Beautiful Luggage

Before leaving on the trip she had checked over the luggage in the attic and concluded they did not have enough, so she had gone downtown and bought three elegant, darkly burnished leather suitcases. They were so beautiful that she was easily persuaded by the salesman to buy a set of canvas covers to protect the leather. These covers, to be sure, were ugly—as coarse as Boy Scout pup tents—but she bought them and had them fitted onto the suitcases. The covers remained on the suitcases while they were aboard ship, and as they had been in each city only a few days she had not bothered to remove them, but now she decided to see if the leather was being protected. She unfastened one of the canvas jackets, peeled it halfway off, and there—as beautiful as though still on display—the leather gleamed. Well pleased, she buttoned on the cover.

*

78

Mirror

Mrs. Bridge slept later than she intended to the second morning in Monte Carlo; they had visited the casino the previous night, and while she had not gambled she had found it nonetheless a rather strenuous experience. Her husband was gone when she finally awoke, but this was not surprising because he had gotten so accustomed to rising early in order to put in a full day at the office that he was no longer able to lie in bed past seven o'clock. Probably he was walking briskly around town, and no doubt he would be waiting to check on the Italian reservations as soon as the travel agency opened its doors for the day. She often wondered where he found so much energy.

The clock on the night table told her it was almost noon. She felt a trifle guilty. And yet it was delicious to lie in bed and to feel on her cheek and on her arms the mild breezes drifting up the hillside from the Mediterranean. A few minutes more, she thought, then she really must get up. And so, with eyes half open, she lay motionless and knew how fortunate she was. And she inquired of herself what she had done to deserve all this. There was no answer. All at once she perceived something so obvious and vulgar that she could not imagine why it had failed to escape her attention. She could see herself in the mirror on the wall, the mirror faced the bed, and she had suddenly realized that in every one of their European hotel rooms a large mirror had faced the bed. At the significance of this her blue eyes opened wide and she quickly turned her head on the pillow. In Paris a beautiful ornate Louis Quatorze mirror had frankly revealed her intimacy with her husband, and in London, too, now that she thought about it, they had been mirrored.

Deeply troubled, puzzled, no longer thankful, Mrs. Bridge lay in bed with an expression of listless despair and gazed through the opened doors of the balcony, through the iron grillwork to the distant sea, to the purple clarity and the white sails.

✱

79

Psst!

Wherever they went they were promptly identified as American tourists. From every side street some young man would come gliding, a hand in his coat pocket, murmuring in broken English that he had a diamond ring for sale, a fountain pen, a Swiss watch.

"Psst! Hey, mister," he would begin.

"How on earth do they always know we're Americans?" Mrs. Bridge inquired.

It was not mysterious to Mr. Bridge, who, however, chose to reply bitterly, for the trip was costing twice what he had estimated, "Europeans can smell a dollar a mile away."

*

80

Peculiar Roman

In Rome their hotel was situated near the Via Veneto, which the desk clerk, who had never been to America but who had a second cousin in Manhattan, insisted was the Broadway of Europe. Neither Mr. or Mrs. Bridge was inclined to dispute him, the principal reason being that the day was overcast and the humidity so high it was difficult to breathe.

"Goodness, this is certainly different from the Riviera," Mrs. Bridge remarked as they were unpacking in their room. It had been hot in Monte Carlo—at least the temperature had been high—but in the shadows of the stone buildings it was usually cool, and even in the direct sunlight they had not been uncomfortable.

"This really is awfully muggy," she said, looking through the blinds at the dank, motionless clouds. "I certainly miss that breeze from the Mediterranean."

They showered, changed into their lightest clothing, and decided to sit at a café on the Via Veneto. A weak, hot rain had begun to fall and they selected a table with an umbrella. At the next table sat an Italian man in a white suit and white perforated shoes who soon addressed them in perfect English.

"You are Americans, are you not?"

Mrs. Bridge said they were, again amazed at such prompt identification.

"And how do you find Italy? Do you enjoy yourselves?"

"Well, it's awfully warm," she said hesitantly, not wanting to be ungracious, and was relieved when he was not offended. So many Europeans were excitable.

He asked how long they had been in Europe and how much longer they intended to stay, and when she replied that after visiting Florence and Milan and Geneva they would be returning to Paris and from there to the United States he offered a curious little gesture which somehow expressed sympathy.

"Unfortunate," he added.

"Have you ever visited America?" she inquired pleasantly.

"No, Madame, I have not."

"I suppose you must be dying to go."

The Italian laughed. Lifting both arms in the gesture they had come to know so well, he said, "My dear lady, why go to America?"

Later, when the rain had stopped, he bowed, told them what a pleasure it had been to make their acquaintance, and strolled along the boulevard.

"Don't let them fool you," said Mr. Bridge. "These people would sell their souls to get to the United States."

✳

81

Change of Itinerary

They came to enjoy sitting on the Via Veneto—so much so that Mrs. Bridge said half jokingly, referring to the peculiar Italian who had no desire to go anywhere else, "I really think he has a point."

They were in front of a different café farther up the boulevard, one they had not tried before. The weather being muggy and cloudy as it had been ever since their arrival in Rome, they decided to have some iced coffee. In a few minutes a waiter approached, a very Italian-looking waiter.

"Let's hope this one understands English," she murmured.

"Try him and see."

"What else did you think I was going to speak?" Mr. Bridge replied. He had just finished changing the film in the camera and now placed it on an empty chair and gave the waiter their order.

"Very good, sir. Will there be anything else?"

"No," he said. "Just coffee with plenty of ice." The waiter bowed and went inside the café. Mr. Bridge wiped his forehead with his handkerchief and shook the sleeves of his linen coat. Mrs. Bridge was fanning herself with a sightseeing folder.

"It certainly does make things simpler when they speak English," she said, "but my!—doesn't this one have an accent!"

They waited and waited. The iced coffee did not arrive. They looked around. It seemed that people were gathering inside the café and that an argument or a discussion of some kind was going on.

"They're usually so good about the service," said Mrs. Bridge, still fanning herself with the sightseeing folder.

They waited a while longer. Finally Mr. Bridge got up, saying he would go into the café and find out what the trouble was.

"For heaven's sake, don't let yourself get involved," she said, for it was obvious the Italians were excited about something. Several of them were waving their arms and denouncing one another; however this went on all the time in Italy and Mrs. Bridge was growing accustomed to it. While her husband went inside she studied the folder. They were planning to visit the Vatican later that afternoon and she was hoping their schedule would permit a drive through the countryside. She looked up with a smile when her husband returned.

"We're getting out," he said as he picked up the camera.

Her smile faded. She knew from his expression that he was not angry.

"What is it?" she said. "What's happened?"

"The Nazis are in Poland."

"Oh, my word!"

Two days later Mr. and Mrs. Bridge were on their way home.

*

82

Inside Europe

At luncheon the day after her return to Kansas City she was questioned about the situation in Europe and she replied that it had been frightening and that she really had no idea what was going on. They had not met any Nazis—at least she did not think so—and she could not honestly give an opinion. She felt more sure of herself when asked about the sights they had seen. Inevitably someone asked if they had gone to a bullfight.

"No, thank heavens," she replied. "We wanted to go to Spain, but Walter felt it would be dangerous so soon after the Civil War. But we did hear a great deal about it. Europe seems to be jam-packed with people who fought on the losing side."

"It's hard to understand how the Spaniards can be so bloodthirsty," Madge Arlen remarked.

"It certainly is," said Mrs. Bridge promptly.

"The poverty of the Europeans must be simply appalling."

"Yes, it's simply unbelievable."

"They say there's no middle class at all, just the rich and the poor."

"Yes, it seems so unfair."

"I suppose they're all dying to emigrate to this country."

"Yes, though of course you can't blame them," she replied. "Grace, would you pass the cream?"

Luncheon being over they moved into the living room, where the hostess, Lois Montgomery, had set up card tables. On each table there was a fluted yellow paper basket filled with salted cashews and peppermints, and there were four tasseled tally cards and four tiny pencils.

Being asked what she thought about England, she answered that it was lovely and that the people were quite nice, though rather reserved. The cooking was not as good as French cooking because the English boiled everything. The roast beef, however, was delicious, and the plum pudding. London was foggy and the English accent sounded strange until one got used to it.

"Aren't we lucky to be living in America!" someone said.

"Isn't that the truth!"

"Oh, by the way," said Mrs. Bridge, "all the time we were abroad I kept wondering if that awful hole in the pavement just off Ward Parkway had been fixed."

"They finally got to it last week. We were just about to give it up as a lost cause."

"That was so maddening. I was so provoked with Douglas one day that I forgot to watch for it and ran right over it."

"Well," said Madge Arlen, who was shuffling the cards with a cigarette in her mouth and one eye closed against the smoke, "you can thank Grace. She sent the mayor a telegram."

"You'd think with taxes as high as they are the city could do something about those holes without waiting till kingdom come."

"Well, you know these politicians. Who's ready for more coffee?"

"Buy any art treasures while you were there?"

"Oh, no. I'm afraid I wouldn't know one if it hit me. Three no trump."

"I've been trying to talk Ralph into a trip somewhere, but now with this Polish thing I suppose it'll have to be postponed."

"Yes, I don't suppose it's safe anywhere any more. Honestly, you can't imagine why we have so many wars."

"I'm simply parched!" said Madge. "Lois, do you mind if I scare up some ice water?"

"Oh, sit still. I'll ring for Belinda."

"Is it true the Italian women get awfully heavy?"

"Yes, we saw some who were positively enormous. I suppose it's from eating so much starch."

Late that afternoon as the party was breaking up someone said to her, "I certainly envy you and Walter. It must have been a marvelous trip even if it did end that way."

"I wouldn't have missed it for the world," said Mrs. Bridge, smiling all around, "and I feel awfully lucky. Even so we were certainly glad to see the Union Station. I suppose no matter how far you go there's no place like home." She could see they agreed with her, and surely what she had said was true, yet she was troubled and for a moment she was almost engulfed by a nameless panic.

*

83

Progress, Madness, Defeat

The only one of her friends who might understand how she felt was Grace Barron, and so it was that a few days after the luncheon she telephoned her. The maid answered and said Mrs. Barron was in bed. Mrs. Bridge asked if she was ill. The maid didn't seem to know, saying only that she had gone to bed about noon. This was so strange that Mrs. Bridge decided to drive over and find out what was the matter.

She was sitting up in bed wearing her favorite sweatshirt and a baseball cap and she was reading a monstrous Russian novel. Closing the book on a hairpin she said, "I'm losing my mind."

"This is the first I've heard of it," said Mrs. Bridge with a smile.

"Do stop," Grace said unhappily. "Don't be gay, India. Please, for once, don't."

"Well, it *is* rather a shocking remark."

"Life can be shocking." She took off the ball player's cap and began turning it around in her hands and frowning. "It's just that I do want to be a person. I do, I do!" Mrs. Bridge did not know what to say and presently Grace continued. "Virgil says there's something wrong with me. He says he's never known another woman in all his life who would wear a sweatshirt on the Plaza."

"Well, you do attract attention. Not that I mind, and I

can't see where it's anyone else's business, and there certainly isn't any law against it."

"But I do attract attention."

"Well," Mrs. Bridge answered uneasily, "as Virgil says, you're the only one from this neighborhood who dresses as though you were going to work in the north end."

Grace nodded. "It's true. Yes, it's true."

Both of them fell silent.

"Do you think we'll get in the war?" said Grace after a while.

"I don't know," Mrs. Bridge replied. "I can't understand what's going on. I hate to think about it. It's so senseless."

Again they fell silent.

"Can you tell me what happened, Grace? Being in bed is so unlike you."

"It was the washing machine's fault," she answered without a smile, and went on to explain that she and the machine had never gotten along very well— "We've always despised each other," she said—and on this day it had defied her, it had knocked and trembled, and begun tearing the clothing, and so infuriated her that she had grabbed it by one leg and tipped it over, and the water ran all over the basement. The maid, who was upstairs in the kitchen preparing lunch, heard her screaming and summoned a doctor.

Mrs. Bridge remained silent and was thoughtful, for here was someone less confident of the future than herself. An evil, a malignancy, was at work. Its nature she could not discern, though she had known of its carbuncular presence for many years. Until now, until this revelation of its existence, she had not imagined it could be more than a fanciful illness, nor that there could be other victims than herself. But her friend was ill and suffering and Mrs. Bridge, too, was afflicted. Thinking back she was able to remember moments when this anonymous evil had erupted and left as its only cicatrice a sour taste in the mouth and a wild, wild desire.

One morning she had chanced to meet Grace downtown and Grace had wanted to look around in a toy store, and so, together, Mrs. Bridge amused and puzzled by this whim, they stopped here and there. So much had changed from the years when she used to buy toys for Ruth and Carolyn and Douglas. Everything was more intricate now, more automatic. It seemed you no longer played with a toy, you operated it. Douglas used to spend hours on his knees—ruining his corduroy knickers—pushing a fire engine or a dump truck and making appropriate noises. Now, however, you simply pushed a lever and the toy ran around by itself and the sirens wailed and the lights flashed until you were able to catch the machine and stop it. And Grace had caught it and was trembling so she could hardly reverse the lever.

There was a doll, too, with its little frock tied up around its head in order to display the electronics in the abdomen. There was a booklet tied to the wrist of the doll and they had read the booklet and then Mrs. Bridge turned the doll on. The eyes began to roll, the jaw dropped, and from the loudspeaker in the stomach came a nursery rhyme, and when this ended the doll sat down and a thin, colorless liquid appeared from beneath it and trickled over the counter.

"Can you help me?" Grace was asking, but Mrs. Bridge was too depressed to speak.

✳

84

Robbery at the Heywood Duncans'

The next time she met Grace was at a party given by the
Heywood Duncans. Shortly after ten o'clock, while the two
of them were chatting, just as Mrs. Bridge was reaching for
another anchovy cracker, four men appeared in the doorway
and they did not look like guests. They were wearing plastic
noses attached to horn-rimmed glasses and were carrying
pistols. One of them said, "All right, everybody, this is a
stick-up!" Another of the men sprang to the top of the piano
and pointed his gun at several different people. At first everyone thought it was a joke—it was so typical of a stunt Noel
Johnson might dream up. But it wasn't a joke because the
robbers made all the guests line up facing the wall with
their hands above their heads. Then two of them walked
around pulling billfolds out of the men's pockets and taking
bracelets and necklaces and rings from the ladies. Another
of the men went upstairs and came down with his arms full
of purses and fur coats. Just before the robbers reached Mrs.
Bridge, who was standing obediently with her hands as high
as possible, something frightened them and the one standing
on the piano—she afterward described him to the police as
not having worn a necktie—called out in an ugly voice,
"Who's got the keys to that blue Cadillac out front?"

At this Mrs. Ralph Porter screamed, "Don't you tell him,
Ralph!"

But the bandits took Mr. Porter's keys, and after telling everyone not to move for thirty minutes they ran out the side door. Heywood Duncan immediately phoned the police while Dr. Foster, who had dropped in unexpectedly and who had been robbed the same as the others, feebly seated himself in a corner and urged everyone to be calm, saying the bandits would not get away with it.

The bandits did get away, though, and it was written up on the front page of the newspaper with pictures on page eight, including a close-up of the scratched piano. Mrs. Bridge, reading the account in the breakfast room next morning after her husband had gone to work, was surprised to learn that Stuart Montgomery had been carrying just $2.14 and that Mrs. Noel Johnson's ring had been zircon.

*

85

No Questions

As if one robbery were not enough, Mrs. Bridge became involved in another—not much of a robbery, and she was detained less than ten minutes; still it was frightening. She was in a department store examining some brocade with the idea of altering the scheme in the dining room when, quite unknown to her, someone looted the cash register not six feet away. The theft was discovered a few minutes later and she, along with several other women, was herded into the manager's office. When it came her time to be interviewed she sat down in front of the desk, adjusted her fur neckpiece, and said, "I surely hope you don't think I'm the guilty one."

The manager raised both hands in a faint gesture of dismay at such a thought. He asked if he might see her driver's license, and when she produced it from her purse he handed it to the police lieutenant who was lounging on the edge of the desk with a felt hat pushed back off his forehead. Mrs. Bridge knew he was a policeman the instant she saw him. She expected him to study the license and ask a great many questions; consequently she was both relieved and slightly ruffled when he barely glanced at her license before handing it back and asked her nothing at all.

"I certainly hope you catch whoever it was," she said.

The lieutenant, who knew a bona-fide country-club matron when he saw one, responded by nodding politely.

The manager opened the door for her.

∗

86

Follow Me Home

Kansas City was apparently headed for an epidemic of crime such as no one could remember since the days of the hoodlums and political bosses. How the latest scare actually started no one knew, although several women, one of whom was a fairly close friend of Madge Arlen, claimed to know the name of someone who had been assaulted not far from Ward Parkway. Some insisted it had happened near the Plaza, others thought farther south, but they were generally agreed it occurred late at night. The story was that a certain

matron had been driving home alone and when she had
slowed down for an intersection a man had leaped from
behind some shrubbery—a clump of spirea, according to
Madge—and had wrenched open the door. Whether or not
the attack had been consummated the story did not say;
the important part was that there had been a man and he
had leaped up and wrenched open the door. There was
nothing about it in the paper, nor in *The Tattler,* which did
not print unpleasant material, and the exact date of the
assault could not be determined, only that it had been one
dark night not long ago.

As this story began to circulate through the country-club
district none of the ladies cared to drive anywhere alone after
sundown; if they did they locked themselves in the car and
drove with great anxiety. And it became customary at the
conclusion of parties where there were "office widows" for
the host to get his automobile out of the garage in order
to follow the unescorted matrons home, which was the
reason there could be seen processions of cars winding
through the country-club district late at night.

So Mrs. Bridge came home on those evenings when her
husband did not get away from the office in time to attend
the party, or when he was too tired to go. At her driveway
the procession would halt, engines idling, everyone watching,
while she drove into the garage and returned along the
driveway so as to be constantly visible until she reached
the front door. Having unlocked it she would step inside,
switch on the hall lights, and call to him, "I'm home!" if
she had seen his car in the garage. If he failed to answer
she necessarily assumed he was asleep or otherwise occupied.
In any event, she would then flicker the lights a few times
to show the friends waiting outside that she was safe, after
which the caravan would move along.

*

87

No Chauffeur

The idea of a chauffeur had begun to appeal to Mr. Bridge. Traffic was getting more congested all the time, and as he did not enjoy driving anyway he thought it would be well worth the expense, so, after they had considered the matter, Mrs. Bridge telephoned an employment agency and the following evening a tall, affable colored man came out for an interview. Both of them were impressed by his manners. He was from New Orleans, he told them, and this somehow added to his stature. He was dignified and courteous. The longer they talked to him the better they liked him, so he was employed.

In the rear seat of the Chrysler, his briefcase in his lap, Mr. Bridge sat erect and tense, expecting an accident at every corner while being driven to the office. It was less exhausting to battle the traffic himself, but now that he had the chauffeur he could not dismiss him without a reason. Then, too, having set his mind to the proposition, he was determined to make a success of it. At the office he got out, very much relieved, and told the chauffeur what time to pick him up. The chauffeur spent the remainder of the day driving Mrs. Bridge around in her Lincoln, or, when she had no use for him, he would loiter in the basement.

During the third week they began to receive mysterious telephone calls asking for Jules, which was his name. Drawling Negro voices would inquire, "Well, whereabout you figure he at?" if it was his day off. Or, "Yes, ma'am, it sho'ly am mighty impo'tant." If, reluctantly, she went to the top of the basement steps and called, "Jules? Jules? Someone wishes to speak to you on the phone," he would not respond, and her patience was severely tested. Eventually they learned that Jules had bought a yellow satin easy chair for his apartment in the north end of the city, but so far he had been unwilling to pay for the chair and these were the creditors who were calling. When a few more weeks had passed an attempt was made to link Mr. Bridge with the payment; a serious talk with Jules having produced no effect, he was dismissed.

Next they interviewed and employed a Japanese called Niki who, with clasped hands, assured them he paid cash for whatever he bought. Mr. Bridge felt more at ease with Niki than he had with Jules, but Mrs. Bridge felt quite the opposite. She was terrified of the way he backed out of the driveway. She asked him to go slower and to pay some attention to where he was backing, and he grinned and agreed to do so, but there was no change. When she became severe about this he looked so grieved by the reprimand that she became ashamed of herself. Still he would not slow down. He never actually struck anything but there were some near misses, the worst when he roared over a pile of burning leaves and almost killed a boy with a canvas bag around his neck who was throwing circulars onto the front porches. It was such a close call that Mrs. Bridge refused to ride with him any more, so there was nothing to do but dismiss him.

After Niki came another Negro man, but there was always a faint odor of whisky around him, and Harriet, when asked for an opinion, compressed her lips significantly and shook her head. After this man came another Oriental, who, within the first month, failed to show up five times. And so at last they were obliged to abandon the idea, and Mrs. Bridge, when discussing the matter with her friends, some of whom had chauffeurs and some of whom were considering it, was apt to say, "Well, it does have advantages, but of course there are drawbacks."

✻

88

The Rich and the Poor

The principal advantage, of course, so far as she was concerned, was that in case of difficulty there was a man around to take charge. Occasionally something unfortunate would occur while she was out driving and she then found herself in a quandary, not knowing whether to telephone her husband and run the risk of interrupting him at work or to try to handle the situation alone. One day, for instance, the Lincoln simply stopped in the middle of Ward Parkway. Luck was with her on this occasion, because a tow truck came by and when she had explained what happened the man looked under the hood. He asked how long it had been since the Lincoln was overhauled. She did not know, but thought it had been quite a while. She knew mechanics often tried to take advantage of people who knew very little about automobiles and so she bent over to peer into the engine, holding her fur coat tightly to her breast so it would not touch anything greasy, and after looking at different things for a few seconds she withdrew and said, "Well, do the best you can. About how long do you think it will take? I have a luncheon appointment on the Plaza."

Aside from mechanical difficulties there was always the parking problem; she had been amazed and impressed with the way the chauffeurs could park the Lincoln, and now that she was again on her own she was more than ever conscious of her inadequacy. Douglas, inadvertently, made the situation worse. A few days after taking up the study of geometry he began to measure everything. In his pocket he carried a carpenter's flexible steel tape, a compass, and a scratch pad, and he was obsessed by a desire to calculate all such things as the number of cubic feet in the attic, the radius of the mahogany dining-room table if it had been circular instead of elliptical, and the angle formed by the radio and the sofa and the fireplace. Among other things he measured the chimney, the back porch, the stove, and the wicker laundry basket, and one evening he pedantically announced that the pantry was almost exactly two cubic feet smaller than the Lincoln. The next time she tried to park the car she was reminded of his calculations. She pulled on one side of the steering wheel with both hands, backed up a few feet, pulled on the opposite side of the wheel, moved forward, backed up, and so on, gasping for breath in her efforts to maneuver the formidable machine, and she was not assisted by the knowledge that it would have been easier to park the pantry.

*

89

Paquita de las Torres

Douglas liked it, though, and he had no more than gotten his first driver's license when he began asking to borrow the car. She was glad enough to let him have it, only cautioning him to drive carefully; if she had to run an errand while he was using the Lincoln she did not mind catching a bus, and if the weather was bad she could telephone one of her friends. She often wondered where he went and what he was doing, but she did not worry much about him because he was growing to be rather conservative, which gratified her, and furthermore he seemed to be using his head more effectively than he did as a child. He was even taking a reasonable amount of interest in schoolwork. In short he was becoming a sober, self-reliant young man, a bit too mysterious, perhaps, but otherwise agreeably normal.

She was, therefore, almost startled out of her wits to encounter him on the Plaza with the wildest-looking girl in the world. He had borrowed the car to go bowling and Mrs. Bridge had later decided to go shopping for some cocktail napkins and so, quite unexpectedly, they met. The girl was a gypsy-looking business with stringy black un-combed hair, hairy brown arms jingling with bracelets, and glittering mascaraed eyes in which there was a look of deadly experience. She was wearing a sheer blouse of burnt orange silk and a tight white skirt, and Mrs. Bridge did not need a second glance to realize that was practically all.

"How do you do, Paquita?" she said, smiling neutrally, after Douglas had sullenly mumbled an introduction. The girl did not speak and Mrs. Bridge wondered if she understood English. The hairy arms and the rancid odor were almost too much for Mrs. Bridge to bear. "I hope you two are having a nice time," she said, and heard a bracelet jingle and saw Douglas and Paquita exchange a deep, knowing look.

"Dad will be home early this evening for a change, so Harriet is planning on dinner at six sharp. I hope you won't be late. It's nice to have met you, Paquita." And she could not be sure, but it seemed to her that a moment after she turned away the girl spat on the sidewalk.

On the bus going home with the cocktail napkins she tried to make sense of it. She tried to be fair. Why would he want to go bowling with someone obviously from a different high school when there were so many nice girls at Southwest? Why would he want to see this girl at all? What could they possibly have in common? Where could he have met her?

"You'd think I was poison," she said to him that evening, jokingly and very seriously, as they entered the dining room. "Why not tell us when you're beau-ing someone new? Your Dad and I are interested in knowing your friends."

Douglas, having pushed her chair in as usual, went around the table and seated himself without a word.

"Paquita certainly jingles."

"She likes bracelets," he said trenchantly.

Mr. Bridge entered, and in passing behind Douglas's chair gave him a solid, affectionate rap on the skull with his knuckles.

"Well," said Douglas, grinning, "you must have had a

good day today. You make another million bucks or something?"

Mr. Bridge laughed and picked up the carving knife, and while examining the roast he said, "I hear you're turning into quite a basketball player."

"Who told you that?"

"Never mind who told me."

"Oh, I don't know," Douglas said, blushing. He played forward on the church team and was trying to make the high-school squad but so far had been unsuccessful.

"Maybe you should butter up the coach's daughter," said Mr. Bridge, busying himself with the roast.

Douglas groaned in elaborate agony. "Anyway, I don't even know if he's got a daughter. And besides, that's no way to make the team."

"Well, how else are you going to do it?"

"Oh, you have to play just the way the coach likes. I mean he likes real smooth dribbling and things like that that really aren't important. I guess I told you about our church team skunking the Southwest second team, didn't I?"

"Yes, you did. Pass your mother's plate."

"Well, doesn't it stand to reason that if we can beat the second team we ought to be at least as good as the first team? I mean, this coach has got his favorites, see? And if you aren't one of his favorites, well, you just don't have a chance."

Mr. Bridge glanced at him and said calmly, "You're joking about that, so I don't mind. But don't let me catch you whining seriously. This million dollars you referred to —if I had earned it I wouldn't have earned it from being the judge's favorite. This country operates on the principle that the more industry and intelligence a man applies to his job the more he is entitled to profit. I hope it never changes."

"Yuh, okay," Douglas muttered, trying to end the conversation before it turned into a lecture.

"Remember that."

"I will. Okay. Okay."

The telephone rang at that moment and Harriet came into the dining room to say it was for Mr. Bridge. No sooner was he out of the room when Mrs. Bridge remarked, "I saw Patty Duncan the other day. She asked how you were."

"Tell her I'm still alive and kicking."

"She's such a lovely girl. And they say she's becoming quite the pianist."

"Okay," said Douglas, who had found himself assaulted from both ends of the dinner table. "For the love of Mike, I mean can't I live my own life?"

For the remainder of the meal she said no more about the encounter on the Plaza, but it had so disturbed her that she waited up until he got in late that night.

"Were you out with Paquita?" she asked, gazing at him earnestly.

In silence, face averted, Douglas took off his leather jacket.

"Does she live around here?" Mrs. Bridge asked, following him to the closet and picking a bit of lint from his sweater.

He hung up the jacket and walked into the living room, where he took a comb from his hip pocket, stooped a little in order to see himself in the mirror, for he was now almost six feet tall and still growing—soon he would be taller than his father—and began combing his long red hair straight back in the style he had recently adopted. His hair would not lie down, it grew stubbornly in various directions, and the more he combed it the more rebellious it looked, but he would not give in and the hair would not lie down.

"You're just like your Dad," she said, observing him, and there was not only love but vexation in her tone. Douglas, scowling, combed his hair and mashed it with his palms. As soon as he lifted his hands the hairs began to rise.

"Dear," she said, having followed him from the closet. She now stood a little way in back of him, looking at his face in the mirror. He slipped the comb in his pocket and bent a look of deep hatred against the mirror.

"What is it?" he asked brutally.

"Oh, I don't know."

"Well, good night," he said and turned to go upstairs, but she reached out and caught his arm.

"Douglas, why do you want to go around with that sort of person?"

At this he jerked his arm free and went to the closet, where he got his jacket and left the house again. She remained with one hand resting on the banister and was sick with anxiety, not so much because of the girl, for she knew he would outgrow her, but because she did not want to lose his friendship. She had lost his love, she knew not why, as she had forfeited that of Ruth, and the thought of losing her son entirely was more than she could endure.

90

Extra-sensory Perception

The next night he borrowed the Lincoln to escort Paquita to a basketball tournament in the municipal auditorium. While driving down Troost toward the north end of town, where she lived with her sister, who was a burlesque dancer, he passed a drive-in restaurant. He neither stopped nor slowed down, but as he went by his attention was caught by a singularly voluptuous carhop, with the result that when the traffic light changed he did not see it because he was looking backward. He drove into the rear of the car ahead of him. No one was injured, but all parties were somewhat dazed and Douglas got himself a lump on the forehead. The grille of the Lincoln was dented and a wheel knocked out of alignment.

At home, when asked how the accident occurred, he replied without hesitation that it was because of a woman.

"Oh-ho!" said Mr. Bridge, who was of the opinion that traffic problems would disappear on the day women were no longer licensed to drive. "What have I been saying all these years?" He asked his son no more questions, only took the paper on which Douglas had written the license number of the other car, and said he would notify the insurance company.

Douglas wisely volunteered no further information and believed he had gotten out of the embarrassing accident rather cleverly until he chanced to look at his mother. Although she had not said a word, he perceived that in some fantastic manner she sensed the complete truth, and he reflected that in matters however distantly related to sex she possessed supernatural powers of divination.

*

91

Frayed Cuffs

Ordinarily Mrs. Bridge examined the laundry that Ingrid carried up from the basement every Tuesday afternoon in a creaking wicker basket, but when she was out shopping, or at a luncheon, the job fell to Harriet, who never paid much attention to such things as missing buttons or loose elastic. Thus it was that Mrs. Bridge discovered Douglas wearing a shirt with cuffs that were noticeably frayed.

"For heaven's sake!" she exclaimed, taking hold of his sleeve. "Has a dog been chewing on this?"

He looked down at the threads as though he had never before seen them; in fact he hadn't.

"Surely you don't intend to *wear* this shirt?"

Since he was already wearing the shirt this struck him as a foolish question, but he said, "It looks perfectly okay to me."

"Why, just look at these cuffs! Anyone would think we were on our way to the poorhouse."

"So is it a disgrace to be poor?"

"No!" she cried. "But we're *not* poor!"

*

92

Sex Education

Thereafter she kept a sharp eye on the laundry, going through it piece by piece to see what needed mending, after which she separated it into three stacks: one for the master bedroom, one for the room which Ruth and Carolyn had shared and which now was Carolyn's alone, and a third for Douglas's room. One by one she carried these piles of clothing into the proper room and there divided them further, handkerchiefs, underwear, blouses, and so forth, and arranged them neatly in the proper drawers.

One afternoon she carried Douglas's laundry into his room as usual and placed it on his bed as she always did in order to sort it. She put the newly laundered shirts on top of the others in his dresser and was about to go on with her work when it occurred to her that in all likelihood he was wearing the same shirts again and again; probably the ones in the bottom of the drawer were never being worn, and with the idea of reversing the order she took them all out and beneath the final shirt she found a magazine. Although she had never before seen one like it she knew instinctively what it was.

Mrs. Bridge sank to the edge of the bed and gazed dismally at the wall, the unopened magazine in her hands. She could hear Harriet singing hymns in the kitchen while peeling green apples for a pie, and the fervency of those good shrill

Christian notes caused Mrs. Bridge to feel more desolate and abandoned than ever. She closed her eyes and shook her head in disbelief. The last thing on earth she wanted was to look into this magazine, but it had to be done. She looked at one page. There was a naked woman. That was enough. She looked no more. Never in her life had she been confronted with a situation like this and she did not know what to do. She was under the impression that these magazines had been legislated against and were not available. She asked herself where she had failed. With him, as with Ruth and Carolyn, she had adroitly steered around threatening subjects; in no way had she stimulated his curiosity—quite the contrary. Where, then, had she failed? She had let him realize, without her having to say so, that there were two kinds of people in the world, and this was true, she knew, for it was what she had been taught by her father and mother.

She kept expecting Douglas to say something about the magazine—which she burned in the incinerator—but if he noticed it was gone he gave no indication. Weeks passed. She did not want to rush him. She wanted him to come to her and confess of his own free will. Carolyn was now a freshman at the university, which was located in the town of Lawrence, about forty miles distant; she often came home on week ends, but during the week she was gone, with the result that Mrs. Bridge and Douglas were sometimes the only members of the family at the dinner table. These dinners were silent and unpleasant for them both; they tended to avoid looking at each other. She waited patiently for the moment when he would give a sign—a single deep look would be enough—and she would know then that he wanted to have a talk. Still time went by and, since he made no move, she began to fasten her eyes on him. These mute invitations had a singular effect on Douglas; whenever he became conscious of her mournful, wretched gaze he would leave the house. She thought he was touched and full of remorse at the unhappiness he was causing and so she continued to gaze deeply at him whenever they were alone. However, more time went by and for some reason he failed to come to her.

One evening, therefore, she walked upstairs to his room and tapped on the door with her fingernail. The door was closed but she knew he was at his desk and that he was staring at the door. She was right, because after she had waited a few minutes she heard the chair creak and then his footsteps on the carpet. He jerked the door open and found her there smiling miserably. She glided past him into the room and to his desk where, without a word, she placed on the blotter a slim, musty pamphlet with a gray cover and sepia pages which she had gotten from a trunk in the attic. The pamphlet had a faint dried odor, like the crumbled wings of moths, and the elaborate typography related a little story about the marriage of a sperm and an ovum. On the frontispiece, beneath an attached sheet of tissue, were two circular photographs taken from laboratory slides.

He had followed her across the room and was now standing on the opposite side of the desk with his fists clenched behind his back. Seeing him so tense she thought that if she could only manage to rumple his hair as she used to do when he was a small boy everything would be all right. Calmly, and a little slyly, she began easing toward him.

Seeing that she was after him he also moved to keep the desk between them.

*

93

Words of Wisdom

A few days later on his return from high school Douglas saw, beneath the hairbrush on his dresser, a page torn from a magazine. On one side of the page was an automobile advertisement, and on the other side was a picture of an elderly Chinese gentleman called the Old Sage, together with a list of maxims:

¶ It is as easy to grin as to growl.
¶ Hatred is self-punishment.
¶ Rotten or decayed wood cannot be carved.
¶ Have no care for the future and you will sorrow for the present.
¶ Life is a mirror that gives back as much as it receives.
¶ A record is often broken when competition gets keen.
¶ A good cure for drunkenness is while sober to see a drunken man.
¶ Courage at the critical moment is half the victory.
¶ Words show the wit of a man, actions his meanings.
¶ The anvil lasts longer than the hammer.
¶ The pleasure of doing good is never tiresome.
¶ Contentment is an inexhaustible treasure.
¶ A handful of common sense is worth a bushel of learning.

Douglas went through these more and more rapidly. Having finished, and not knowing exactly what to do with the list, thinking she might want it back, he put it in a desk drawer and paid no further attention to it. In the days that followed their eyes occasionally met and locked, inexpressively.

He knew she was waiting for him to comment; she knew he had read the maxims.

✻

94

Very Gay Indeed

Ruth did not write home as often as Mrs. Bridge had expected, nor was it possible to guess from her letters what sort of a life she was leading in New York; however she seemed to be getting along all right and did not sound unhappy. She wrote that she had moved into an apartment near the Hudson, that she was now working for a fashion magazine, and that she hoped for a promotion before long. In April she was promoted; she became an "assistant editor," whatever that meant, but it did sound important and Mrs. Bridge was very proud and let her friends know about Ruth's success. That same month they were surprised and delighted when she flew home for a visit. She had changed a great deal; she had become very sophisticated.

Carolyn came home from the university that week end, and Mrs. Bridge was struck by the difference in the girls. It was hard to believe they were sisters—Ruth so dark and sleek, and really too thin, angular, sauntering about and smoking one cigarette after another and having cocktails with her father as though she had been drinking for years;

Carolyn so active and blond and determined, and rather sturdy-looking in low-heeled golfing shoes, for she had begun playing golf in high school and was now getting exceptionally good.

Ruth was undeniably more mature and Mrs. Bridge noticed an odd fact: Ruth and Douglas liked each other very much. There was no reason they should not—in fact they certainly should like each other—but she could not get over a sense of astonishment when she heard them laughing together, or saw them earnestly talking in the breakfast room, drinking pots of coffee and discussing she did not know what. They appeared to have developed a new relationship. They were no longer just brother and sister, and Mrs. Bridge felt a little thrilled and more than a little sad.

She and Ruth did not have much time alone, and all at once, so it seemed, Ruth was on the telephone checking her plane reservation to New York. On her last evening in Kansas City the two of them remained in the dining room after Douglas and Mr. Bridge had left the table. They had only a few minutes because a young man named Callaway Rugg was coming to take Ruth to a Little Theatre production of *Cyrano*, but while they were talking at the dinner table she mentioned that one of the men who worked in her office in New York was a homosexual.

"Just what do you mean, Ruth?" asked Mrs. Bridge soberly. She had picked up a spoon and was slowly stirring her coffee.

"Why, he's gay, Mother. Queer. You know."

"I'm afraid I don't know," said Mrs. Bridge.

Ruth could not tell whether her mother was serious or not. The idea of her mother not knowing was too incredible, and yet, thinking back, and having talked with Douglas about things that had happened recently, and after a long, probing look into her mother's eyes, Ruth knew her mother was speaking the truth. This realization so shocked her that she said coldly, "Then it's time you found out." Feeling cruel and nervous and frightened she continued, in the same tone, "I'm very fond of him, Mother. One morning he brought me a dozen long-stemmed roses."

From the hall came the sound of the front door chimes. Immediately Ruth jumped up and hurried to open the door, leaving Mrs. Bridge as isolated as she had ever been in her life, as she had been isolated by her husband that day on the rue Auber.

*

95

Local Talent

Seldom had anyone from the country-club district attracted national attention, but there had been a few. A girl named Catlett, whose mother Mrs. Bridge knew slightly, went off to the Bahamas for a summer vacation and came back triumphantly engaged to a senator. Then there were the twins who were featured in a toothpaste advertisement, and occasionally one of the older men would be mentioned. But of the younger people the most celebrated was Callaway Rugg. He was a few years older than Ruth, but he had known her in high school and used to take her on long drives through the country; he would speak of the brevity of human affairs and of how vital it was to live as one wanted to live. He himself did not know how he wanted to live, but after playing in some dramatic productions staged in a barn on the outskirts of the city he was picked up by a talent scout and sent to Hollywood, where for the first two weeks

they were under the impression he was a lion tamer. After
this was straightened out he was put into a movie. *The
Tattler* spoke of "Kansas City's own Carleton Reynolds,"
which was what Hollywood named him. Surprisingly, or so
Mrs. Bridge had thought, the fact that he was a Kansas
Citian did not noticeably increase the run of the picture.
She had gone to see it. Rugg had appeared in only one
scene: on the stroke of midnight, arms bound behind his
back and a sack over his head, he fell out of a grandfather
clock.

"Of course his part was small," she had remarked while
discussing it with Madge Arlen, "but I do think he's quite
talented."

However Hollywood must not have thought so, for Rugg
was next heard from selling encyclopedias on the Plaza.

*

96

Exchange of Letters

The new *Tattler* came out a few days after Ruth returned
to New York and Mrs. Bridge mailed a clipping to her:
"Found holidaying at the charming home of her parents,
Mr. and Mrs. Walter Bridge of Crescent Heights Drive, was
the lovely eldest, Ruth, now setting Gotham aflame. Scores of
admirers hope the fascinating and exotic editoress-to-be
won't become a permanent Manhattanite." On the back of
the clipping was the conclusion of an article of advice to
hostesses: ". . . jungle the natives simply peel and eat, and

so should we! No more worry about knives and forks, left-hand or righthand." And below this was the first line of a quotation from Thoreau.

Mrs. Bridge wrote that Carolyn was playing golf every afternoon and had beaten one of the boys who was on the university team, that the weather in Kansas City was awfully pleasant this time of year, that some man named Genaro had telephoned just after she returned to New York but hadn't left a message, that the city was finally widening the street in front of the Junior League clubhouse, and that her visit to Kansas City had seemed awfully brief. Ruth had remarked on the graft in New York, so Mrs. Bridge wrote, "Isn't it awful there's so much graft? We have it here, too. It just makes you wonder about people."

She also mentioned what had been going on socially and what events were on the calendar. "Wednesday evening the Arlens are staging a cocktail party for Anne who's off to Europe and it sounds quite intriguing. Thursday, Madge and I are off to a recital given by some folk singer who plays the dulcimer, and then on Friday there's to be a church doing (at which a Moslem will talk!) but I'm not sure I'll be able to make it. I've been having a siege of headaches and they just don't seem to be able to make heads or tails of them. Dr. Stapp told me it's all mental but that doesn't make sense. Dr. McIntyre (he's so nice!) thinks it may be an allergy but if so I wish they'd hurry up and get together, whatever it is. Then next Monday there's a reception at Crestwood for the McKinney girls who're just back from a month at the Royal Hawaiian. That must have been grand. . . ."

Ruth chose to answer this letter one night while she was in bed with a man named Dowdey, whom she had met the previous week. She wrestled the pillow away from him and put it behind her back in order to sit up more comfortably, and with an airmail pad on her knees she began:

"The weather in New York has been lovely, but otherwise there isn't very much news. I can't stand my boss because he's an absolute tyrant, but everybody else is nice, and we're trying a new format that I like better. A man who works in the next office"—and she dropped one hand to give Dowdey a pinch on the buttocks—"has been awfully sweet although I don't know him very well yet. I haven't been going out much lately. I usually come home after work and get to bed early. It was marvelous seeing everybody in Kansas City." Here she paused and tapped the pen against her teeth, and finally added that she hoped to visit Kansas City again before long.

Dowdey, having rolled over and raised himself to one elbow, was reading the letter with his chin propped on Ruth's shoulder.

"Jus' like I aim to get back to San Antone," he said, and began kissing her throat.

"Hush," she said. "And stop. You're bothering me!"

"Come on down here and le's bother all over," said Dowdey, "on account of you can write yo' little mama in the mornin'."

"Cut that out," said Ruth. "Now cut that out!"

"Yo' mama look like you?" he asked, sliding his arms around her waist.

"She's my sister's mother!"

And as if by hearing these words she realized what she had said, Ruth touched her lover gently and looked down into his unblinking hazel eyes. She caressed the wind wrinkles of his leathery face; he became solemn and expectant.

"I'll only be a little while," she said. For a few minutes she sat with her knees drawn up to her chin and gazed across the river and the buildings on the western shore, and she was able to see her home, not as it was now, but ten years before, at a time in her life when she would never have thought to say her mother was not her own: when she had been as tall as the new evergreen trees in the yard, when her brother was a baby. Now this was gone, and it was gone forever. She wondered why she was in New York, why she would soon give herself to this man for whom she had no feeling.

"I don't think it's her fault," Ruth whispered, with her head on her knees, and when Dowdey asked what she had said she did not answer. Presently she sighed and continued with the letter, thanking her mother for sending a box of oatmeal cookies Harriet had baked, and said they were wonderful, though in truth they had arrived broken and crushed, and she had sprinkled them on the window sill for the pigeons. Having signed the letter with love, as she always did, she ordered Dowdey to open his mouth and hold out his tongue to lick the envelope.

"That all?" he asked, grinning, as she leaned across him to place the letter on the night table.

"It depends on what you mean," Ruth said. She turned out the light. When he covered her she was looking across the dark river, gravely thinking of her home.

97

Frozen Fruit

With Ruth gone and with Carolyn at home only an occasional week end, with Mr. Bridge continuing to spend long hours at the office, and with Douglas appearing only for meals, Mrs. Bridge found the days growing interminable; she could not remember when a day had seemed so long since the infinite hours of childhood, and so she began casting about rueful and disconsolate for some way to occupy the time. There were mornings when she lay in bed wide awake until noon, afraid to get up because there was nothing to do. She knew Harriet would take care of ordering the groceries, Harriet would take care of everything, Harriet somehow was running the house and Mrs. Bridge had the dismal sensation of knowing that she, herself, could leave town for a week and perhaps no one would get overly excited. At breakfast—lunch if she chose to call it so—she would consider the newspaper with sober apathy, sighing at the events in Europe, lethargically eating whatever Harriet prepared—toast and orange juice, chipped beef and cinnamon rolls, fruit salad, bacon and tomato sandwich, a dish of sherbet; whatever it happened to be Mrs. Bridge would eat some of it though it seemed tasteless. Summer had come again, another summer, another year.

One warm windy morning in June she could hardly open her eyes; she lay in the stuffy bedroom and listened to the wind in the trees, to the scratching of the evergreen branches against the house, and wondered if she was about to die. She did not feel ill, but she had no confidence in her life. Why should her heart keep beating? What was there to live for? Then she grew cheerful because she recalled her husband had told her to get the Lincoln waxed and polished. In fact he had told her that three weeks ago but she had not yet gotten around to it. Now, in any event, there was something to do; she would do the work herself. She would drive to the Plaza to an auto-supply store and buy a can of wax and some polish and a chamois, or whatever the salesman recommended, and she would spend the day working on the Lincoln. It had been years since she had done any work, with the exception of puttering in the garden, and it would be refreshing. But then, still in bed, she became doubtful and more reasonable. She had never attempted to polish an automobile, she knew nothing about it, nothing whatsoever, and if she should ruin the finish of the Lincoln what on earth could she say to her husband? He would be amazed and furious because it was so nonsensical; he would manage to control his temper but he would be infuriated all the same, and want to know why she had done it. Could she explain how the leisure of her life—that exquisite idleness he had created by giving her everything—was driving her insane?

However, she reflected, as she got out of bed holding a hand to her brow to prevent herself from collapsing, she could at least drive to the Plaza and wander around while the Lincoln was being polished. She could look into Bancroft's; perhaps they had some new imports. She could have a late luncheon in the tea shoppe. Surely something else would come to mind by then and soon the day would be over.

Once out of bed she felt more alive, and while getting dressed she thought of telephoning Grace Barron. Perhaps they could spend the day together. No one answered the Barrons' phone. After a few minutes she tried again with no success and then dialed Madge Arlen. The line was busy. She knew from past experience that Madge stayed on the telephone for hours, but now the Plaza idea had begun to sound exciting with or without company and she began to hurry around getting ready to go, and was annoyed with herself for having wasted the entire morning. It was fifteen minutes to one when Mrs. Bridge came downstairs. Harriet was vacuuming the hall. Mrs. Bridge signaled her to stop the machine, and when the roaring died away she said, looking quickly into her purse to see she had not forgotten anything, "I've got to run to the Plaza to have the car taken care of. It needs waxing. If anybody calls, tell them I'll be home about five."

Harriet replied that Mr. Bridge had had the car waxed and polished the previous Saturday.

Mrs. Bridge stopped and looked at her in stupefaction. "He did? I wonder why he didn't mention it."

Harriet did not say anything.

"Are you sure?" asked Mrs. Bridge.

Harriet nodded.

"Oh. Well, then," she said doubtfully, "I suppose it doesn't need to be done again. Isn't that strange? He must have forgotten to tell me." She noticed Harriet looking at her without expression, but intently, and she became embarrassed. She dropped the car keys back in her purse and slowly took off her hat. She had driven the Lincoln several times since Saturday and it was odd she had not noticed the difference.

Harriet turned on the vacuum.

After changing into more comfortable clothes Mrs. Bridge wandered to the kitchen, fixed a sandwich for herself, and sat in the breakfast room for about an hour watching the sparrows in the garden. Finally she managed to get Madge Arlen on the telephone.

"Lord, I'm glad you called!" her friend exclaimed. "I'm out of my wits for something to do."

"Come on over this minute," said Mrs. Bridge.

"Are you in the same fix?"

"I should say I am!"

And now the day took shape and Mrs. Bridge was no longer embarrassed. She had found she was not alone, and if others felt as she felt there was no reason to be depressed. The hours no longer loomed ahead; it was just another warm June day. A few minutes later Madge Arlen was coming in the front door, wearing a loose lavender gaucho blouse, chartreuse slacks, and cork wedgies that made her nearly six feet tall. She was smoking one of the English cigarettes she liked but which were now so hard to obtain. Harriet made some coffee, for Madge Arlen drank coffee all day, and they sat on the porch and talked. The British were concluding the evacuation of Dunkirk, and for a while Mrs. Bridge and Madge Arlen discussed the war.

"So many of the boys are joining up," Mrs. Bridge remarked. "It certainly changes things. I notice the difference everywhere. Piggly Wiggly still delivers, thank heavens, but the service is so much slower than it used to be and I was so surprised the other morning to see they have a girl driving the truck."

"Just wait till Congress passes a draft law. Lord, we'll see the difference then!"

"Oh, I hope not! I'm sure the war will be over soon, and of course we're doing everything humanly possible to stay out of it."

And they talked about people they knew. Grace Barron's son, David, had been taking violin lessons for a number of years and wanted to make a career of music. His father disapproved of this and, as everyone knew, the Barrons were not getting along well. Madge Arlen mentioned that the situation was worse.

"Being a professional musician does sound exciting," Mrs. Bridge observed. "But I just wonder how practical it would be. Oh, my word, it's four o'clock already! I don't know about you, Madge, but I'm simply famished."

They went to the kitchen and Mrs. Bridge looked into the refrigerator.

"Strawberries and whipped cream?" she suggested. "These are frozen, of course. They don't really taste the same as the fresh, but they certainly are a time-saver."

✱

98

Reflections on Montaigne

The Tattler killed many an interminable hour. She read it, not avidly, but thoroughly, from Bancroft's full-page ad inside the front cover to Mr. Alexander's striking floral ad on the back.

Of all the things in *The Tattler* she was most impressed with the philosophy. Between snapshots of country-club residents enjoying themselves at their favorite swimming pool, or on the golf links, and items of gossip regarding prominent Kansas Citians, the editors of *The Tattler* customarily sandwiched a thought or two—preferably cheerful, affirmative at the very least. Emerson and Saint Francis were frequent contributors; Oliver Wendell Holmes was a great favorite. The observations of such eminent men were set in italics and were apt to be followed by, "I wonder if the scion of a certain well-known *famille* doesn't realize his many conquests are causing talk among the younger set."

Mrs. Bridge, being considerably interested in these maxims, had at one point thought of beginning a nice scrapbook with the idea of handing it on to the children. Though she had not found time for this she continued to try to memorize certain quotations, despite the fact that there never seemed to be an appropriate occasion to re-quote them. A line from Montaigne set her to thinking.

I have always observed a singular accord between super-celestial ideas and subterranean behavior.

In less crystalline style she had observed somewhat the same thing and was puzzled by it: she recalled the strange case of Dr. Foster, who had been positively identified at the burlesque, not once—which could have been attributed to his gathering material for a sermon—but several times. Furthermore he never mentioned it.

Over the wisdom of Montaigne she brooded, eventually reaching the conclusion that if super-celestial ideas were necessarily accompanied by subterranean behavior it might be better to forego them both.

*

99

Gloves

She looked forward to Saturdays because on that day she was occupied with the distribution of used clothing at the Auxiliary charity center on Ninth Street. Usually she went with Madge Arlen. One week they would drive to work in the Arlens' Chrysler, the next week in the Lincoln, and when it was Mrs. Bridge's turn she drew up before the garage where her husband parked. There she honked the horn, or beckoned if someone happened to be in sight, and shortly an attendant whose name was Hal would come out of the garage buttoning on a white duster and he would ride in the rear seat to the charity center. There he would jump out and open the door for Mrs. Bridge, and after that he would drive the Lincoln back to the garage because she did not like it left on the street in such a neighborhood.

"Suppose you come by for us around six, or six-fifteenish, Hal," she would say.

He always answered that he would be glad to, touched the visor of his cap, and drove away.

"He seems so nice," said Mrs. Arlen as the two of them walked into the center.

"Oh, he is!" Mrs. Bridge agreed. "He's one of the nicest garage men I've ever had."

"How long have you been parking there?"

"Quite some time. We used to park at that dreadful place on Walnut."

"The one with the popcorn machine? Lord, isn't that the limit?"

"No, not that place. The one with the Italians. You know how my husband is about Italians. Well, that just seemed to be headquarters for them. They flocked in there by the dozen to eat their lunch and listen to some opera broadcast from New York. It was just impossible. So finally Walter said, 'I'm going to change garages.' So we did."

The charity center had not yet been opened for the day. Mrs. Bridge and Mrs. Arlen walked between the counters piled high with sour, unwashed clothing, past the reform-school boys who were emptying sacks of clothing on the floor, and continued into the back room, which was reserved for Auxiliary members. Lois Montgomery was there, and Mabel Ong and Rebecca Duncan, along with several other ladies. They were having coffee and eclairs as they always did before starting work. Mrs. Bridge and Mrs. Arlen joined them.

After a while the doors were unlocked and the first of the poor entered. Behind the counters waiting to assist them were Mrs. Bridge and her friends, all wearing gloves.

*

100

Marching with Dr. Foster

For a few months Grace Barron worked at the charity
center; then she quit, abruptly, without offering an explanation. Mrs. Bridge was hurt by this, for it seemed un-
like Grace Barron to be inconsiderate. Then, too, Mrs.
Bridge reflected, she had always been so concerned about
the welfare of others; still she did have streaks of peculiarity,
as, for instance, her attitude toward Dr. Foster, whom Mrs.
Bridge considered not only one of the nicest men she had
ever met, but also one of the most intelligent. Grace, in-
explicably, was amused by Dr. Foster.

Mrs. Bridge regretted having told her about a rather
unfortunate slip of the tongue which occurred at the start
of the benediction on Palm Sunday. Dr. Foster had said,
"With eyes bowed and heads closed . . ."

True, this was unfortunate, but, as she promptly added
in defense of the minister, "It could happen to anyone."

Grace probably didn't hear; she was laughing hysterically.
"I knew I should have gone last Sunday," she said, wiping
the tears from her eyes, "Oh, I'm so sorry I missed that!"

Then there had been that awful day when the elevator
plunged into the bargain basement. It was a dark, rainy
afternoon and Mrs. Bridge had gone downtown and was
browsing through the basement of one of the department

stores in search of something humorous to give as a booby prize at a forthcoming card party. She was examining some celluloid toys when all at once there was a noise like a shot and a shrill singing whine and a rumble, and before she could understand what it was all about the elevator crashed not ten steps from where she stood. Later it turned out that the elevator had not fallen as far as everyone thought; in fact it had only dropped about six or eight feet. Even so, it made a great noise and most of the passengers dropped their parcels and one or two fell down. Mrs. Bridge had not yet recovered from her surprise and was only looking rather blankly at the people in the elevator, who themselves were stunned into momentary silence and were looking blindly out of the cage, when someone began to scream for help. It was someone in the rear of the elevator, and presently this person fought his way through the other passengers and got to the front where he grabbed the cage and began shaking it.

"Why, Dr. Foster!" said Mrs. Bridge, and then there was so much confusion and so many people rushing around that she lost track of him.

He was not badly injured, as she had supposed he was; he had a sprained ankle. He went about on a cane for quite a while afterward—longer, in fact, than she had ever seen anyone employ a cane for a sprained ankle—and for several weeks more he hobbled and alluded dryly to his accident. Mrs. Bridge was a little disappointed in him without knowing just why. However there was certainly nothing funny about the accident, and she was quite put out with Grace for laughing when she heard of it.

Her entire attitude toward religion was flippant, and Mrs. Bridge did not think it was in very good taste. After one of the Auxiliary meetings she chanced to be nearby when Grace got on the subject of religion and said there was a rumor

that after Christ was sentenced to death He turned to one
of the soldiers and said, "When am I going to learn to
keep my big mouth shut?"

Mrs. Bridge smiled courteously, as she never failed to
do when someone told a joke, and though she did not
believe God was planning to strike Grace dead, still she
could not see there was anything to be gained by asking
for trouble.

Frequently she attempted to interest her in religion, or
at least in the habit of attending church, but the attempts
were unsuccessful. It was a rare Sunday when she encountered Grace among the crowd on the church steps after
services.

In the center of the church lawn stood a green wooden
cupboard with a glass front. Each Thursday morning the
janitor came out with a manila envelope full of white
celluloid letters about two inches tall, and with these he
composed the title of Dr. Foster's forthcoming sermon. Mrs.
Bridge was pleased to see the Barrons' Cadillac parked in the
lot one Sunday morning when the sermon was entitled:
Should We Go to Church?

Naturally no one believed Dr. Foster would decide in
favor of the negative, yet Mrs. Bridge could not help being
irked when Grace whispered that she could hardly wait to
find out. In a few minutes Dr. Foster appeared and ascended
to the pulpit. He was growing more stout and more dignified
every year. Solemnly he gazed down upon the congregation.
At such times Mrs. Bridge thought he looked every inch the
Man of God. She remembered seeing him one day on the
Plaza; he had been studying himself in the mirror of a
cigarette machine and she thought she had never seen him
look more impressive. It was only at cocktail parties that
he seemed unable to avoid little belches, after which he
would stare with severity at the sandwich or cocktail in his
hand.

"Should we go to church?" asked Dr. Foster of his audience. He allowed a few seconds for everyone to ponder. "Should we go to church?" he repeated. He cleared his throat, placed his hands on the sides of the lectern, and began.

The sub-title of the sermon was "Unexplored Warehouses of the Cliff Dwellers." The parable had to do with the fact that in plentiful years the Mesa Verde Indians stored part of their harvest in cliff houses and in time of famine they ate what they had saved.

A few minutes after noon Dr. Foster was winding it up. "We, of this more enlightened age, can surely benefit from the wisdom of those ancient savages. They learned to store their surplus against the time of dire necessity, and so it is when we go to church. . . ."

A few minutes later he descended and strode magnificently through the swinging doors. The last they saw of him was the tail of his black and royal purple cassock. To Mrs. Bridge he had seemed unusually eloquent and moving, and it was very strange, she thought, that throughout the sermon Grace was inattentive and listless. Afterward, on the steps, they talked for a little while.

"Grace," Mrs. Bridge said impulsively, and took her by the hand, "is something troubling you?"

"No," she whispered, with her eyes tightly shut. "No, no, *no!*"

"There is!" cried Mrs. Bridge. "I know there is!" But at this point they were interrupted by the arrival of the men and whatever might have been revealed was lost.

*

101

Quo Vadis, Madame?

That evening, while preparing for bed, Mrs. Bridge suddenly paused with the fingertips of one hand just touching her cheek. She was seated before her dressing table in her robe and slippers and had begun spreading cold cream on her face. The touch of the cream, the unexpectedness of it—for she had been thinking deeply about how to occupy tomorrow—the swift cool touch demoralized her so completely that she almost screamed.

She continued spreading the cream over her features, steadily observing herself in the mirror, and wondered who she was, and how she happened to be at the dressing table, and who the man was who sat on the edge of the bed taking off his shoes. She considered her fingers, which dipped into the jar of their own accord. Rapidly, soundlessly, she was disappearing into white, sweetly scented anonymity. Gratified by this she smiled, and perceived a few seconds later that beneath the mask she was not smiling. All the same, being committed, there was nothing to do but proceed.

102

Joseph Conrad

She was wakened by the chimes of the grandfather clock in the hall. It was three or four in the morning. Her husband was sleeping easily, but gravely, as though exhausted. She awoke simultaneously with the knowledge of one morning many years before when she had been dusting the bookcase and came across an old, old red-gold volume. Taking it down she found on the flyleaf in dry, spidery script the name of Shannon Bridge, who was the uncle of her husband—an unambitious, taciturn man who had married a night-club entertainer and later died of a heart attack in Mexico, and upon whose death they had inherited a few books and charts. She had no idea what the charts were about, for she had not unrolled them, only stored them in the attic, and then one day, absently, since they were useless, she had discarded them; and as for the books, no one had read them, so far as she knew, though later she found Douglas examining them, and now at four in the morning she was lying completely awake, thinking of the time she had taken a book down from a shelf and had begun turning the brittle, yellowed pages. She stood beside the bookcase for quite a while, growing absorbed in what she read, and wandered, still reading, into the living room, where she did not look up from the book until someone called her, because she had come upon a passage which had been underlined, no doubt by Shannon Bridge, which observed that some people go skimming over the years of existence to sink gently into a placid grave, ignorant of life to the last, without ever having been made to see all it may contain; and this passage she had read once again, and brooded over it, and turned back to it again, and was thinking deeply when she was interrupted.

And Mrs. Bridge remembered now that she had risen and had said, "Yes, all right, I'm on my way," and had placed the book on the mantel, for she had intended to read further. She wondered what had interfered, where she had gone, and why she had never returned.

*

103

Psychotherapy

Mabel Ong was going to an analyst. Mrs. Bridge was surprised to learn this because Mabel in her tailored suits and with her authoritative masculine manner had always seemed the very picture of confidence. At luncheon club not long after Dr. Foster's eloquent sermon on church attendance she found herself sitting next to Mabel, and by the time luncheon was over Mrs. Bridge was convinced that she, too, needed analysis. She had, in fact, privately thought so long before her talk with Mabel. More and more it had occurred to her that she was no longer needed. Ruth was gone, so very gone—even her letters said so little—and Carolyn was almost gone, and Douglas, though still at home, was growing so independent, more like his father every year. Soon he too would be leaving home. What would she do then? It had been a long time, she felt, since her husband truly needed her. He accepted her, and he loved her, of this she had never had a doubt, but he was accustomed to and quite unconscious of love, whereas she wanted him to think about it and to tell her about it. The promise of the past had been fulfilled: she had three fine children and her husband was wonderfully successful. But Mrs. Bridge felt tired and ill. She wanted help.

She surmised her husband would not be sympathetic to her idea of being psychoanalyzed, so, for a number of weeks before mentioning it, she planned the conversation. She meant to open with the direct, positive, almost final statement that she was going downtown the first thing in the morning to arrange a series of appointments. That certainly ought to settle the matter—he ought to be able to understand the situation. Possibly he was going to inquire how much it would cost, and she was uneasy about this, suspecting it was going to be expensive, with the result that she avoided finding out what it would cost. After all, in spite of his complaints, she knew, and he was aware that she knew, that they had plenty of money.

She tried to imagine all his objections to her idea, but really there was nothing he could say. He would simply be forced to agree. It had been years since she had asked him for anything, no matter how slight; indeed, every once in a while he would inquire if there wasn't something she wanted—anything for the house, or for herself. No, there was nothing. It was difficult to find things to buy. She had the money, but she had already bought everything she could use, which was why she often spent an entire day shopping and came home without having bought anything except lunch, and perhaps some pastry during the afternoon.

Having solved whatever objection he might make in regard to the expense, she concluded that all she had to do was let him know her intention. She kept putting it off. She rehearsed the scene many times and it always came out satisfactorily.

The difficulty lay in finding the opportunity to begin. So it was that several weeks slipped away, then one evening after supper, as they were settling themselves in the living room, she with a bag of knitting and he with the stock-market page of the newspaper, she knew the time had come. She pretended to be straightening her knitting, but she was greatly occupied with marshaling her thoughts. He always got to the heart of a matter at once, wasting no energy on preliminaries, and she had to be ready for this. Just then he lowered the paper and she was terrified that somehow he had been reading her mind. Quite often he could, and this more than anything else was the reason she found it exceedingly difficult to defend her ideas. He was glaring at the newspaper.

"Listen to this: The Central has asked the ICC to investigate the circumstances of the sale of eight hundred thousand shares of stock, owned by the Chesapeake and Ohio Railway, to Murchison and Richardson last week." He looked across the paper at her as if she were responsible.

"Well!" said Mrs. Bridge in what she thought an appropriate tone. It would be unwise to annoy him at this point, but until he made it clear whose side he was on she could not say anything specific. Her expression remained intent and neutrally expectant, as though she wanted to hear more.

"What in God's name do those people think they're doing?" he demanded sharply.

"It certainly doesn't seem right," she answered, still not certain whether the scoundrels were Central, or Chesapeake and Ohio, or Murchison and Richardson. Or, of course, he could be angry with the newspaper for having publicized it.

Mr. Bridge had taken off his glasses and was staring at her.

"I don't know a thing in the world about it, of course," she added hastily.

He resumed reading. A few minutes later he said, "Allied Chemical: up four! Great Lord! What's going on here?" After this he was quiet for a long time, coughing once, shaking the paper into shape. Mrs. Bridge, having noted it was almost time for bed, decided she must speak.

"Walter," she began in a tremulous voice, and went on rapidly, "I've been thinking it over and I don't see any way out except through analysis."

He did not look up. Minutes went by. Finally he muttered, "Australian wool is firm." And then, roused by the sound of his own voice, he glanced at her inquisitively. She gave him a stark, desperate look; it was unnecessary to repeat what she had said because he always heard everything even when he failed to reply.

"What?" he demanded. "Nonsense," he said absently, and he struck the paper into submission and continued reading.

104

Pineapple Bread

The following day being Thursday, Harriet's day off, Mrs. Bridge prepared supper for herself and her husband. Douglas had telephoned a few minutes after school let out to say he was at a fraternity meeting and that as soon as it was over he and a couple of friends were going to get a hamburger somewhere and then were going downtown to a track meet in the municipal auditorium.

"What about your homework?" she asked.

"Homework," he replied, giving a very final opinion of it.

"Well, I don't think you should stay out late," she answered. "After all, it's a week night."

He said he would be home early, but early could mean any hour.

"All right now, don't forget," she said. "Your grades haven't been worth boasting about."

"I'll get by," said Douglas. "Holy Cow!"

"Yes, well you just might Holy Cow yourself right out of graduating."

With that the conversation ended and she went into the kitchen to start preparing a casserole, as she had done many, many times before. She moved around the kitchen slowly. She had plenty of time. The house was so quiet that she began to think of how noisy it had been when all the children were there, how very much different everything had been, and presently, remembering the days when she used to cook the meals, she went to the cupboard where the old recipe books were stored. Harriet occasionally referred to them, but otherwise they had lain untouched for years. Mrs. Bridge began looking through them, seeing pencil notations in her own handwriting, scarcely legible any more. Her husband liked more pepper in this, no bay leaves in that—whatever he wanted and whatever he did not like was expertly registered in the margins, and as she turned through these recipes she thought how strangely intimate the faded penciled notes remained; they brought back many scenes, many sweet and private memories; they brought back youth.

Mrs. Bridge grew thoughtfully excited. A glance at the electric clock on the stove panel told her there might be time enough to alter her plans for supper. She was thinking of fixing spaghetti for him, with the special sauce he had so often said was the best in the world. She had not fixed it for years. Harriet could not sense just how long to let it simmer, and without that particular flavor to the sauce there was not much point in eating spaghetti. A quick search of the refrigerator and of the cupboards disclosed there were not the right ingredients. She found some canned sauce and thought about improvising from it, but it would not be the same. He would taste the difference. And so, regretfully, she admitted it was going to be the casserole again. Next week they would have spaghetti. A little sadly she turned on through the cookbooks, and once more she had an idea. She had come across the recipe for pineapple bread and there was time for that and she was certain they had the ingredients—not only the pineapple but the chipped pecans, the raisins—yes, yes, she could do it.

She carried the bread to the table wrapped in a towel because it was still hot from the oven, and Mr. Bridge, who, as he unfolded his napkin, had been looking at the casserole with resignation, now glanced with puzzled interest at what she was bringing him. His expression began to brighten. He smiled.

"Oh-ho!" said Mr. Bridge, rubbing his hands together, "What have we here?"

She placed it before him, too thrilled to speak, and hurried back to the kitchen for the bread knife.

"Well, well!" said he, accepting the knife, and he smacked his lips and shut his eyes for a moment to inhale the fragrance of the small plump loaf.

"Go ahead and cut it," she said to him intensely, and waited beside his chair.

The first slice fell down like a corpse and they saw bubbles of dank white dough around the pecans. After a moment of silence Mrs. Bridge covered it with the towel and carried it to the kitchen. Having disposed of the bread she untied her little ruffled apron and waited quietly until she regained control of herself.

A few minutes later she re-entered the dining room with a loaf of grocery-store bread on a silver tray. She smiled and said, "It's been a long time, I'm afraid."

"Never mind," said Mr. Bridge as he removed the lid of the casserole, and the next day he brought her a dozen roses.

✱

105

Carolyn's Engagement

Time was passing more rapidly than she thought; she was almost overcome when Carolyn appeared in the middle of the week with an engagement ring she had gotten the night before from a thin, shaggy boy with protruding teeth whose name was Gil Davis. He was a junior at the university. He was studying business management and working part-time in the dean's office.

Mrs. Bridge, seeking a moment to recover from the shock, looked at Carolyn's ring and said, "It's an opal, isn't it?"

"Gil doesn't have much money," Carolyn explained. "He told me he thought diamonds were absurd. And you know, Mother, he's worked for everything he owns!"

She was fascinated by this. She had never known a boy who was poor. In high school she had known boys who worked during summers and some who worked after school in order to have spending money, but none of them had been forced to work in order to eat and buy clothing. "Well, I think it's lovely!" said Mrs. Bridge, squeezing her hand. "Does your father know?"

"No," said Carolyn.

"Well, I'm afraid you'd better tell him, don't you think so?"

"Why don't you call him?" Carolyn suggested.

"This isn't my engagement," replied Mrs. Bridge.

Mr. Bridge, being informed of his daughter's engagement,

was outraged. He had never heard of any Gil Davis, and who did Gil Davis think he was? And as for Carolyn, there was to be no more of this ridiculous nonsense. She was to return that ring to that upstart boy, whatever his name was, and that was to be the end of the matter. Carolyn immediately burst into tears and threw her ring on the carpet. Her father had never talked to her like that before. When she returned to the university the ring was in her pocket. She had promised to give it back.

Gil Davis, being informed that his suit had been rejected, was also outraged. He was twenty years old and never before in his life had he been the cause of any trouble. He looked at the ring, he looked at Carolyn, and then he ran out of the dean's office and ran all the way to the bus station, where he bought a ticket to Kansas City. He pushed his way past the secretary who wanted to know what his business was and he walked into Mr. Bridge's private office without bothering to knock. He emerged at eight o'clock that night in company with his intended father-in-law; they ate sausage and buckwheat cakes together in a lunch wagon, both of them exhausted, and they had agreed he was going to marry Carolyn. So, for the second time, Gil Davis placed his opal ring on her finger and she wore the ring with a truculent expression.

"I know you two are going to be very happy," Mrs. Bridge said, hugging her. "I'm so relieved everything worked out all right."

Carolyn said, "You do like him, Mother, don't you?"

"Why, of course, dear! He's awfully nice. It's just that he's so different from the kind of boys you've been used to."

Gil Davis was aware of this fact; he quit the university because he saw he would need steady money and quite a lot of it as soon as he married Carolyn. He returned to his home town, which was located near the Oklahoma border in southern Kansas, and there he went to work for his uncle, who owned a dry-goods emporium. Carolyn wanted him to work in an aircraft factory where he could get overtime wages, but saw the sense of his decision when he told her his uncle was considering retirement.

The friends of Mrs. Bridge were avid for information about Carolyn's engagement.

"Is her ring a blue or a white?"

"It's a lovely opal," Mrs. Bridge replied, facing the inquiries with her best smile.

"What a nice idea!"

"It's what Carolyn was hoping for," Mrs. Bridge countered.

"I understand he's not a Kansas Citian."

"From Parallel," she replied serenely, and scored a point by not explaining where Parallel could be found.

"It sounds quite far."

"They'll be driving up for visits, I'm sure."

"What does the father do?"

He was a plumber. Mrs. Bridge had confronted herself with this fact a thousand times; there was simply no way around it. She imagined herself replying to this question, which, inevitably, would be asked, replying evasively that he was associated with a company that did household installation, and yet she knew in her heart she must speak the truth. It seemed to her that Carolyn's happiness depended on the acknowledgment of this condition, and, for better or worse, the acceptance of it.

Said Mrs. Bridge—and her throat was so constricted she was afraid the words would lodge there— "Mr. Davis is a plumber." She was astonished to see she had very nearly scored again, for she had spoken with such ease that one might almost believe everybody nowadays was marrying the sons of plumbers.

"I hear the boy is a Beta."

"Well, no. As I understand the situation, Gil is of the opinion fraternity life can be a liability."

"Oh, how true."

"And how does he stand with the draft?"

His feet were as flat as ironing boards and his teeth were bad; he had been rejected as generally unsatisfactory. There was no sense going into detail, such details as Carolyn had given, and so she replied that he had been exempted for medical reasons. She believed he had had rheumatic fever when he was a child. In any event this sounded plausible, and was acceptable.

"You say he's in Parallel now?

Mrs. Bridge knew what was next. She nodded.

"I see. I didn't realize he'd already graduated."

"According to what Carolyn tells me, in his opinion a four-year university education is actually less worth while than a certain amount of practical experience." It had been badly put, she knew, and it was a retreat, but the business of the plumber had broken her composure.

106

Present from Douglas

Wedding gifts arrived. Day after day they arrived and Carolyn received enough silver to open a shop. She tore open the packages greedily and her blue eyes gleamed more brightly than the richest plate. Mrs. Bridge, meanwhile, seated at her writing table with a notebook and fountain pen, dutifully jotted down what it was and who had sent it. Carolyn would be expected to memorize this list in order to be able to thank everyone personally and specifically: she would be expected to, but would she? Mrs. Bridge was uneasy. She, herself, no matter how long it took, no matter how arduous the job, would have learned to identify every gift. She could only hope Carolyn would be as considerate.

There were a few awkward presents—a green bronze frog to be used as a doorstop, a queer desk lamp that resembled a pagoda, two or three novels and a book of Persian poetry, and from cousin Lulubelle Watts in Memphis a lifetime subscription to a magazine no one had ever heard of. There was one gift, however, worse than these. It was a present from Douglas. It was a toaster.

Douglas had delayed until the last moment because he hated to give or to receive presents. He liked his sister but he did not see where spending fifteen or twenty dollars would prove he wished her happiness. In deference to custom, however, on the next to last day he decided to buy a toaster because she had said she would need one. He walked to the Plaza— "Nobody's using the Lincoln," she had said, but he replied that he felt like walking—and on the Plaza he looked them over, hands in his pockets, while a salesman demonstrated. He was shown the most elaborate toasters that money could buy, but he was not pleased. The dials were set, the pointers turned, the levers pressed, the machine plugged in, the concealed tray that collected crumbs was removed, all for his benefit, but he was not pleased. At the conclusion of the demonstration he walked across the street to a dime store and bought a primitive toaster such as his parents had had when they were first married.

No one criticized the gift. Carolyn thanked him. Mrs. Bridge exclaimed over how simple it was to operate, and indeed it was simple. Neither of them mentioned the four magnificent automatic toasters which had been delivered that same morning.

Of course the amount of money spent was not the important thing, everyone admitted that, and everyone said something really should be done to make wedding gifts more reasonable;

all the same, people would want to know what Douglas had given his sister, and either Mrs. Bridge or Carolyn would be obliged to point it out. Clearly it had not cost more than two dollars. Mrs. Bridge was absolutely baffled by her son. Never in her life had she so wanted to shake him.

*

107

Carolyn Marries

To southern Kansas Carolyn moved after the ceremony and a one-week honeymoon at Excelsior Springs. Mr. Bridge had offered them a wedding trip to the Bahamas, but Gil refused, saying they would honeymoon on the money he himself had earned, so Excelsior Springs was the extent of it. Carolyn had wanted to see the Bahamas ever since she could remember. The wedding gift metamorphosed into one hundred shares of expensive, conservative stock.

Gil began working nights in order to convince his uncle that it was feasible to retire and leave the dry-goods business in his hands, the result being that Carolyn was lonely and bored, and became petulant, and frequently drove to Kansas City for the night after leaving a note pinned to the tablecloth. She would stay in her old room and, if there chanced to be a party that week end, she might remain in Kansas City until Monday. From the beginning she disliked Parallel and could not make up her mind whether she could stand living there.

"The golf course is pathetic, Mother," she said one evening. "It's a nine-hole public course—and by public I mean *any-*

body, but anybody, even if they never *saw* a golf club before, can play there. I mean, really, how does Gil expect me to accomplish anything there? It'll absolutely ruin my game. The greens—there aren't any greens, Mother, they're as hard as wood and the grass is burnt to a crisp. It isn't any fun. Anybody can hit the ball three hundred yards, just about—they just go on rolling. My God! I mean, actually, Mother, you should see that place! I had no idea it would be like that."

Mrs. Bridge was extremely anxious for Carolyn to be happy. "I should think it would be nice for a change," she said.

Carolyn was not listening.

"Gil's a type, really. He *is.* He's a small-town boy, and it shows, Mother. He got simply furious when I tried to tell the barber how to cut his hair. I got so mad I wouldn't speak to him for three days."

"Dear, I wish you wouldn't argue with him."

"Listen, Mother, no man is ever going to push me around the way Daddy pushes you around."

*

108

Alice

Subsequent events proved that Carolyn and her husband had their reconciliations, no matter how brief, for she very soon was pregnant.

She drove up from Parallel one snowy afternoon and said as she came in the door, stamping snow from her galoshes,

"You'll never believe this, Mother, because it's too perfectly incredible." And she said this repeatedly, as if to convince herself it was a dream. It was less than a dream, or more, depending, though she continued to exclaim for about three months, "I mean, this is just insane!"

Eventually she grew accustomed to her situation and it appeared to Mrs. Bridge that the marriage was going to work out all right. Gil and Carolyn were looking for a house in Parallel; their apartment would be too small when the baby came.

"But everything is so high," said Carolyn. They were in the kitchen. It was Harriet's day off and Mrs. Bridge was baking some oatmeal cookies to send to Ruth, and Carolyn was helping. "We want something with a decent yard," she went on, sliding a spatula under a row of hot cookies and transferring them to a towel spread on the drainboard. "And Gil insists on a dry basement. That's the first place he goes. The real-estate agent no more than has the door open when Gil heads for the basement and I'm left standing there as big as an elephant. He's gone mad on turning out salad bowls on a lathe. A friend of his has a lathe. He says it calms his nerves, and so that's why he has to have a dry basement—so it won't rust the goddamned lathe. Really, how berserk can a man go?"

Mrs. Bridge, carefully drawing a second tray of cookies from the oven, observed that there should be lots of pleasant homes in Parallel.

"Oh, there are, there are," Carolyn mumbled, "but you've got to check the neighbors."

"I don't understand what you mean."

"The niggers are moving in."

Mrs. Bridge slowly put down the tray of cookies. She did not know just what to say. Such situations were awkward. On the one hand, she herself would not care to live next door to a houseful of Negroes; on the other hand, there was no reason not to. She had always liked the colored people she had known.

She still thought affectionately of Beulah Mae and worried about her, wondering if she was still alive. She had never known any Negroes socially; not that she avoided it, just that there weren't any in the neighborhood, or at the country club, or in the Auxiliary. There just weren't any for her to meet, that was all.

"That reminds me, Carolyn. You'll never guess who I bumped into the other day. Alice Jones! We got on an elevator together."

"My God! I'd absolutely forgotten that girl."

"Don't you remember how you two used to play together? You were practically inseparable. I almost had to pry you apart at lunch time."

"Did she recognize you?"

"Oh, right away."

"What's she doing?"

"She's married now and she's working as a maid in one of the downtown hotels."

"How many children does she have?"

"She didn't say."

"Does she look the same?"

"Heavens, no! She's almost as tall as Douglas and she looked so black. It's such a shame."

Carolyn became thoughtful, and finally said, "I think I'd like to see her. Which hotel is she working at?"

"I've been trying to think. I knew you'd want to see her. And she told me which one it was."

"Well, it doesn't matter, I guess. I don't know what we could say to each other, it's been so long."

"How many years has it been?"

"Quite a few," Carolyn answered, biting her lip. "It's been quite a few years, Mother."

Mrs. Bridge turned off the gas in the oven and shut the doors.

✳

109

Winter

The snow fell all night. It fell without a sound and covered the frozen ground, and the dead leaves beneath the maple tree, and bowed the limbs of the evergreens, and sifted out of the high, pearl-blue clouds hour after hour. Mrs. Bridge was awakened by the immense silence and she lay in her bed listening. She heard the velvet chimes of the clock in the hall, and presently the barking of a dog. She had a feeling that all was not well and she waited in deep expectancy for some further intimation, listening intently, but all she heard before falling asleep was the familiar chiming of the clock.

110

Death and Life of Grace Barron

The next morning Lois Montgomery telephoned to say that Grace Barron had committed suicide.

In the days that followed Mrs. Bridge attempted to suppress

this fact. Her reasoning was that nothing could be gained by discussing it; consequently she wrote to Ruth that there was some doubt as to what had been the cause of Mrs. Barron's death but it was presumed she had accidentally eaten some tuna-fish salad which had been left out of the refrigerator overnight and had become contaminated, and this was what she told Douglas and Carolyn.

To intimate friends, to those who knew the truth, which was that Grace Barron had swallowed over fifty sleeping tablets, Mrs. Bridge talked more openly. They asked one another familiar and similar questions because, in many ways, Grace Barron was indistinguishable from anyone among them. Their problems had been hers, their position, their wealth, and the love they knew, these also had belonged to her.

"It came as such a shock," Mrs. Bridge heard herself say again and again. "It's awfully hard to believe."

She often wondered if anyone other than herself had been able to divine the motive; if so, it went unmentioned. But she herself had found it instinctively less than an instant after hearing the news: her first thought had been of an afternoon on the Plaza when she and Grace Barron had been looking for some way to occupy themselves, and Grace had said, a little sadly, "Have you ever felt like those people in the Grimm fairy tale—the ones who were all hollowed out in the back?"

111

Old Acquaintance

The country was now at war. Douglas had graduated from high school and wanted to join the Army. Ruth was gone; she seldom wrote. Carolyn, unable to get along with her husband, was coming home more frequently. And Mrs. Bridge, lost in confusion, often lay down to rest awhile, and thought back to happier times. She saw that it was inevitable these things had come to pass, and she could not escape a feeling of unreality. One day, while shopping on the Plaza, she had recognized someone who used to live next door to her when she was a child. The woman was now evidently verging on old age, and Mrs. Bridge, counting down the years as she observed, from a distance, the conclusion of the youth which was her own, felt a growing sense of despair and futility, and ever after that day she herself moved a little more slowly.

112

Carolyn Comes Home

Sometime in the middle of the night Mrs. Bridge awoke and knew Carolyn had come home. The house was absolutely still and yet she had no doubt; rising quietly so as not to disturb her husband she pulled on her quilted satin robe, found her slippers, and went along the hall to the room where the girls had lived. Sure enough the door was closed; ordinarily it was open. Mrs. Bridge hesitated outside, listening, but heard nothing; she had expected to hear Carolyn sobbing.

"Dear, may I come in?" she asked. There was no answer, but she pushed open the door and saw Carolyn lying on the bed fully dressed with her hands clasped beneath her head. She was staring at the ceiling.

"Did you and Gil have another argument?" she asked, seating herself on the edge of the bed.

"I can't stand him," she answered after a while.

"What was it this time?"

"He hit me."

Mrs. Bridge caught her breath.

"He did," she repeated, with no apparent anger. "He slapped me so hard I lost my balance and fell down."

"You must have done something to provoke him. Didn't you?" she asked.

"Are you on his side?"

"I'm trying not be on anyone's side, dear," she said, and

reached out to stroke Carolyn's head. "It's just that I don't think Gil is that sort."

"Oh, no? If you lived with him you'd find out different." Tears had sprung into her eyes, and seeing them Mrs. Bridge felt herself ready to weep.

"Do you know what he did afterward, Mother? He tried to make it up the way men always do."

"Carolyn, there are some things about marriage that a woman has to—"

"Oh, no, don't tell me that! I don't want any part of that myth—I don't! Why, Mother, he didn't even know it was me. Do you know what I'm saying?"

"Why don't you tell me how it all started?" she replied, pulling the robe more tightly around her throat.

"It started at breakfast because I'd forgotten to get butter the day before, so he got sarcastic, and then he decided I didn't know how to feed the baby, and then he began yelling when he couldn't find his blue suit. Mother, he's been hounding me about that suit for two weeks. It's been at the cleaners and I've been so rushed with the baby and with the qualifying rounds at the club that I haven't had time to pick it up. He could have picked it up himself because he comes right by the cleaners every day, but he keeps saying that's my job. So, anyway, next he began shouting at me that if I spent less time playing golf and more—oh, hell, what's the use? I mean, anyway, after he finally went to work I thought maybe it was partly my fault and so in order to make it up to him I got a baby-sitter to come over while I went to the beauty shop to have my hair set, and they couldn't take me right away and by the time I finally got through it was late and I didn't get home till after he did because I had to pay some bills and stop at the club to see if my entry had been posted. Well, I guess you can imagine what a foul temper he was in when his dinner wasn't ready for him, and he'd called the club and they'd told him I was there, even after I'd given strict orders to say I wasn't. Well," she went on, after drawing a deep breath, "he was furious and swearing. He'd thrown clothes all over the bedroom and even jerked out some of the drawers and turned them over on the bed because he couldn't find what he wanted. I told him the stuff hadn't been washed and he knew perfectly well the washing machine was broken. I guess he expected me to hand-wash everything. I mean, really, Mother, that's what he expected."

"Well, I don't think it would hurt you to do some washing."

"Oh, Mother, honestly! All he has to do is get the machine fixed."

"Yes, I understand, dear, but perhaps if both of you were to try a little harder—"

"He said I didn't have the faintest idea what it meant to have to work."

"Why, that's absurd!"

"He said I was spoiled, Mother. Is that the truth?"

"Of course not, dear. Why should he say a thing like that? Now I'm sure everything is going to work out all right, so why don't you get some rest? You'll feel better in the morning."

"And do you know whose fault he said it was, Mother?"

113

Mr. Bridge Adjourns

Mrs. Bridge was caught between wanting Carolyn home again for good, and wanting the marriage to succeed. The world was reeling, so it seemed, and she lost faith in tomorrow. Her ears rang with the frenetic song of war. She could not understand the slaughter and she was often frightened now that Douglas was gone. He had persuaded his father to let him join the Army before the draft caught up with him and now he was somewhere in Arizona. He wrote to her every week—cheerful, airy letters, as though he had gone camping for the summer and would be back in time for college, and she could almost believe this was true. Then, without warning, she would be struck by the actual truth and she would feel lonely and helpless, and guilty over the happiness she experienced whenever Carolyn appeared. With Carolyn in the house—even in a foul humor so that she smoked and cursed without regard for anyone else—even then Mrs. Bridge was comforted, for her presence was an arch to the past, and Mrs. Bridge never tired of dreaming of the days when the children were small, and there had been peace, and so much to anticipate.

Often she sat up with a start, and after a desperate glance at the clock she would be ashamed to learn that two or three hours had gone by while she was thinking. She had given up working at the charity center; there were more than enough volunteers, particularly among the younger women, and the staring eyes of the people on Ninth Street had begun to haunt her. She often saw them in the middle of the night, the hungry, lost people.

And she was haunted, too, by recollections as inanimate and soulless as these unfortunate people, which surrounded her with undemanding, relentless attention, like a perfect circle of question marks—incidents, for the most part, comments she had offered, replies, attitudes, trivial circumstances which by all logic should have long since passed into obscurity, but which recurred persistently to trouble her. And always, or very nearly so, she overcame these doubts; and yet, even as she arose, secure in her convictions, she was aware she had not triumphed over them, nor destroyed them, nor pacified them, but only pushed them away for a little while, like nagging children.

Douglas came home on furlough; he got out of the taxicab

looking much older. There was another soldier in the taxi to whom he waved good-by, and Mrs. Bridge, waiting to embrace her son, heard him call in a resounding voice, "Save a Jap for me, sergeant!"

"Who was that?" she asked.

"Fellow I met on the train," he replied briefly.

"Didn't you want to ask him in?"

"I did, but he's on his way," Douglas said, and throwing his duffel bag across one shoulder he pushed open the door and strode into the house.

"You've gained some weight," she said, and she noticed, too, that he stood erect now, and there was a frankly adult look in his eyes. The most remarkable change, however, was the fact that he was beginning to grow a mustache—a reddish burr looking somewhat like a patch of sandpaper. Mrs. Bridge thought it looked very silly, and not wanting to hurt his feelings she avoided mentioning it.

Mr. Bridge, however, was neither reticent nor considerate of Douglas's feelings.

"For the love of Mike, what's that?" he asked, on first catching sight of the new mustache, but Douglas, very much to the surprise of his mother, neither flushed in embarrassment nor dropped his eyes.

"You think you could do any better?" he solemnly replied.

Mr. Bridge laughed and clapped him solidly on the shoulder. "How about a drink before dinner, soldier?"

"I could use one," said Douglas, and away they went to the kitchen. Mrs. Bridge heard them laughing, and Harriet's shrill laughter joining in.

Although she could not understand her son she was so pleased to have him home that she continually found excuses to be near him. So it was that she knocked on his door to ask if his socks needed mending. He told her to come in and look. She entered and found him standing in front of the bathroom mirror lathering his jaw. He was not wearing a shirt, only an olive green undershirt and khaki trousers, and she noticed a metal chain around his neck that he had never worn before.

"What on earth is this?" she inquired, approaching hesitantly, full of love and tenderness.

"Dog tags," he said. He was amused.

She drew the chain up from beneath the undershirt, strangely and deeply moved to discover there was hair on his chest, and she held the tags in trembling fingers. She inquired about the data stamped on the dull brass disks, and he told her that one was his serial number, another his blood type, and so on.

"What is this 'P'?" she wanted to know.

"Protestant," he said. "I told them I was a Buddhist, but they insisted I was a Protestant."

"You did *what?*"

"We have to fill out forms all the time. Every form has a blank where you write down your religious affiliation. I always write Buddhist, but somebody always types it up Protestant. I don't know why."

"Well, for goodness' sakes, that's an awfully odd thing to write. You're not a Buddhist."

Douglas dipped his razor in the water. He was looking gently down on her in the mirror, white and foamy almost up to his eyes. She thought he looked inscrutable. She was bewildered.

"Well, I suppose you know what you're doing. Now hurry and finish shaving; Harriet will soon have dinner ready."

She expected him to shave off the mustache, but he did not, and so several days later while he was leaning against the bookcase with Omar Khayyám in hand she remarked, "You look like a perfect stranger."

Douglas glanced down at her in a friendly way and said, without having asked what she meant, that he thought he would keep his mustache nonetheless.

But next morning, seeing it across the breakfast table, she

knew it would have to go. Without a word she set down her orange juice and went upstairs to his room, where, in the closet, she found his Army cap. She put this on her head, and having touched up her graying curls at the mirror she marched downstairs and into the breakfast room swinging her arms stiffly. Douglas was not there. Harriet, stacking the dishes, gazed at her in astonishment. Mrs. Bridge smiled at her bravely, and as serenely as possible under the circumstances. Just then she heard Douglas cough. It sounded as though he were in the living room. She turned around and marched through the hall and into the front room where she came to a halt in what she considered a military manner, and tried to click her heels.

"Attention, Private Bridge. March right upstairs this very minute and shave off your silly mustache."

Douglas had been looking at the photograph on the dust jacket of Dr. Foster's book of essays. He dropped the book on the sofa and crossed his arms. When it became obvious that he did not intend to speak, that he was simply waiting for her to leave, she pulled the cap from her head and stood in front of him uncertainly, rather humbly.

He was to leave from the Union Station at four o'clock the next afternoon, but a few minutes after three the telephone rang. It was Mr. Bridge's office and the secretary was on the phone. Mr. Bridge was dead. He had hurried into the office immediately after lunch and resumed work with a dictaphone. Sometime after that he rolled out of his swivel chair and sprawled on the carpet as dead as he would ever be. When the dictaphone cylinder was played they heard him say, "It appears, therefore, the defendant—" and the squeak of the swivel chair.

"It was awfully good of you," Mrs. Bridge said, standing at the half-open door, telling each visitor good-by. "Everyone has been so kind."

*

114

Letter from a Buddhist

Douglas, having exchanged telegrams with the commandant of his camp, remained in Kansas City till after the funeral. Ruth had flown home from New York and Carolyn had driven up from Parallel; both of them were struck by the change in Douglas. Ruth had no difficulty accepting him as the new head of the family, though he was nearly five years younger than she. Carolyn challenged him once or twice, half-heartedly. Neither of them expected their mother to make decisions. And to Mrs. Bridge herself it seemed natural that he should become the authority. Harriet, keenly attuned to every situation, asked Douglas if she could have a raise; he said no. From that moment on she stopped calling him by his first name and referred to him as Mr. Bridge, and his mother, hearing this for the first time, began to weep.

Soon, like birds abandoning a tree, they flew off in different directions. Ruth went back to New York, Carolyn to southern Kansas, and Douglas to the Army. The functions of the house were carried on by Harriet, and Mrs. Bridge was left alone. She often went to Auxiliary meetings, and she went shopping downtown, and to the Plaza for luncheon, and to a number of parties, but she could no longer lose herself in these activities; the past was too much with her, and so she was frequently content to stay at home, waiting for the mail, or waiting for someone to call, remotely conscious of the persistent roar of the vacuum cleaner, no longer caring if Harriet smoked in the kitchen.

When she received the first letter Douglas wrote after returning to camp she thought how intimately it resembled the letters her husband used to write when he was out of town on business. There had been something quaint about her husband, an old-fashioned inclination which had caused him to begin his letters to her with, "My dear wife . . ."

How strange that Douglas should write:

My dear Mother,

My father loved you above all else, and if he was apt to be rude or tyrannical it was because he wanted to protect you. He wanted so much for us all. He did not ever realize that what we needed was himself instead of what he could give us. On more than one occasion he and I discussed the family and its problems and in these talks I felt his constant preoccupation with your welfare after he was gone. I guess he knew he was not going to live much longer. He said he had never told you about the trouble with his heart.

There is nothing at all for you to worry about. You made him very happy during his life. I am quite certain that never once was he interested in another woman. My love to you, Mother, and to both my sisters. Tell Ruth when next you write her that I am anxious to hear from her.

Well, we have to go out on maneuvers now, but I'll write you again pretty soon.

With love, as always,
Douglas

*

115

All's Well

Not long after this she was window-shopping on the Plaza
when a young man in civilian clothes stopped and addressed
her by name. At first she did not know him; then she saw it
was Jay Duchesne.

"Why, I thought you were in service!" she said with a
smile. Then she noticed he was missing an arm.

"I was," he said, shrugging the shoulder where the arm
had been.

"Oh, I'm sorry, Jay. I must have been asleep."

"That's all right," he answered cheerfully, and after a
pause he said with a rueful grin, "I'm one of the clowns
you read about in the comics—the ones who never do anything right. I was always clumsy." He took a package of
cigarettes from his pocket, expertly shook one between his
fingers and lighted it. "How's old Red Dog these days?" he
asked, blowing a stream of smoke.

"How is who?"

"Old Red Dog Doug. Gosh, I haven't seen the bum in
years. What a character he is!"

"Why, he's in the Army," she replied. She was disconcerted by the news that Douglas was a character; he had always seemed very normal to her, though a little more laconic
than most boys.

"They bagged him, too? No kidding?" Duchesne laughed, puffed on his cigarette, and said, "He'll give 'em fits."

"He seems to enjoy it and he's doing quite well." She was positive Duchesne was about to say he never heard of anybody doing well in the Army.

"Kidding aside," he said. "How times change. What about Mr. Bridge? Dead and gone these many years, or still raking in the jack?"

"Mr. Bridge passed away not long ago," she replied stiffly.

Duchesne observed her for a minute, smoke curling from his nostrils. "I'm sorry to hear that," he said finally. "He was a nice guy—once you got underneath the crust he was a real soft touch. Is Ruth still in the big city?"

"Yes. She's been there quite a while and is doing very well."

"I can believe it. I always figured she'd wind up in Hollywood. She was sort of a glamour type, you know, but mysterious, like in these secret-agent movies."

"Oh?"

Duchesne studied his cigarette. "Look, Mrs. Bridge, how's Cork?"

"Why, she's just fine."

"Still married?"

"Of course!" Mrs. Bridge laughed in displeasure. She noticed that Duchesne seemed rather disappointed.

"Why should you ask, Jay?"

"No reason," he said, flipping the cigarette in the street. "I think about her a lot, that's all. Tell her hello for me."

"I certainly will. It's been nice seeing you again, Jay. You're looking quite well."

"Things could be worse, Mrs. B. In the hospital I couldn't go for it, but I know better now." He took a deep breath and straightened up. "So, anyhow," he added, just before walking away, "do give her the word."

＊

116

Remembrance of Things Past

Her album provided many comforting hours. There she could find her children once again, and her husband, too. He was standing in bright sunshine with one hand on the fender of the new Reo and Carolyn was sitting on his shoulders. There was Douglas showing off the baseball bat they had given him for his birthday. And there was Ruth in her first high heels, standing pigeon-toed and earnestly determined not to fall on her face. There, too, were her friends—Grace Barron waving from the high diving board at the country-club pool, Mabel Ong outside the Auxiliary clubhouse with hands thrust in the side pockets of her tweed jacket, Madge one snowy day in a Persian lamb coat with her galoshes unzipped, and Lois Montgomery looking presidential. Mrs. Bridge wished she had taken more snapshots.

She had quite a few of the European trip. She had spent more than one enjoyable morning with a damp sponge on which to wet the mounting corners, the huge album lying open on the writing desk and the carpet all around her feet littered with negatives and with yellow drugstore envelopes. In went Trafalgar Square, Buckingham Palace, Piccadilly, the Thames, the changing of the Guard, and the ravens she had seen at the Tower of London. In went the Seine, the Arch of Triumph, an awning of Maxim's, Notre Dame, and Mr. Bridge buying the *Herald Tribune* in front of the American Express. The pictures of the Riviera had not turned out well, though she could not imagine why, unless the light meter had not been working properly; the Riviera, whenever she thought about it, seemed so foreign, really more foreign to her way of life than Paris had been. Often she remembered the cliffs, the harbor, and the shining sea.

"I don't know whether this would interest you or not," she would say to guests, picking up the album in both hands, and as she deposited it on her visitor's lap she would say, "Now, just look at them until you get bored, but for heaven's sake don't feel obliged to go through them all." And she would then hover nearby, anxious to know which pictures were being looked at. Often she would be unable to sit still; she had to look over the visitor's shoulder, reaching down now and then to say, "That's the famous old cathedral you're always hearing about." Or, "That's the ocean, of course." Or, "This was taken from the steps of the National Gallery, and right there—directly behind the man on the bicycle—is where we ate lunch."

But the pictures to which she returned most often for her own pleasure were those of her family: they evoked what she had known most intimately, and all she had loved most profoundly.

*

1 1 7

Hello?

One December morning near the end of the year when snow
was falling moist and heavy for miles all around, so that the
earth and the sky were indivisible, Mrs. Bridge emerged
from her home and spread her umbrella. With small cautious steps she proceeded to the garage, where she pressed the
button and waited impatiently for the door to lift. She was
in a hurry to drive downtown to buy some Irish lace anti-
macassars that were advertised in the newspaper, and she was
planning to spend the remainder of the day browsing through
the stores because it was Harriet's day off and the house was
empty—so empty.

She had backed just halfway out of the garage when the
engine died. She touched the starter and listened without
concern because, despite her difficulties with the Lincoln,
she had grown to feel secure in it. The Lincoln was a number
of years old and occasionally recalcitrant, but she could not
bear the thought of parting with it, and in the past had resisted this suggestion of her husband, who, mildly puzzled
by her attachment to the car, had allowed her to keep it.

Thinking she might have flooded the engine, which was
often true, Mrs. Bridge decided to wait a minute or so.

Presently she tried again, and again, and then again.
Deeply disappointed, she opened the door to get out and
discovered she had stopped in such a position that the car

doors were prevented from opening more than a few inches on one side by the garage partition, and on the other side by the wall. Having tried all four doors she began to understand that until she could attract someone's attention she was trapped. She pressed the horn, but there was not a sound. Half inside and half outside she remained.

For a long time she sat there with her gloved hands folded in her lap, not knowing what to do. Once she looked at herself in the mirror. Finally she took the keys from the ignition and began tapping on the window, and she called to anyone who might be listening, "Hello? Hello out there?"

But no one answered, unless it was the falling snow.

Connell, Evan S
Mrs. Bridge.

Wilmington Public Library
Wilmington, N. C.

___

RULES

1. ~~Books marked 7 days may be kept one week. Books marked 14 days, two weeks. The latter may be renewed, if more than 3 months old.~~

2. ~~A fine of two cents a day will be charged on each book which is not returned according to the above rule.~~ No book will be issued to any person having a fine of 25 cents or over.

3. A charge of ten cents will be made for mutilated plastic jackets. All injuries to books beyond reasonable wear and all losses shall be made good to the satisfaction of the Librarian.

4. Each borrower is held responsible for all books drawn on his card and for all fines accruing on the same.